Risky PLAY

DANICA FLYNN

RISKY PLAY

A PHILADELPHIA BULLDOGS NOVEL

DANICA FLYNN

RISKY PLAY

ISBN: 978-1-957494-27-2
Cover Art: Qamber Designs
Editor: Charlie Knight

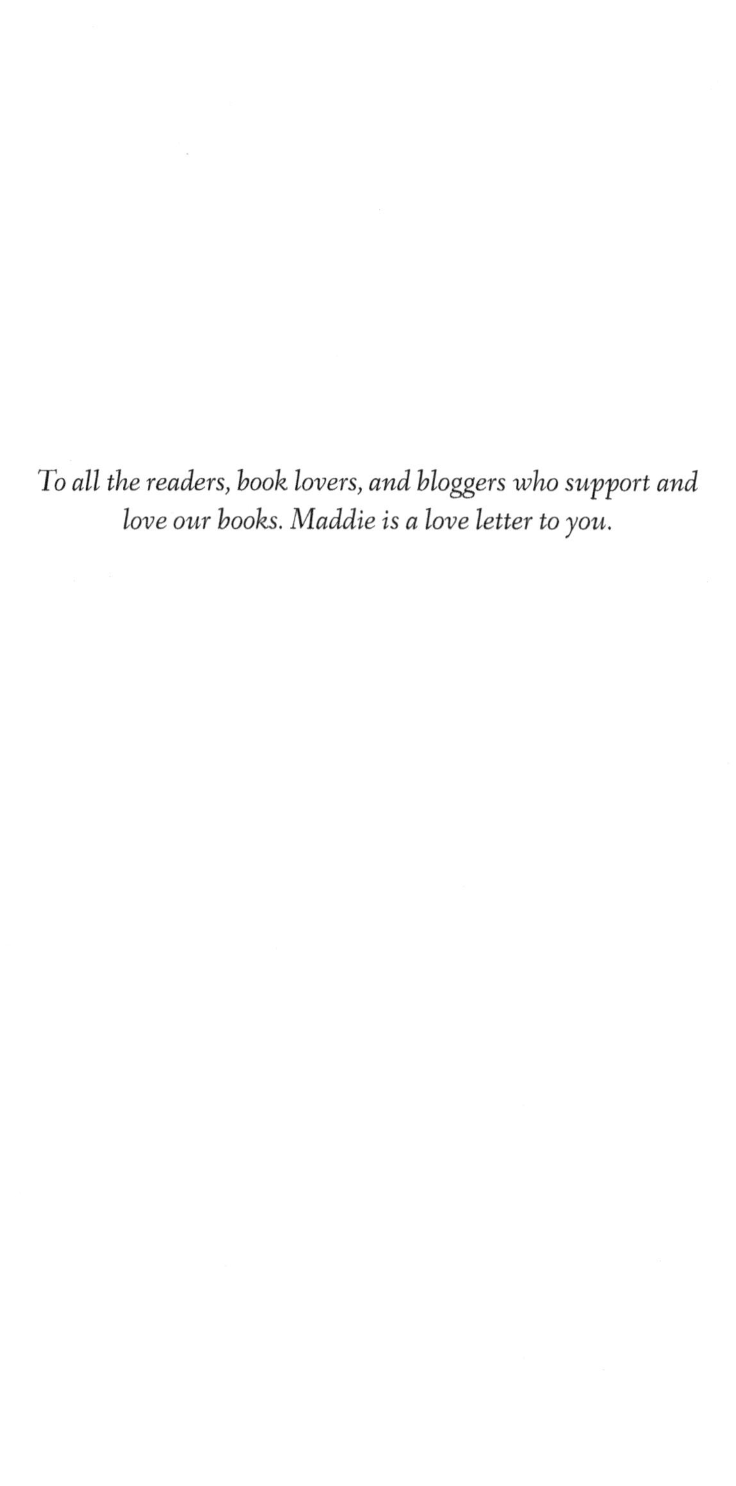

To all the readers, book lovers, and bloggers who support and love our books. Maddie is a love letter to you.

PLAYLIST

"Feel Good Inc." By Gorillaz
"The Night We Met" By Lord Huron
"We're Going To Be Friends" By The White Stripes
"Seeing Red" By Best Coast
"Need Your Love" By Tennis
"Crush Culture" By Conan Gray
"Heat Waves" By Glass Animals
"Closer" by Tegan and Sara
"Uncover" By Zara Larsson
"About A Girl" By The Academy Is...
"Dirty Little Secret" By The All-American Rejects
"Water Fountain" By Alec Benjamin
"Secret Love Song" By Little Mix, Jason Derulo
"Weed Party" By Band of Horses
"All I Wanted" By Paramore
"I Want To Be With You" By Chloe Moriondo

AUTHOR'S NOTE

Please note this book deals with a female character who was a victim of revenge porn prior to the beginning of this book.

CHAPTER ONE

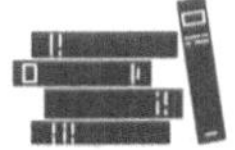

MADDIE

JUNE

"Have you told your brother yet?" Dinah, my soon-to-be sister-in-law, asked as she fixed her veil and touched up her makeup.

She asked me to kick her mother out of the room three minutes ago because she was about to explode. Dinah, not her mother. This wedding was supposed to be super low-key, but with my brother being a hockey player and Dinah coming from a large Italian family, it had morphed into a huge affair.

I handed her the flask again, and she took a generous swig. I didn't care if she was drunk at the altar; all my big brother asked of me was to make sure his bride didn't have a meltdown. Even though it was totally his fault since he insisted this wedding be perfect.

"Mads?" Dinah asked again.

I sighed. "No."

"You should have told us you were transferring to Franklin!" she exclaimed. "We would have let you come live with us instead of having to deal with the dorms."

I shrugged. "I wanted the American Ivy League experience."

I also didn't want to be under the constant scrutiny of my overprotective older brother, but I didn't tell Dinah that. I couldn't bear to tell her the real reason I transferred to Franklin. When Noah found out about my move, he'd do everything in his power to make me move in with him.

Dinah's bestie and her matron of honor, Fi, flipped her gorgeous red hair over her shoulder. "You're going to Franklin?"

I nodded.

"My friend Katie's a professor there. English."

"Katherine Fitzgerald?" I asked.

Fi thought for a moment. "Yeah. She used to be at UPENN, but she likes Franklin better."

"I think I have her for one of my communications classes," I said and wracked my brain for confirmation.

"You'll love her," Fi reassured me and squeezed my arm.

"Are you nervous about transferring?" Dinah asked.

"A little, but at least my brother's here, so it's not a completely foreign country."

They both laughed, and then Roxanne Desjardins came rushing back into the room and looked annoyed. "Okay, D, I get it now. Your mom asked me when Benny and I are getting married."

"Did you tell her the fifth of never?" Dinah joked.

"Of course!" the tall, curvy woman answered with a laugh.

"Okay, D, are you ready?" Fi asked.

"I'm nervous," she admitted and took the flask from me

again. She took a large gulp that made Rox cheer her on. Rox could hold her liquor like no woman I'd ever seen. It made me want to be her when I grew up.

"D, it's gonna be fine," Fi told her gently.

"You love my brother, right?" I asked.

My brother never gave me the whole spiel, but I knew it was a bit of a challenge when he and his next-door neighbor finally got together. Dinah had been married before, but her husband died, so I think she had some hang-ups about it and the fact that she was eight years older than him. Even though nobody gave a shit about that. My mom was five years older than my dad, and it had never affected their relationship.

"I love him so much. I didn't think I would ever get married again. And..." she trailed off and held a hand against her stomach. "I never thought he'd want me knowing I can't have children."

"Oh, D! He loves you, and that doesn't matter to him," Fi said.

Ooh, right. Noah had mentioned *that* to me. It broke my heart for Dinah because she would have been such a good mom. None of that ever mattered to my brother, though. He just wanted her to be happy.

"Noah loves you for *you*," I reassured her. "So we're all going to go out there and watch you say your vows and have your happily ever after."

"Okay..." Dinah whispered, but she still looked unsure.

"Girl, come on, you two are so sickeningly cute!" Rox encouraged. "Let's get you married."

"You're next," Fi teased.

Rox made a face. "Hard pass!"

Fi led us out of the bridal suite, and we began the procession down the aisle. She walked with her hot, blonde, hockey-playing husband, while I walked with Noah's best friend TJ. TJ's fiancée wasn't a bridesmaid because she had been pregnant for most of the wedding planning, and now she had her hands full, literally, with twin babies. I took my place behind Fi and watched as Rox and Benny walked down the aisle next.

My brother had his long hockey flow down but out of his face, and his beard was freshly trimmed. I was glad he had listened to me about the beard but not about pulling his hair back into a fashionable man-bun. He hated those.

I gave him a thumbs-up when he caught my eye.

Panic was etched across his face, and he looked like he was sweating in his tux. Oh, poor guy.

Noah wanted everything to be perfect for his wife, but Dinah would have much preferred getting married in a pair of jeans and a hockey jersey at the courthouse. She was doing all of this for him and her family. I guessed that was what love was like—sacrificing things for your partner even when you didn't want them. I'd never known that. Never got far enough with anyone to feel that way about someone.

The music switched to the bridal procession, and I was pretty sure Dinah was gritting her teeth in annoyance behind her veil. Rox nudged me with an elbow so I wouldn't laugh. My brother turned, and his face broke out into a big smile. He looked so happy, and I loved that for him.

I watched as Noah bent down to his pint-sized partner and lifted the veil over her face. She reached up a hand to brush across his beard, and their love poured out between them. A spike of jealousy ran through me. My brother and Dinah were so freaking cute together. I wanted that one day, but I wasn't sure I'd ever find that if my brother disapproved of every guy I was interested in. Not that he didn't have his reasons. I wished he'd forget about what happened with my ex last year.

I daydreamed during the ceremony until the preacher announced them married, and the happy couple kissed. I made a face. I didn't need to see Noah's tongue in Dinah's mouth.

"They're so extra," Rox chided beside me.

Fi barked out a laugh. "You have no room to talk."

Rox shrugged with a mischievous look.

We spent an hour getting pictures done while everyone else was enjoying cocktail hour. I was grateful I was twenty-one and could legally drink here in the States.

"You okay?" Dinah whispered in my ear when we settled at the long table in the banquet hall.

I nodded.

"You sure?" she asked.

I nodded again and took a sip of my cranberry vodka. "I'm so happy you're my sister-in-law now."

She squeezed my hand. "Me too."

I looked down at my plate, and when I looked back up, my eyes locked with the hottest man I had ever seen.

His dark hair was styled back with the ends curling around his ears. He was clean-cut and looked sharp in a blue pin-striped suit that stretched across his broad chest. He smiled at me, and when I saw a full row of pearly white teeth, I got excited, thinking that meant he wasn't a hockey player.

Dinah nudged me. "He's cute."

Cute didn't even cut it.

"Who's that?" I asked.

"Oh, that's Cally. I forgot we didn't introduce you yet."

I groaned.

Cally. That was one hundred percent a stupid hockey nickname.

Because of course he was a hockey player at my hockey-playing brother's wedding. If he played with Noah, that meant he was off-limits. Or rather, *I* was off-limits. Hockey players didn't break the code. If they did, there was hell to pay. I'd seen it so many times before growing up in hockey culture.

Dinah squeezed my arm. "Ask him to dance later."

"What? No! Noah would flip out."

At the sound of his name, my brother turned to us with a smirk. "What are you two scheming about over there? What would I flip out about?"

Dinah gave him a sweet smile, and it was like a light switch got flipped because my brother looked like he would do anything she said. Holy shit, Dinah was the alpha in their relationship. "Oh, babe, Maddie told me great news."

He furrowed his brow. "What?"

I opened my mouth, not sure what she was playing at, but she beat me to it. "She's moving to Philly."

"What?" Noah snapped, and I immediately had my hackles up.

"I'm transferring to Franklin U," I explained.

The crease in his brow deepened. "What?"

"C'mere you," Dinah ordered, and she pulled his face to hers to meet him in a long kiss. I gagged because I'm pretty sure I saw some tongue again. Ew.

When I quit trying to throw up in my mouth, I realized what she was doing. She was distracting him for me. Dinah was the best! Rox figured out what was going on, too, because she grabbed my wrist and led me over to the bar to grab herself another drink.

"So your brother does that whole big brother protective bullshit thing?" the older woman asked.

I sighed. "Rox, he scares every dude away. Every single one!"

She tried not to laugh.

"How did TJ take it when he found out about you and Benny?" I asked.

Hockey players not breaking the code? Yeah, Rox's partner Benny did that with her.

She grimaced and took a sip of her drink. "Terribly. He heard us having sex."

I felt my eyes bulge out of my head. "What?"

She shrugged. "Whatever, it was good sex. I'm not ashamed of it. But then he punched Benny in the stomach and drank him under the table. The next day, TJ and my dad made him bag skate while Benny was hungover. He said it was worth it."

"Aw!" I cooed.

She smiled. "He's a big softie."

"Who's a big softie?" a deep voice rumbled behind us.

"You are," she told him with a big smile as he leaned down to kiss her. Benny was the biggest guy on the team, but Rox was on the tall side, so he didn't have to bend that far. Not like my brother and his pocket-sized wife.

Benny eyed the two of us as he wrapped his arm around Rox from behind and kissed her neck. I was so jealous. I wanted a guy to look at me the way Benny looked at Rox. Like he couldn't wait to peel her out of her clothes later. Why couldn't I have that?

"What are you two up to?" he asked.

"Getting Maddie out from under Noah's watchful eye."

He snorted. "Noah? The nicest person I've ever met?"

I groaned. "Not to any guy I've ever been interested in."

Benny furrowed his brow. "I hate that shit."

"I know, love," Rox muttered to him and brought him down for another kiss.

I turned away from them, not wanting to intrude on their moment.

My eyes traveled over to the man I had spied earlier, and he had definitely been staring at me like he liked what he saw. I could work with that. I was ready to take my V card out of my back pocket, and it didn't matter to me who it was with. Besides, a wedding one-night stand could be fun.

CHAPTER TWO

MATT

I felt a tap on my shoulder and turned to see the smoking hot bridesmaid standing in front of me.

"Hi," she greeted and pushed a strand of her dark hair behind her ear.

I plastered on my signature cocky smirk. "Hey there."

I had my eye on this girl all night. She was a rocket with an awesome bod, wearing a dark blue bridesmaid dress that fit her like a glove. She wasn't subtle, eying me up all night long, either.

The pretty brunette smiled at me and bit her lip. I loved when chicks did that. It was sexy as hell, especially when they did it right before they wrapped their lips around my cock.

Okayyy...maybe I needed to get laid.

My dry spell was no joke. Kinda hard to meet anyone when I was on the road with the team all the time. Especially when I wasn't sure about my place on the team. Most people I met had dollar signs in their eyes when I told them

I was a professional athlete. Yeah, sorry, I was on an entry-level contract, and I didn't get paid as much as the older guys.

She wrung her hands. "Um..."

"You wanna ask me to dance?"

She nodded. "Yes. Sorry. I'm usually not this forward."

I grabbed her hand. "Let's dance."

That made her laugh, and she let me lead her onto the dance floor. I didn't even know this chick's name, but if this hottie was giving me the time of day, I wouldn't waste it.

I twirled her around and ran my hands down her sides. She was tall for a woman, which I liked because, at six-foot-two, it was annoying to almost break my neck to kiss a girl. I eyed my teammate Noah, who was dancing with his new wife. I didn't know how he did it with her being a whole foot shorter than him. I didn't get guys that liked petite girls they could put in their pockets. A leggy Amazon was more my speed.

The mystery brunette wrapped her slender hands around my neck, and I was doing everything in my power to not get hard on the dance floor. She had a body that wouldn't quit, and the way she danced with me made it hard not to think about peeling her out of that dress.

"What's your name?" I asked.

"Maddie."

"I'm Matt."

She gave me a sly smile, but over her shoulder, Noah glared at me.

That was odd. He was the nicest guy you'd ever met. The other guys on the Bulldogs gave him grief for being such a Canadian stereotype. But he was glaring at me like he wanted to stab me. I'd only ever seen his expression darken like that when someone cross-checked him into the boards.

His wife, Dinah, pulled him down to her and kissed him, and I turned away, not wanting to spy on their sweet moment. Maddie's hand played with the ends of my hair, and I bit back a moan. How did women always know that doing that felt good?

I leaned down and whispered in her ear. "You better stop that."

"Why?"

I ground my hips against her, and her ocean-blue eyes got wide as she felt my hardness press against the material of her dress. Then she gave me a sultry look. "Oh, I can work with that."

My lips curled up into a wicked grin. "You think so?"

She nodded. Her eyes were big but hungry, like she wanted to hop on my dick right here if I let her. Hell yeah—I loved a woman who was in tune with her sexuality and wasn't shy about it.

"I've got a room upstairs. You wanna get out of here?" she asked.

"I'm ready if you are."

She took a quick look around, and then she grabbed my hand, dragging me out of the ballroom of the swanky hotel. I put my hand on the small of her back as we walked toward the elevator.

Once inside, I pinned her against the wall. She looked up at me through her big lashes, looking so innocent and sweet. I dipped my head down to meet her lips with mine. She sighed into the kiss, her hands coming up to thread through my hair while she opened her mouth to me. I darted my tongue inside, reveling in her letting me take the lead.

The sound of the elevator dinging forced us apart, and we laughed as we walked out of it and down the hall to her room.

I pressed myself against her perfect ass and kissed the back of her neck while she fumbled with the room card.

"Oh my God, stop. You're distracting me!"

"You really want me to stop?" I purred into her ear, nosing across her soft skin.

"No," she answered truthfully when the card reader lit up green and she opened the door.

She let me inside, but once she closed it behind her, I was on her again, lifting her up into my arms and kissing her hard. She wrapped her heels around my back as we deepened the kiss. I pressed her against the back of the door, pinning her there while I licked inside her mouth. We were a tangle of lips and tongues as we kissed like we needed it to breathe.

I kissed down to her neck to that soft spot I knew drove women wild. "Tell me what you need."

"To come," she moaned.

"I can do that."

She wrenched my head back up to her lips. "Can you?"

I liked this girl. She didn't play around, and by the way she was rubbing my dick through my pants, she was hungry for it. I liked that a lot.

I set her down on her feet and led her to the bed. Then I turned her around so her back was against my chest.

I pushed her hair over her shoulder and kissed her soft skin. "Can I take this off?" I asked as I fingered the zipper of her dress.

She nodded.

"Maddie, be a good girl and say yes."

"Yes," she stuttered out.

I held the fabric of her dress taut while I slid the zipper down her back, revealing inch-by-inch of her summer-kissed skin. I kissed down her spine, smiling against her skin as she giggled at the sensation.

I bit back a moan when her dress fell to the floor and she was only wearing the tiniest black see-through thong I'd ever seen. Damn, did she have a nice ass. A nice everything.

I spun her around. "Look at you."

"What about me?"

I fingered the string of her thong. "So sexy. Where can I touch you?"

"Everywhere?"

I lifted my hands up to cup her tits and bent my head to take one nipple in my mouth. She made a little noise of enjoyment while I switched to the other one.

"Can I take this off too?" I asked, pulling at her thong again.

She nodded enthusiastically. "Uh-huh."

I dropped to my knees and slid the small piece of fabric down her legs until she was completely bared to me. Maddie had a rocking body. She was fit and toned like an athlete. That should have given me pause, but I was more interested in getting my mouth on her pussy.

"You don't have to," she told me while I spread her legs and looked up at her with desire-hooded eyes.

"Yeah, I do," I growled and nipped at her toned thighs.

"You don't...oh..."

She quit arguing when I licked her like she was mine. Like I was marking her for nobody else but me. I lapped at her clit and pressed a finger inside her entrance. She tensed at that.

I lifted my head to gauge her reaction. "You okay? You're really tense."

She grimaced but then nodded. "I'm fine. You have thick fingers."

I pressed a second finger inside her. "Relax."

"I…"

"Please?" I begged from below her. "I want to make you feel good."

She ran her neatly manicured hands through my hair. "Are you gonna lick it again or what?"

I gave her a cocky smirk and did exactly that. The tension left her body when I focused on her clit, licking and sucking while I thrust my fingers inside her at the same time. She clenched her hands hard in my hair, but I didn't mind a little pain.

"Matt!" she screamed as she went over the threshold.

Hell yeah.

I held onto her legs so she didn't fall over while I licked and sucked her through another orgasm. When I looked up again, her eyes were closed in ecstasy. Chicks were the sexiest after I made them come.

"Maddie."

"Hmm?"

"Can you let go of my hair?"

Her eyes snapped open, and a crimson blush came across her tanned skin. She unclenched her fingers and brushed my hair back in a gentle caress. "Sorry."

I stood up and gripped her jaw in my hand. "Don't be. You're cute when you come."

She blushed again, but then she trailed a finger down my dress shirt to land on my belt. She rubbed a hand across the bulge in my pants. "You have too many clothes on."

"You want to help me out of them?"

Her deft hands undid my tie and threw it across the room. I laughed, but then she undid the buttons of my dress shirt. I shed my suit jacket and peeled the shirt off my wide-set shoulders. Her hand feathered across my chest, trailing down my abs until it was on my belt again. Her hands felt like light kisses across my skin, and I really wanted to know where this chick was gonna take me tonight.

She undid my belt buckle and then the zipper. My pants dropped to the floor, and her eyes widened. "Oh. Commando?"

I gave her a wink. "I like the breeze."

Lie. I forgot to do laundry, but I wasn't gonna tell a chick that.

She smirked and surprised me when she stroked my dick. I held back a moan. It had been months since someone other than me had touched my junk. I forgot what it was like to have soft, tentative hands on me. I closed my eyes at the sensation and tried not to blow my load.

She stoked it in gentle pumps at first, like she was feeling me out. My eyes snapped open when I felt her swirl her tongue around the head. I looked down, and she peered up at me with wide, innocent-looking eyes. She took me inside while her other hand stroked me.

"So good," I groaned and reached down to hold her hair out of her face.

Not to be a gentleman or some shit. It was so I could watch her bob on my dick, seeing it sliding in and out of her mouth while she licked and sucked me until I came.

"Maddie," I warned.

But instead of pulling off, she looked up at me innocently and continued to suck me off.

She was a brat, and I was into it.

"Fuuuckkk," I groaned.

I jerked my hips, fucking her face while I came in hot spurts down her throat. She sucked until it was all gone and then stood up like it was nothing. I gripped the back of her neck and kissed her roughly.

I backed her up until her knees hit the bed, and then I tossed her on it like she didn't weigh a thing. It was in that torturous moment while she was spread out waiting for me that I realized I didn't have a condom.

Fuck me!

CHAPTER THREE

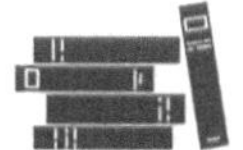

MADDIE

"Maddie, wait," Matt sighed. He sat on the bed, but he wasn't getting in next to me. Or climbing on top of me like I wanted.

"What?" I whined.

"I don't have a condom."

I groaned. "Seriously?"

"Sorry. Wasn't expecting this tonight. We could do more oral?"

I was tired of oral sex.

I loved oral, giving, or receiving, but I didn't want to be a horny virgin anymore. I wanted to get railed by a man while he growled in my ear, letting him take me until I was screaming his name. I wanted to be held down on the bed while he nailed me from behind.

"I want to have sex," I growled.

He sighed in equal frustration. "I always wrap it up."

I pulled the cover over me. Now that we wouldn't have

sex, I felt self-conscious being naked around him. "You're right. Being safe's important. But I want to finally get laid."

He turned back to me with a dark eyebrow raised, his brown eyes searching mine. I had been so focused on getting it in that I hadn't noticed his whiskey-colored eyes or how nice they looked when the light hit them at the right time. Right now, they were wide with terror.

"What do you mean?" he asked.

I bit my lip. "I've never...you know."

"What?"

"Had sex. Penetrative sex, at least. I've been finger blasted and eaten out a lot."

His face paled and he climbed off the bed in a hurry. I sat up in alarm and watched him put his clothes back on in a hurry.

"Matt?"

"I...I'm sorry, Maddie."

"You're gonna leave?" I cried.

He rubbed the back of his neck. "I'm not gonna take your virginity."

"Why not?"

"You should reserve that for someone special!"

"Why should I do that?"

Why did people think virginity was this sacred thing? I wanted to get it over with, and it didn't matter who it was with. I had no illusions that Matt and I would fall madly in love after one night; I would have been content with never seeing him again.

"If you waited this long, you should save it for someone who means something," he explained.

I rolled my eyes. Again with the idea of virginity being something special. "My brother drives away every single guy I'm interested in. I want to get it over with."

He frowned. "Wait, which brother? I thought you had three?"

I shook my head. "No, just the one. It's great being constantly known as 'Noah Kennedy's baby sister.' 'Don't go out with Maddie Kennedy. Her brother might drop the gloves on you.' It's been super fucking great."

He looked green. "Your brother's Noah Kennedy?"

"Yeah? Who did you think I was?"

"Fuck me," he sighed and rubbed a hand across his clean-shaven jaw. "I thought you were Dinah's little sister. No wonder Noah was staring daggers at me."

"You thought I was Dinah's little sister? Why? Because we both have dark hair? Are you serious?"

How could he think Dinah was my sister? Sure, we were both white girls with dark hair, but I was tan and lanky, whereas Dinah was petite and paler than a ghost. He did come off as a cocky hockey player, though, and sometimes they didn't pay that much attention. That was mean, but I was a jock, and I recognized that some of us...fulfilled the stereotype.

He pulled his pants back on, and I wanted to cry that he was rushing out of here—not because we didn't have a condom, but because I was his teammate's virgin sister. Why did I let that slip?

He didn't say goodbye. He let the door slam behind him as he literally ran away from me.

At least he made me come when he went down on me. That was better than nothing.

I lay in the bed, staring up at the ceiling and thinking about how my life got to this point. Would I ever get out of the shadow of my older brother? Probably not. Maybe moving to the same city as him wasn't the best idea.

I let tears roll down my cheek. I understood why Matt

freaked out about Noah being my brother. It was the same story I'd dealt with my whole life. No guy wanted to break the stupid hockey code. It didn't mean I couldn't be pissed about it.

I let myself wallow for a bit until I decided I wasn't going back downstairs. I had grabbed my purse off the back of the chair before we snuck up here, so there was no need to return. I changed into my pajamas and checked my phone.

I saw a ton of social media notifications. Earlier, I forced Dinah to let me post a selfie together on her profile. I loved Dinah, and she was a talented writer, but the admin stuff, like posting on her socials, was not her forte. I, however, had amassed a big following in the book community, so I was trying to teach her my ways.

I scanned down the list of comments on her post.

Can't wait for your next book!

OMG you look amazing!

OMG is that MaddieKReads?!?

I logged out of her account and went to my own, where I reposted the photo and wrote my own caption.

Not so secret secret for you all! You know that one of my fave authors is Dinah Lace, but she's also my new sister-in-law. I don't know what she sees in my brother, but I love them both so much.

Almost instantly, I saw a text come through from said writer.

DINAH: Your brother's asking where you went, but I just saw Cally come back into the ballroom and then flee.

ME: I don't want to talk about it. Tell Noah I wasn't feeling well.

She didn't answer, so I thought that meant she had dropped it until ten minutes later when there was a knock at my door. I sighed and opened it, only for it to be pushed open by a meddling bride and her two friends.

Rox held up a bottle of whiskey, and Fi pulled red solo cups from out of nowhere. Who were these women?

"Spill!" Rox demanded while she poured large cups for us. I took it from her and sat back on the bed.

"What are you all doing up here?" I grumbled.

"What happened?" Fi asked.

Dinah gave them a look, and she sat next to me. She pulled me into her arms and gave me a big hug. I leaned into her, and the floodgates opened up. The tears of frustration spilled out while my new sister-in-law rubbed my back and told me it was going to be okay.

I pulled away and wiped the tears away.

Rox looked pissed off. "What the fuck did he do?"

"Down girl!" Fi laughed and took a swig of her whiskey.

I chugged mine, too. "I'm gonna die a virgin."

Dinah blinked at me while Rox and Fi shared an amused look. "Come again?" my sister-in-law asked.

"We didn't have a condom—"

"You didn't go without, right?" Rox cut me off. "You should always wrap it up."

"Paranoid," Fi teased.

"Looking out for the girl," Rox explained with a glare.

Dinah shushed them. "Maddie... I didn't realize you weren't experienced. I wouldn't have encouraged you to hook up with Cally had I known."

"Why not?" I cried and gulped down more of my whiskey.

Dinah pursed her lips. "Your first time should be special."

Fi snorted. "My first time was a quickie with Riley in my parents' basement. It doesn't have to be special, D."

"True," Rox agreed. "Pretty sure I got fucked in the backseat of a car. Or was it underneath the bleachers? I forget. But it wasn't great."

"I want to have sex!" I exclaimed.

Rox busted up laughing. "Holy shit! I forgot that you're not all timid and shit like Noah."

I laughed with her. "It's not like I'm completely innocent. I'm pretty good at blowies."

That made all of them laugh.

Rox put her hands up in the air. "Okay, hold up. Let's discuss this. So you've had oral sex?"

I nodded. A lot of oral sex. Always got to third base but never got to run home. Which never made sense to me. These guys were so afraid of my brother, they didn't want to deflower me, but they were fine with me giving them head. Men had weird logic.

"That's still sex," Rox said. "Virginity's a social construct, and it's heteronormative to assume sex only means with a dick in a pussy."

"Okay..." I agreed with her. "But I want to get railed by a hot guy who knows how to use his dick."

Dinah snorted. "I love how ridiculous you are."

I pinched her side. "Because you're exactly the same way."

"Yeah, this is the girl that says 'Eat pussy. Don't cheat' when the boys ask for dating advice," Rox said with a laugh.

Dinah shrugged. "What? Am I wrong?"

"NOPE!" the other two cheered.

I was pretty sure my sister-in-law was a little drunk. Drunk Dinah was hilarious and said inappropriate things. I loved that my quiet and serious brother got this loud-mouth

Philly girl to bring him out of his shell. I especially loved that she wasn't afraid to say what she was thinking.

"But maybe D's right. You don't have to force it. Did you have a good time with Cally?" Fi asked.

I nodded. "He's bomb at eating pussy."

"To men who are superb muff divers!" Rox cheered and raised her cup.

"Eat pussy..." Dinah started and raised her cup, too.

"And don't cheat," Fi finished and repeated the action.

"To men who know how to find the clit!" I chimed in.

"Hell yeah!" Rox laughed and downed her cup. "You want another?"

I shook my head and tossed back the rest of the drink. Rox was liberal with the pouring. Supposedly, she could drink the entire hockey team under the table. She was the coolest.

"Okay, so you had a good time, and you didn't find a condom, then what? He left?" my sister-in-law asked. Her mouth was a thin line, and that meant she was on edge about this situation.

I shook my head. "Accidentally spilled the beans, then he freaked out, and oh, he thought we were sisters."

"Ohhh. It's about the code," Rox said while she refilled her cup.

"Bullshit code," Dinah muttered. "Honey, I talked to your brother about letting you make your own choices. I know he's protective, but at least you only have one brother and not three like I do. I reminded Noah about that."

"Does he know I went off with Matt?" I asked.

I didn't want Matt to suffer because my brother thought it was his duty to protect me against every dude who wanted to stick their dick in me. As if I wasn't a sexual being who wanted that.

"Nah. They had a quickie in the bathroom, so Noah was none the wiser," Rox explained and downed another swig of her whiskey.

"Rox!" Dinah hissed.

The curvy woman shrugged. "What? That's literally what you told us. Gleefully, I might add."

Fi laughed. "She's got you there. You were all like, 'BRB, bitches, I'm gonna go get my pussy licked.' "

Dinah swatted Fi's arm, but the redhead darted away from her. I really liked these women and how they ragged on each other. It reminded me of my friends back home.

"She doesn't want to know that," Dinah scolded her bestie.

I made a fake gagging sound in my throat, but I was happy that my brother found someone who knew how to take the reins. Noah might look like a badass alpha male on the ice, but he was timid and unsure of himself with women. Which was probably why it took him two whole years to put the moves on his now-wife. I was glad he finally did and met this woman who said what she was thinking and didn't care what anyone thought of her.

Dinah squeezed my hand. "Sorry, honey."

Fi gestured to my pajama-clad state. "What's this all about?"

"I'm up here for the night."

Fi shook her head. "Nope. Get your ass out of the bed, put your bridesmaid dress back on, and Rox will fix your makeup."

"Why?" I whined.

Fi arched a red eyebrow at me. "Honey, we're all gonna go back downstairs and have a good time so you can forget about Cally bailing on you."

Dinah gave me a smile that said 'What can you do?' I

sighed and got back into my bridesmaid dress, even though I didn't want to go with them.

"You're all pushy," I sighed.

The three of them shared a conspiratorial look.

"Hurry up!" Dinah urged. "It's my wedding, and I want you to have fun tonight."

"Come on, have another drink with us downstairs," Rox nagged.

Having these three women egg me on made me hope I'd find a similar friend group once I got to Franklin. This year was supposed to be a fresh start. As soon as I got to school, I'd forget all about Matt and this disastrous night. It wasn't like I'd run into him all the way in West Philly. But first, I was getting shit-faced with my sister-in-law.

CHAPTER FOUR

MATT

OCTOBER

"High sticking!" I yelled from the bench, watching my teammates trying to set up another play on the ice. I squirted water into my mouth and put my mouthguard back in, waiting for the change-up.

Of course the ref missed that call while the Pittsburgh Miners took every chance they could get.

"Simmer down, rookie," Benny teased as he slid down the pine with me.

Being on the line with the big dude and Hallsy had been a blessing these past couple of weeks. Especially since I was still worried I'd wake up one day and find out I was put on waivers. I had to prove to the Bulldogs that I had earned my spot on the team.

On the change-up, I hopped over the boards, and I took the face-off against Pittsburgh's Sanderson. I got possession of the puck and tried to break it out of our zone. I passed to Hallsy, who got it into Pittsburgh's zone and was looking for the setup.

I was in the corner open for the puck again, but Hallsy passed to Benny, who slapped it back to him. Hallsy deked around a Pittsburgh defenseman and took the shot. I groaned at the pinging of the pipes. I scrambled at the net, trying to get the rebound, but Pittsburgh's goalie covered it.

I hung my head and spied the scoreboard again. 1-0 us with five minutes left in the period, and we needed this W. While it was still early in the season, we had been in a slump the past week, and sinking a win right now was what the team needed.

I got into position while Benny took the face-off this time. Pittsburgh got a hold of the puck, and we raced down the ice after it. Riley and Logan were hitting our opponents hard, trying to block the slot in front of Metzy, but Pittsburgh wanted this win, too. I had to do everything in my power not to let that happen.

We went back and forth from end-to-end of the ice, both teams trying to get another puck deep, but it was no use. The hockey gods were on the Bulldogs' side because even though we didn't get another puck to the net, we ran the clock out and won the game. Not pretty, but I'd take another point in the win column over another L.

By the time we headed back to the locker room, I was drenched in sweat, but the team was in high spirits. I hoped we could keep this momentum going for the rest of the season.

Noah nudged me as I was stripping off my jersey.

"Nice job today," he complimented me.

Noah had great hockey sense, so it was nice to hear that

from him. I still felt super awkward around him because of what happened at his wedding.

When I got called up to the big leagues last season, Noah offered me a place to stay in the house he and Dinah had just bought. He had taken me under his wing, helping me with my trouble spots in my game, and gave me girl advice when my ex and I were still on and off. There was no way I was repaying him for all that by fucking his little sister behind his back. I didn't care about 'the code,' Maddie could make her own decisions, but I couldn't do that to my mentor.

"Thanks," I muttered and finished getting undressed.

I hit the showers before he could say anything else. He noticed something was off with me, but I kept waving him off, petrified I'd blurt it out if he pressed me.

Truth was, try as I might, I hadn't gotten Maddie Kennedy out of my head. She was gorgeous and bomb at giving head, but she was my teammate's sister. His virgin sister. It was a relief that she lived in Canada, and I wasn't likely to ever run into her again. Otherwise, I might have some explaining to do.

Noah was brushing out his beard at his cubby and shooting the shit with TJ when I got out of the shower.

"You coming to the bar later tonight?" TJ asked me.

Today was a rare afternoon game, so we had a free night. If the game was during our regular time, we didn't get home until well after midnight. Normally, I'd say yes, but I promised my friend Ty I'd meet him at Franklin U. His girlfriend dumped him for the last time, and he needed a drinking buddy.

I shook my head. "Nah."

"Come on!" TJ whined.

"Leave the kid alone," Noah told him. "I'm not coming out either."

"I thought D wasn't gonna make you a boring married dude."

"I'm not boring," Noah argued.

I pretended not to listen to them bicker while I got dressed.

I appreciated that Noah and Dinah let me live with them, but I worried I was cramping their style. I caught them kissing in the kitchen this morning, and Dinah laughed it off, but Noah got that tomato-red shade across his face. I didn't blame them since they were newlyweds, but it sure made things awkward.

"Ready to go?" Noah asked.

I nodded.

"Boring!" TJ teased as the three of us walked out of the locker room together.

"Then come to the house, bro," Noah tried to convince TJ.

TJ gave him a lopsided smirk. "Nah. Max's having a day with the twins. I'm not sure she'll let me out to play anyway."

Noah shoved his shoulder. "Then stop being so annoying."

TJ laughed and headed to his sports car while I got in the passenger side of Noah's SUV. The nice thing about living with Noah was that his house wasn't that far from the arena in South Philly, so it was never a long drive.

We were both quiet on the drive over. Noah was likely categorizing all the mistakes he made tonight while I was still thinking about his sister.

"You looked good tonight," he told me as he pulled his car into the garage, tearing me away from my thoughts.

"Not good enough," I muttered.

I got out of the car before he could argue. He pressed onward toward the door to the steps upstairs, and I followed behind him.

"Don't be too hard on yourself. You're doing well on the second line with Benny and Hallsy. Coach wouldn't put you there if he was trying to get rid of you."

I knew I should listen to him, but I wasn't so sure he was right. The Bulldogs drafted me early at eighteen, and I spent a couple of years with the minor affiliate in Reading. Then, last year, I got the call up when our former captain was out with an injury. Pretty sure the only reason I made the team again this year was because G decided to retire last season.

I raised my eyebrow at my teammate when we heard two female voices laughing in Dinah's office on the second floor. My ears perked up at the other voice that sounded vaguely familiar.

Noah shed his suit jacket across the couch, and that's when the two women came down the stairs. I felt all the blood rush to my head when I saw the statuesque brunette beside Dinah. Standing next to her was Noah's sister Maddie. Her crystal blue eyes met mine, and we both froze.

"Cally, you met my sister at the wedding, right?" Noah asked.

"I think so," I lied.

"Yeah, we danced together until you left because you said you ate something that didn't agree with you," Maddie answered for me. She leveled me with an icy glare that pierced me in the chest.

My dick thickened against my leg because I knew exactly what I ate that didn't agree with me. And we both knew that was a big, fat lie. I had feasted on her until she cried out, the sound a permanent echo every time I closed my eyes.

"What are you doing here?" I snapped more harshly than I meant to. My mouth moved too quick for my brain to scream at me to shut up.

Noah fixed me with a glare, and Maddie arched a perfectly sculpted eyebrow at me as if testing me.

I ran a hand through my hair. "I thought you lived in Canada."

"Nope," was all she gave me, but then she turned to Dinah. "I gotta head out. I have lots of studying to do. Work on what we talked about today and let me know how I can help you next week."

"What would I do without you?" Dinah asked.

"Be terrible at marketing! Your publisher doesn't do enough for you."

Noah begrudgingly put his jacket back on.

Maddie shook her head at him. "Noah, put your jacket away. I know how to get back to campus."

The tall, bearded man glared at his little sister. Compared to his tiny wife, Maddie was an Amazon, but not as tall as Noah. She put her hands on her hips and glared up at her brother.

"Mads," Noah sighed and scrubbed a hand across his beard. "It's late at night. Just let me drive you to West Philly."

"Babe..." Dinah tried to cut in, but the siblings gave her a look that said, 'Stay out of it.'

Maddie curled and uncurled her fists but then stomped out of the house.

I sighed and slunk away to my room in the basement.

Noah and Dinah said I didn't have to stay in their finished basement since they had guest rooms upstairs, but I liked having my own space. The basement was fully furnished, complete with a full bath and bedroom, making it feel like my own. There was even a door that led to the garage, so I could come and go as I pleased. They were great about respecting my privacy and never came downstairs unless invited. In truth, it was a kickass living arrangement.

I got out of my suit and changed into a pair of sweatpants and a t-shirt before flopping down on my bed.

I scrolled through my phone absent-mindedly and ended up searching through Dinah's social media feed. Which was mostly stuff for her books until I went far enough back and found the selfie she posted with Maddie at the wedding. Then I scrolled through Maddie's profile. She posted a lot about books with half-naked dudes on the cover, but every once in a while, there was a rare selfie. She looked amazing in each and every one. But it didn't explain why she was here tonight.

Dinah knocked on the door to the basement. "Hey! You want something to eat?" she called through it.

"Did you cook?" I yelled up to her.

I heard her loud laughter, and a smile stretched across my face. Despite being from a large Italian family, Dinah wasn't much of a cook. Noah said he'd worry about her forgetting to eat while he was on the road if it wasn't for her overprotective older brothers coming over and checking the fridge.

I pocketed my phone and went up the steps into the kitchen. Dinah sat at the kitchen table with her laptop open, nursing a beer. She slid a plate of lasagna over to me when I took my seat. I shoved food in my mouth, but I felt awkward as hell. I was pretty sure she knew I had hooked up with

Maddie. Which worried me because the guys ragged on Noah all the time about how he told his wife everything and vice versa.

"What's up, honey?" she asked but didn't look up from her work.

"Um. I should find my own place."

"Why? I thought you were unsure about if they were keeping you on. I know the two-way contract doesn't pay as well."

I rubbed the back of my neck. "Well...I don't want to cramp your style."

She laughed, shut her laptop lid, and peered at me with her shrewd emerald gaze. "We like having you here. You're not a burden, okay?"

"I don't want to get in the way of you two starting a family."

She stiffened for a second, and then she took a swig of her beer. "That's not a problem."

"Oh. I didn't realize you didn't want kids."

She sighed, and I realized I had hit a nerve. "Can't."

I cringed. "Shit. Dinah, I didn't know. "

"It's okay, honey. I don't like to talk about it. I wasn't sure I ever wanted kids, but I had a surprise pregnancy after my first husband died. I miscarried, and they said there was a slim chance of ever carrying another pregnancy to term."

I reached across the table to put my hand on hers. "I'm sorry. I shouldn't have asked."

"It's okay! I made my peace with it. I wanted to try for a little, but..." she trailed off and frowned.

"But what?"

"I almost died during that miscarriage. Noah found me and saved my life. He doesn't want me to go through that again. Plus, I know how painful it was for him to watch me cry over a negative pregnancy test month after month."

"Oh, Dinah," I sighed.

God, I felt like such an asshole for bringing up kids. After everything my parents went through to get me and my sister, I should have known better.

She waved me away. "We talked about it a lot before we got married. We considered adoption and surrogacy. But... he's my home and all I'll ever need. Besides, I have a feeling we'll start taking in more strays. I'll just adopt a bunch of man-children."

"Like me?" I asked with a grin.

She gave me a knowing look. "After we bought the house, Noah offered Logan a place here too, but with him having custody of his nephew, he didn't want to impose. We offered it to McCarthy, too, after he and his girl broke up, but I think he's rooming with one of the other guys."

"I shouldn't have brought up you having kids. I was my parent's miracle baby."

She smiled at me. "Matt, it's okay. You have bigger problems than insulting me." She got up from the table, grabbed another beer out of the fridge, then placed it in front of me.

"You know?" I asked.

"Yup."

I took a swig of the beer. "I didn't know she lived here."

"She transferred to Franklin this fall. Noah's been trying to get her to move in with us, but she needs to live her own life. He's too protective of her."

"So he doesn't know—"

"That you know what her pussy tastes like? No."

"Jesus, Dinah!"

She grinned. "What?"

"I didn't know she told you everything!"

She laughed.

Noah wasn't an open book. He kept things close to the vest, but not his wife. She didn't give a fuck. Normally, I liked her candor, but right now, not so much.

"You should see your face right now! Don't worry—that's between you two. I'm staying out of it."

I wasn't sure I believed her on that one.

CHAPTER FIVE

MADDIE

"Why was he there?" I asked my brother once I begrudgingly got into the passenger seat of his SUV.

Noah turned on his car and backed out of his garage. "Who Cally?"

"Yeah, Matt."

"Oh, he lives with us."

I felt like the floor dropped out from underneath me. Matt lived with Noah and Dinah? Okay, that explained a little more of why he freaked out when he found out I was Noah's sister.

But what the fuck? Why didn't Dinah mention that to me?

My brother clenched his teeth as he sped off to the other side of town.

Noah didn't like that I was living on campus, but I wanted that American university experience. I was even playing on the women's hockey team. It wasn't the same as back home in Winnipeg; it was just club hockey, but that made it more fun since there was less pressure. I wasn't known as Noah Kennedy's baby sister here, and I was hoping to keep that quiet.

"Why are you so agitated?" I asked.

He sighed. "D doesn't want to quit her job."

Oh. Yeah, I knew why she didn't want to quit her day job. Her last book didn't sell. Like at all.

Despite my efforts to hype it up and reception from other book bloggers, her publisher wasn't happy with the sales. That was why I came over. I was helping her ramp up her social media presence and brainstorm her next series. I even offered to do admin work for her. She wasn't doing the bare minimum important things she should be doing. I loved Dinah, but she needed a personal assistant to do all the shit she didn't want to do. Her focus had to be her writing, and she couldn't do that if she was bogged down with admin work.

"Did she tell you why?" I asked.

Noah shook his head. "No. She's being stubborn."

It was obvious she hadn't told him she felt like her writing career was in jeopardy. Dinah's brand was sweet young adult novels, but she showed me a steamy novel she was writing in secret. Only Fi knew about it because she dared Dinah to write it. It was such a departure from her normal stuff, but it would sell. Maybe not under her current name, but it could be successful. She said it was a fun project to help her get through writer's block. I needed to work on her more because she had something fantastic she needed to explore.

"What?" Noah ground out.

"She wants to do it when she can afford it herself."

"But I—"

I held up my hand. "She's not making enough on her books alone to go full time. If you weren't married to her, it wouldn't be a possibility for her."

"But I make a ton of money, and she doesn't have to stay in her shitty job that makes her cry."

I frowned. "It really makes her cry?"

Noah tightened his grip on the steering wheel. "I can't stand how unhappy she is, and I can't do anything about it. I..." he sighed again. "I love her, Mads."

"I know! And she knows that, too. Just...support her. Let her come to her own decision."

I wished I could find a man to love me the way my big brother loved his wife. Someone who wanted to fix all my problems because he could. One day. Definitely not today, especially if my brother never approved of any guy I was interested in.

"Will you reconsider moving in with us?" Noah asked when he found a parking spot on the street near my dorm building.

I shook my head. "I already paid for this year."

"I'll pay for it, Madison," he grumbled.

"Why does it bother you?"

He shot me a glare. "Because you up and transferred here without saying anything to me."

"I needed to leave Winnipeg, okay? I applied on a whim. I didn't think they'd accept me."

"Is this about what happened last year?"

I wanted to run out of his SUV. Of course, this was about what happened last year. Being the subject of revenge porn was never fun. I couldn't show my face at my old university without someone recognizing me. Or my boobs. Wished I didn't have to learn the lesson to never put your face in racy photos, but there was no going back now.

The worst part about the whole situation? I felt like I disappointed Noah.

Last year, I met a great guy, and when I told him I was still a virgin, he said we'd take it slow. Then I saw him with his tongue down another girl's throat at a party, and I broke up with him. Next thing I knew, someone had plastered the sexy photos I sent him all over social media. No surprise who did it.

My best friend Ally thought I was making a mistake transferring to get away from the gossip. Especially when I told her there was only club hockey at Franklin. But I didn't have aspirations for any of the fledgling women's leagues out there. Club hockey was fun and let me focus more on my studies. It meant I could play hockey for fun again.

"Madison," Noah said sternly, still waiting for my answer.

"Yes," I muttered. "Okay? Is that what you want to hear? Do you want to shove it in my face that I made a bad decision? Like perfect Noah Kennedy's never made a mistake before. Can't be Noah! Bow down to the hockey god!"

He rubbed his temple. "Mads, I'm not blaming you. That guy sucks, and if I ever see him again—"

"I can handle my battles myself!" I snapped. "I was the one who transferred here to solve my problem. It had nothing to do with you."

He was pissing me off. I loved my brother, I really did, but his overprotectiveness had got to go. Yes, I trusted the wrong person, but Noah didn't have to keep rubbing it in my face.

I got out of his car in a huff.

"Maddie!" he called after me.

I spun around. "What?"

"I love you, okay? D and I are here for you—that's all I'm trying to say."

Of course they did, and I knew that, but I wanted to make my own choices. Not mooch off my older brother.

"Can you let me fight my own battles?"

"Okay, " he relented. "Okay."

I waved goodbye to him and tried not to be agitated. Noah wanted the best for me, but it was annoying. I complained to Mom last night on the phone, but she said it was because I was his only sister, and he hated seeing me hurt. Noah cared, but in a very irritating big brother way that made me want to drop the gloves on him.

I rode the elevator up to my seventh-floor dorm room and thought of everything I needed to do for the coming week. I worked ahead and already had a draft of a paper that was due in two weeks, so I was in good shape.

When I moved to Philly, it surprised me to find I had a private bedroom but shared a bathroom with another student in a suite-style room. I had been expecting to share a room with another student. I had chatted with my suitemate Ari a little already. She was a third year, too, but she wasn't a transfer like me.

She was shy but stood out in a crowd with her brightly colored hair in a mix of blue, purple, and pink. Even though we had separate rooms, we got along great, and she was one of the first friends I made at Franklin. We had bonded over our love of smutty romance books. I was still trying to find my place on the hockey team, and when I wasn't doing that, I was burying myself in my studies, so it was nice to have one person to hang with. Even if it was just to get dinner.

When I walked into our suite, I saw Ari's bedroom door open, but alarm ran through me at the sound of her sniffling. "Hey, you okay?"

She shook her head.

I walked into her bedroom and saw her eyes rimmed with tears. "What happened?"

"I told Jack I was bisexual, and he broke up with me."

"What?" I snarled.

Ari confessed she was bisexual a couple of weeks ago. Her parents were a little confused at first but said they'd love her no matter what. She had been working up the courage to tell her boyfriend. To be honest, I met him once, and he seemed like a douche.

"Why did he break up with you?" I asked.

"He said he didn't want to be with someone who was more likely to cheat," she blubbered.

"What an asshole! That's not how bisexuality works."

Being a female athlete, I've had many teammates who were gay or bi or even pan over the years. Her ex being biphobic pissed me off. I always believed you should love who you love and not care what people think.

"I know," she agreed.

"I'm sorry, Ari."

"I really loved him."

"You wanna grab a drink and complain about the shitty men in our lives?" I offered.

She wiped her eyes. "Maybe. What shitty ones are in yours?"

I groaned. "Remember I told you about the guy I hooked up with at my brother's wedding?"

"Right, the hockey player who didn't want to help you with 'operation lose it.' "

I laughed. I had told her about my unfortunate virginity problem, and she made a joke about it being 'operation lose it.' Which so far had been unsuccessful. Not that I had been trying all that much.

"He lives with my brother."

Her mouth dropped open. "No wonder he didn't want to piss him off."

I groaned. "You know what's the worst part?"

"What?"

"He's still so fucking hot!"

That made her laugh, and I was glad I could make her smile. I couldn't stand when any of my friends were in pain. Fuck her ex. She'd find someone better. I was sure of it.

She wiped her eyes. "Thanks, Maddie. I think I'll take you up on that drink."

"Local Hangout?" I asked.

She nodded. "Gimme a few."

I went into my room and dropped my bag off. I wanted to change if we were going out. I was wearing yoga pants and a hoodie, fine for lounging around, but not if we were going out. And hey, maybe I'd find someone at Local Hangout to take away my pesky virginity. Probably not, though. That would be rude to do to Ari.

I changed into a pair of jeans and an off-the-shoulder top that was casual but not too much. I checked my phone and noticed a couple of social media notifications. I swiped through them, but there was one notification that gave me pause.

MCally14 started following you.

I stared at the notification and then clicked through to the profile. It didn't shock me when the first image was of Matt Callahan wearing that pinstriped suit at my brother's wedding. In the photo, he had his arm around my brother, and they wore big smiles. I touched my heart when I read his heartfelt caption.

Congrats to my boy Kennedy on his wedding! Your friendship and mentorship on and off the ice mean more to me than you'll ever know. Thanks to you and D for basically adopting me!

Matt was much more eloquent in his words than I gave him credit for, assuming he was just another dumb jock. No wonder he didn't want to piss off Noah by sleeping with me.

That hadn't stopped him from liking a bunch of my photos, most of them from the wedding. Which meant he had to go far down my feed to look at them. I scrolled down his own feed, but he didn't post all that often.

Ari walked into my room. "You ready?"

"Yup!"

We rode the elevator down to the lobby and walked the few blocks to Local Hangout. Yes, that was literally the bar's name. You'd expect something divey for a college bar, but it gave off hipster vibes. Ari loved it because they had great vegan offerings and craft beer. Eh, beer was beer to me, but I'd admit it was better than the swill they had at any kegger.

The bar was packed when we got there, but we muscled our way through and found two spots at the bar. Ari looked sad, so I bought the first round. I felt eyes on me as Ari asked me to tell her something good, and I told her about trying to convince my sister-in-law to publish her adult romance.

"Oooh. I liked her other books. They were cute, but not my usual thing," Ari said.

"They're great, but this would be off-brand for her."

Ari pinned me with a curious look. "You're a marketing major, right?"

"Guilty! I wrote a paper last year on influencer marketing and impressed my professor."

I felt someone nudge me, but I ignored it and continued telling Ari my dreams of owning a PR company or working for a major publisher one day. I loved books, and if I got to work in the industry, it would be a dream come true.

"Hey, can I buy you a drink?" a voice purred in my ear.

I reared back, noticing that the drunk guy next to me was too close for comfort.

"No. Thank you," I told him, polite and firm.

I tried to go back to my conversation, but the guy grabbed my arm. Before I could push him away, a dark shadow crossed over his face.

"Hey, sweet pea. Sorry to keep you waiting," a familiar voice said from behind me.

Sweet pea? What?

Before I could even register what was going on, muscular arms spun me around, and soft lips pressed against mine. I melted into the familiar kiss, not even thinking about who they were attached to.

CHAPTER SIX

MATT

Damn, her lips on mine felt good. Forgetting this was a ruse, I slid my hands through her silky dark locks and deepened the kiss. She let me taste inside her mouth and pressed up against me like she yearned for it. It was the kind of kiss that had my body tingling and desperate for more.

I had only walked over and ambushed her with this kiss because I saw that guy bothering her. I might not have noticed her if it wasn't for her friend's bright purple hair. Once my buddy Ty pointed it out, I stilled at the sight of the gorgeous brunette, salivating at her painted-on jeans and sun-kissed skin peeking out from her off-the-shoulder top.

Then I saw that guy put his hands on her, and my resolve buckled. I forgot why I needed to stay away, but instead, I needed to mark her as mine. Forgetting that her brother would kill me if he ever found out about this.

The thought of Noah was the blood-chilling reminder that forced me to tear my mouth from hers. Her eyes fluttered open, and once the shock wore off, her mouth turned into a hard line. Yeah, she was pissed at me.

Her eyes scorched across me, putting distance between us and silently telling me where to shove it.

Despite Local Hangout being a college bar, I hadn't expected to run into her tonight. It surprised me when Ty said he wanted to go to the bar rather than join the rager his teammates were throwing. But he knew I preferred it here because it was more chill, and I rarely got recognized. Now if Noah or TJ walked through the door, it would be a different story. Not for a rookie like me struggling to get ice time.

I looked over Maddie's shoulder, and that creepy guy had moved on to another girl already. "He's gone."

"Good. You can go," she said, dismissing me as she took a sip of her beer and turned back to her friend.

"Hey, asshole, you gonna introduce me, or what?" Ty asked me.

Maddie's friend laughed, her colorful hair bouncing with her motions. Now that I looked at her, her hair wasn't exactly purple. It was a collage of blue, pink, and purple. I think chicks called that 'mermaid hair' or some shit. She was tiny next to Maddie's statuesque figure, but she was cute in that art school kind of way.

"I'm Ari," she introduced herself.

"Matt. This is Ty," I told both girls and gestured to my friend. Ty was a pale guy with short king energy and the life of the party.

Maddie squinted at Ty. "Aren't you dating my captain?"

Captain?

Ty hung his head. "Who Elsa? Nah, she dumped my ass."

Oh. Right. Ty's ex was the captain of the women's hockey team here. I had no idea Maddie played hockey.

Maddie's eyebrows rose at Ty's downtrodden expression. "Umm."

Ty bellowed out a laugh. "Don't worry about it, dude! E's great, but she's too serious to keep this player tied down."

I rolled my eyes.

Ty could be such a douche, but he was my best friend, so I let him slide. Also, it was one hundred percent a front.

"I got dumped, too," Ari said with a frown.

"Let me buy you a beer in solidarity," Ty said and gave her his signature grin. Ari smiled back at him, leaving Maddie and me standing there, pretending not to notice the tension surrounding us.

Maddie crossed her arms over her chest. "Sweet pea? Really?"

I grinned. "Sorry, that slipped out. It worked to get that asshole to leave you alone, right?"

She tipped her head down in agreement.

"Maddie, can we..." I trailed off.

I couldn't blame her for hating me. I had zero regrets about hooking up with her, but there was no way in hell I was going behind Noah's back. I had an excuse at the wedding since I didn't know she was his sister, but not now. That would be a betrayal.

"What, Matt?" she barked out, anger laced in her tone.

"Can you two grab a drink and resolve whatever this is?" Ty asked.

Ari's mouth dropped open. "Oh! You're him."

I felt my brow crease, and I looked between the two women.

Maddie shrugged. "Yeah, the douche who ran away. Literally."

I turned to her. "Can we start over?"

She ground her teeth together. "Fine."

I held out my hand. "Hi. I'm Matt Callahan."

She stared down at my hand, and her friend nudged her. She rolled her eyes but gripped my hand in hers. "Madison Kennedy. Call me Maddie."

"Buy you a drink?" I asked, giving her my winning smile.

"Fine."

I eyed Ty and Ari, and he was already putting on the charm, twirling a strand of Ari's colorful hair while she laughed at a joke that probably wasn't funny.

I sighed.

"Problem?" Maddie asked.

I gestured to Ty. "He's laying it on thick already."

Maddie peered at her friend and shrugged. "Maybe she needs a good rebound to get over her ex. I didn't like him. At least someone's getting laid." She mumbled that last part under her breath, hoping I wouldn't hear it.

"D said you transferred to Franklin," I said, trying to change the subject.

"Yup. I needed to get out of Winnipeg. This is a good school."

She was right about that. It impressed me she got in because Franklin was an Ivy League school. That must have meant her grades were killer. That was the only reason Ty went here. He was pre-med, and Franklin had an amazing medical program. He wouldn't be playing club hockey if the school wasn't so good.

"Don't sell yourself short. This is an awesome school."

She beamed at that, and maybe I softened her a little

with the compliment. "I didn't know you lived with my brother. I get that it's complicated."

"Your brother's a good friend. I..."

"I know. I get it," she finished for me.

If I didn't live with her brother, maybe I'd be more inclined to break the code. Hell, Benny did it with Rox. Although Rox was scary, and I don't think there was anything her twin brother could have said to her to make her back down.

Maddie finished her beer, and I flagged the bartender down to grab her another one. She gave me a small smile in thanks, and we looked amused as Ty pointed to a curvy blonde. "What about that one?" he asked Ari.

"What are you doing, asshole?" I asked.

Ari laughed. "He's trying to guess which women are my type."

"Oh."

Ari laughed it off and shook her head back and forth, which made Ty laugh.

"You don't put enough power in your shot," Maddie said to me, pulling me away from our friends' conversation.

I nearly choked. Her brother said the same thing last week. "Excuse me?"

"Well, if we're gonna be friends, you'll take my friendly hockey advice, right?" she asked, giving me an evil grin.

"That's what Noah said," I grumbled.

"He's right. But he always says that to me too, so don't feel special," she said and made a face.

I grinned.

Noah was the most talented hockey player I'd ever met. That was why it was so great he took me under his wing when I got the call up to the big leagues.

"You gonna come to the game tomorrow and give me more pointers later?"

She shook her head. "Nope. I got practice and a night class."

"Saturday?"

"I've got a game."

"Well, shit sweet pea, how's this friendship gonna work?"

She laughed, and when the smile spread across her face, I knew I was wearing down her walls. Yeah, it was a dick move to run away, but holy shit, I couldn't date Noah's sister. He would kill me. Dinah seemed on board, though, but that didn't matter. As much as it pained me, I couldn't start anything with Maddie.

But fuck me, did she smell good—and look good too.

Get your shit together, Callahan.

"Again with the sweet pea?" she asked, but her eyes twinkled.

I took a pull off my beer and winked at her. "So, you play hockey too?"

She nodded.

"What position?"

"Center."

"Like me. And your brother."

Her chin jutted up in agreement. "Taught me everything I know."

My gaze roamed down her body. Her lean, long legs looked powerful from skating, and she had small but defined muscles in her arms. She was lean but athletic, and I hadn't recognized that the night we met. It all made sense now.

"Matt," she warned.

I snapped my head up, realizing I got caught staring. "Hmm?"

"Stop looking at me like that."

"Like what?"

She sucked her bottom lip into her teeth. God, she looked sexy like that.

NO! Get your shit together, Callahan. She is off-limits. Very much so.

But she couldn't answer because she turned to Ari, and I mirrored her movement, only to find Ty with his tongue down Ari's throat.

I rubbed a hand down my face. Goddamnit, Ty. "Bro, come on!"

Ty pulled away and gave me a grin. "Come on, Cally, you know what they say. 'The best way to get over someone is to get underneath someone else!' Right, Ari?"

Ari gave him a flirty laugh.

"Must be nice," Maddie muttered into her beer.

I frowned and gave Ty a look, but he shrugged and went back to kissing Ari.

I blew out an annoyed breath. "I'm sorry."

Maddie laughed. "For what? They're both single and can do what they want."

I shook my head at my best friend's antics, annoyance clawing its way up my chest. Maddie picked at the label on her beer and avoided my gaze. The awkward silence between us felt like it could stretch on forever.

"What were you helping Dinah with today?" I asked.

I needed to change the subject to anything that would get me to stop thinking about her lips on mine again.

Maddie brightened. "Oh! I'm helping market her books. She's awful at it."

"Oh? You know anything about doing sponsored

content? My agent set me up with an athleisure brand. I'm supposed to post stuff, but I keep forgetting to do it."

"MATT!" she chastised. "I can help. Did they give you photos or ad copy to use in your posts? What are the guidelines?"

I rubbed the back of my neck. "Uhhh."

I was pretty sure that was in an email my agent sent me that I was ignoring. He kept yelling at me about it. I wasn't even sure why this company reached out to me. I wasn't big like Noah or TJ. Or even Riley. My agents said some buzzwords about breakout younger players. Whatever that meant.

She pulled out her phone and began typing away. "I can help. I'll come over tomorrow before you leave for the game and set something up."

I blinked back at her. "Really?"

She nodded. "I'd love to work for a PR firm or do social media. I work with a lot of them for books, but this could be great practice for my future career."

I had no clue what she was talking about, but it was cute to see her face light up when she talked about it. The sexiest thing of all was when someone was passionate about their work.

"Hey," Ty interrupted. "We're getting out of here."

I gave him a warning look, but he gave me that goofy grin of his.

Maddie had a perplexed look on her face, and I saw her mouth, 'are you okay?' to her friend, who nodded back at her in confirmation. Ty and Ari left hand in hand, leaving Maddie and I at the crowded bar with matching confused looks on our faces.

"Did we just get ditched?" I asked.

She shrugged. "Good for her. Her ex was a dick. He broke up with her because she came out as bisexual."

"Fuck that guy. One of my teammates is bi. Who gives a shit?"

"Right, Blaise. And so is Rox," she reminded me.

"And Rox," I agreed, and I downed the rest of my beer.

Maddie set her empty beer on the bar. "I better get going."

"Let me walk you home."

She shook her head. "That's okay."

"Maddie, your brother wouldn't forgive me if something happened to you.'

She groaned. "I'm fine."

"It wasn't an offer. I'm walking you home," I said firmly.

Noah might not like me hanging with his sister, but he'd freak out if I let her walk home alone at night. No fucking way.

"Fine," she said but stomped away.

I cashed out, shaking my head that Ty left me to pay for his drinks. I'd give him that one since he just got dumped. Not a shock he jumped onto the first woman he met.

Maddie was waiting outside for me, and as soon as she saw me, she walked on. I had to jog to catch up to her. She had legs for days, and I found my eyes lingering on the sway of her hips. I chastised myself before catching up to walk beside her, weaving through the busy streets of West Philadelphia. It wasn't a far walk until we came upon a high rise with a lot of people wearing Franklin U apparel coming in and out.

"Well, this is me," she said. "I'm coming over to help D tomorrow anyway, so we can work on the stuff you need to do."

"You'd really do that?"

"Sure! I love doing that."

"That's awesome. I don't know how to thank you."

She wrinkled her nose. "There's one thing you can do for me."

The color drained from my face. "Maddie, I'm not taking your virginity."

She scowled. "That's not what I was going to say!"

"Then what?"

"I need a wingman."

I arched an eyebrow. "Why me?"

"I want a guy's perspective. I know you're super busy with hockey, but maybe one night you could help me pick out someone decent."

"Maddie, it should be with someone you love. You should want it to be special."

She shook her head. "I don't care who it's with. I want it to be done so I'm not this virgin loser anymore."

"You're not a loser. But if that's what you want, I'll help you. Find a nice guy who will treat you right."

She beamed and reached out to squeeze my arm. Shock went through me at her touch, and if she felt it too, she ignored it. "Thanks, Matt. I'll see you tomorrow."

I watched her walk away, making sure she got into her dorm okay. Definitely wasn't watching her ass. Not at all. I wasn't sure what I was getting myself into, but I had a feeling this was a terrible idea.

CHAPTER SEVEN

MADDIE

I glared at Matt. "You're giving me an 'I don't want to be here' look."

He rubbed a hand across his clean-shaven jaw. I made him shave when I got here because he had too much stubble, and I wanted him to look the part. His image was clean-cut, with that luscious thick hair styled impeccably. He didn't rock the flow like my brother, but it was the kind of hair you wanted to sink your hands into.

Dammit. I couldn't think about that. Despite our kiss the other night, he made it clear where we stood. Unfortunately.

"I don't want to do this, but my agent made me," he growled.

I raised an eyebrow at him.

He gave me a pained look. "Sorry."

I pulled my camera away from my face and peered at him. I had him sitting on the staircase at my brother's house. Noah and Dinah had a gorgeous modern townhome, and the open staircase looked like a perfect place for photos, but Matt was being difficult.

"How about we do this outside?" I suggested.

He furrowed his brow. "Why?"

"I think it would be better. The exterior has the brick-yet-modern look. It would make the photos come out great."

"Fine," he grumbled.

For me doing him a favor, he sure was grumpy about it.

"Listen to her!" Dinah called down from her office on the second floor.

A grin spread across my face at D coming to my aid, but then I frowned. "Get back to your edits!"

I smirked when I was met with silence.

When I got here, I told Dinah to get working on her word count, and once I was done with Matt, we'd talk marketing. Someone had to crack the whip. My brother gave in to her demands too much, despite him trying to get her to work, too.

Once outside, I instructed Matt to sit on the steps; he obliged but still looked irritable. I set down my camera and repositioned him, angling his head down a little and having him show off the logo on his hoodie. When he said an athleisure company wanted to work with him, he neglected to mention it was one of the most popular brands. His agent should have a professional from the brand working with him, not me.

I pushed his hair behind his ear, and he flinched at my touch. "Sorry, just trying to make it look good."

"Sorry. I'm grumpy."

"What's wrong? I promise this won't take long. I'll snap a bunch of shots, and you pick the best. Then I can help you schedule this."

I didn't have class until late, so I had all the time to help

Matt with this before he had to get to the arena. But it was like he got up on the wrong side of the bed today.

"Nothing," he muttered.

"Okay..." I trailed off but didn't believe him.

I stepped back, put my camera up to my face, and took some shots. He was still a grumpasaurus.

"Matt, look like you enjoy my company," I said.

The crease in his brow deepened. "Why would you say that?"

"Because you're not smiling in any of these. Like you hate me."

"I don't hate you, sweet pea."

I gave him an annoyed look, especially with that cheesy nickname again. "Doesn't look like it."

"I'm a healthy scratch today."

Oooh. Well, that made sense. Definitely sucked being on the bench for no reason. Sometimes, it was just to shake up the lines. Other times, you pissed off the coach, and he was teaching you a lesson. Or Coach needed to give someone else minutes.

I looked at Matt's stats this morning, and he was doing well. He played two seasons at the minor league affiliate before he got the call up last year when the old captain got injured. He made the team this year, but he was still on a two way contract. He put up points in his last game, so it didn't make sense for Coach to bench him.

"Maybe Coach needed to shake things up."

"I want to prove myself. I belong on the team," he grumbled.

I put my camera down. "Okay...I get that."

"No, you don't."

I tilted my head down in a nod. "Yes, I do. Do you know what it's like being Noah Kennedy's baby sister? Every coach in pee wee assumed I'd be just as good. I love hockey, but people think I should live and breathe it and want to join one of those women's leagues. People put a lot of pressure on you when they learn your brother's a legit hockey superstar."

He held up his hands. "Okay, okay. I'm sorry."

"Geez, now you sound like my brother."

The corner of his lips upturned into a smile, and I quickly snapped a photo of him. Right at that moment, as the afternoon sun glinted across his chestnut-colored hair, he looked like a God. The kind I'd want to worship on my knees.

Fuck, I was horny.

"That's perfect. Don't move," I told him, and I snapped a few more shots. These were going to be awesome.

After taking a couple more, I pulled my camera away from my face and checked my watch. "I got it."

"Really?"

"Let's go inside, and you can pick one. Then I'll do edits on it and send it over to you so you can post with all the ad copy and such."

His gaze clouded over.

Okay...I might have gone into work mode on him. "Help me pick, and I'll do the rest."

We went inside the house and sat on the couch together while I scrolled through my camera and asked him his opinion. Matt's thigh pressed against mine as he leaned over to look at my camera. I had to tell myself to breathe because his big body pressed against mine had my libido thinking naughty thoughts. God, I wanted to be naughty with him so bad.

He pointed at the screen. "Go back."

In the photo, he was smiling like I wasn't taking these to

help with this sponsorship. As if that flirty smile was all for me and he was happy to see me.

He put a hand on my thigh, and I hitched in a breath. "This one?" I asked to quell the nerves.

He squeezed my thigh. "You're amazing. This is great."

I slid away from him and grabbed my laptop. I loaded the photo and opened my editing software.

"Thanks," Matt said.

"Sure," I told him brightly.

Matt stretched his arm over the back of the couch, silently watching me work. This was exactly what I wanted to do with my life. I hoped I could find work with a PR firm after I graduated.

An alarm blared upstairs, and I slid further down the couch. If Noah woke up from his pregame nap and saw Matt and me cozy on the couch, he'd blow a gasket.

"Can you email me that?" Matt asked. "I gotta get dressed for the game."

I waved him off. I sat crossed-legged on the couch and touched up the photo until it was perfect. I then emailed it to Matt and gave him the copy to include with hashtags.

My brother came down the steps wearing a suit, and his face lit up when he saw me. "Hey, I want to talk to you about something."

I closed my laptop and steeled myself for yet another argument. I told him last night I didn't want to move here, but Dinah already warned me he'd ask again.

"What's up?" I asked.

"I want to pay you for the work you're doing for Dinah."

Oh. I hadn't expected him to say that. I hadn't thought about working this semester due to having a bigger course load since some of my credits didn't transfer over.

He frowned. "But...I'm confused about whether you can do that with your visa."

"I'm not on a visa," I reminded him. "I was born here, and Mom made me apply for dual citizenship, remember?"

He glared at me. "That's right. You ruined our family vacation to Disney World by coming early."

I laughed. "Aren't you over that already? You were five!"

He shook his head with a laugh. "So rude."

"Get over it!"

"So, anyway, send me an email with your rates, and we'll figure it out."

"Sounds good to me."

First, I had to figure out what those rates should be. I should reach out to one of my blogger friends and ask for their advice. Maybe look at what some of the publishing PR companies charged.

"You've been here for a while helping her," Noah said.

"I was helping Matt, too."

A scowl formed across his face. "With what?"

"Sponsored content. Like when I helped you with that beard wash ad we did last year. Am I not allowed to be friends with your teammate?"

"He's older than you."

"Noah, he's one year older than me. We ran into each other last night, and I agreed to help him. Don't read into it."

As if on cue, Matt came up from the basement, and I tried not to stare. Even if he was a healthy scratch, he had to dress the part for the game. The sight of him in that blue pin-striped suit from the wedding had the memories of our night together rearing to the surface of my brain.

Noah got up from the couch, brushed off non-existent

lint from his pants, and walked back upstairs to say goodbye to Dinah.

I checked my phone and saw a notification on my lock screen. I opened it and saw I was tagged in something. I beamed that Matt had tagged me as the photo credit for the sponsored ad. I checked his hashtags and then scrolled through all the comments. Jealousy reared its ugly head at all the women commenting on how hot he looked.

"Good?" Matt asked.

"Perfect!" I said with a cheery smile. "Hopefully, the brand likes it. Let me know. I'd love the feedback."

A sly grin spread across his face. "You really like this stuff, huh?"

"It's my calling."

He shuffled his feet but glanced away when Noah and Dinah descended the steps. I watched with a pang of envy in my chest as Dinah stood on the steps and kissed my brother goodbye. He adored his wife so much; I could only hope to find that one day.

"Ready, bud?" Noah asked Matt.

Matt nodded to me, and then he and my brother walked out the door. As soon as the door slammed shut, Dinah crossed her arms over her chest and gave me a 'spill' look.

I grabbed my laptop and followed her up to her office.

"How did everything go with Matt?" she asked.

"Okay. But he was grumpy."

She cringed. "He's pissed he got benched. He thinks he's going to be put on waivers."

"What does Noah think?"

She tilted her head to one side. "Why does it matter to you?"

"Just curious if he's sticking around," I lied.

She narrowed her eyes at me. "Uh-huh."

"You didn't tell Noah, right?"

She shook her head. "I'm not opening that can of worms. Are you interested in Matt like that?"

I put a finger on my lips as I thought about it.

I was pissed yesterday, but when he kissed me, it reminded me of how good he was at it. The fact he didn't want to piss off my brother made me like him more. I may have ulterior motives for asking him to be my wingman. His kiss reminded me of how good we fit together, and I hoped we could hook up again. As long as we kept it quiet and never, ever told my brother.

"Yes," I muttered. "But he's afraid of Noah and breaking the code. He's pretty firm on it."

Her eyes twinkled. "We can warm Noah up to the idea. I'm in your corner, so let me know. I can work my magic on your brother."

I blanched. I didn't want to know what that meant, but I had a feeling it was something sexual. Dinah said what she was thinking. Which I loved, but ew, I didn't want to know about her sex life.

"Anyway..." I drawled out, changing the subject. "Let's talk about you getting your word count done. Noah talked about me doing more work for you."

She let out an agitated breath. "I need a PA. I took off today at the day job because I need to meet this deadline, but I ended up doing all the admin tasks you told me to do."

"DINAH!" I scolded. "Let me do that for you. How many words did you write today?"

"Two thousand."

"Okay, good. I have practice today, so I only have a little while to talk, and then I got to hop back to Franklin."

She frowned. "You're not coming to the game?"

I shook my head. "Like I said, I have practice, and then I have a night class."

"Okay, well, let's talk about it. I need the help."

"Noah wants you to quit your day job."

She rolled her eyes. "I'm not there yet."

"That secret project could really help you."

Her face colored. "I'm not sure I'm comfortable publishing it. It was fun to write, but..."

"It's not your brand," I finished her thought. "That's what having a secret pen name's for."

She chewed on her lip. "That's what Fi said."

"She's right. Let's brainstorm a name."

"You're annoying."

"Persistent!"

I stayed at the house for another hour, brainstorming and helping her talk through plot struggles with her book. Then, I had to jet for practice.

Before I walked into the locker room, I saw a text from Matt.

MATT: Thanks for the help today. You're amazing. I'm grumpy.

ME: Wow. I had NO idea.

MATT: Don't be sassy, sweet pea.

ME: You love it! Sorry you can't play tonight. Let me know if you need help with another sponsored ad. I'm your girl.

"Ooh, does new girl have a secret lover?" Kiira, our goaltender, crooned as we walked in together.

I belted out a laugh at the blonde goofball. "No! Just a friend. Ready for me to fire shots at your head today?"

"Oh, bring it, Kennedy!"

I grinned. "Oh, I will. You're gonna be eating my pucks!"

The goaltender was always the weirdest one on the team, but I loved Kiira. She was fun and, so far, one of the few players I bonded with. That was okay. It took time to get used to a new team dynamic. At least one thing in my life was sorting itself out. I'd figure out the rest this year at Franklin.

CHAPTER EIGHT

MATT

"Bar tonight?" I asked, looking around the room at my sweaty teammates.

It pissed me off that I was a healthy scratch tonight, and I needed to release this tension. Earlier, Riley had pulled me aside and told me not to worry about being benched. He took the mantle of Captain to heart after G retired. He was a good guy, and I appreciated it, but it still didn't make me feel better.

I spent most of the game watching from the executive box and scrolling social media. That was bad. Half the time, I scrolled through Maddie's account like a lovesick puppy, and the other was spent reading all the tweets from fans bemoaning how we sucked.

That was why Noah advised me to not check my mentions and to not, under any circumstances, search my name. I listened to him on that one, but it was hard when you got tagged in stuff. No wonder so many of my teammates didn't do social media.

TJ gave a sad shake of his head. "Nah. Max had a rough day with the kids."

Before I got here, everyone said TJ was the biggest party boy, but lately, he rushed home to his family. Max let him loose on the road—that's when I saw the wildcard come out. But at home, he'd fallen into settling down as a good husband and father. Which meant the boys ragged on him non-stop about it.

"Really?" Benny asked. "I never thought I'd see the day. TJ 'party boy' Desjardins's an old man!"

TJ threw a towel at Benny. "Shut it. Not like you can't wait to get home to my sister. Rather spend time with my family than hang out with you jerkoffs."

"Well, I'm in. Buy me a beer, Cally," Benny told me.

I laughed. "Okay."

"I could use a drink," Noah said.

"Who else?" I asked.

Cully already snuck out of here. He wasn't one to go out for drinks when we were home. He was more content rushing home to his girl and their kids. I roomed with him on the road and knew that was mostly because they were total nerds and he wanted to get some gaming in with her. A lot of the older guys with kids shied away, especially if it was a school night.

"Nope. My wife's pregnant and tired," Riley announced.

We all stared at him at the revelation.

"For real, dude?" Noah asked.

He gave us an infectious grin. "Yup. Baby number two, we're excited."

"D didn't say anything to me," Noah grumbled.

Riley laughed. "Fi asked her to keep it a secret until we were sure."

A scowl formed across Noah's face. "She's not supposed to keep things from me. She knows I can keep a secret."

Panic flared up in my chest because Dinah was keeping something else from Noah. I'd be so fucked if he ever found out I hooked up with his sister. In my defense, I thought she was Dinah's sister, not his. How was I supposed to know that? It's not my fault Noah never introduced us.

Benny clapped Riley on the back. "Congrats, man."

We all gave our captain congratulations and worked out who all wanted to grab a drink at the bar tonight. Naturally, we went to Eileen's Tavern. Even though Blaise moaned about it because it was his dad's bar, and he got razzed by his little brother who worked there.

I could use a drink. Maybe it would soften my grumpy mood. It was one in a million to play in this league, and not everyone came out as a superstar, but I wanted to prove myself. I couldn't do that if I wasn't even riding pine, but sitting out completely.

I drove over to the bar with Noah since he was my ride anyway.

"You're agitated tonight," he said.

I rubbed the back of my neck. "I got benched."

"I don't think it was because of anything you did. Coach is shifting the lines up."

"I don't want to get put on waivers."

"You won't."

"Okay," I muttered, not quite believing him.

Noah was number two in his draft year, and he hit the ice with fire under his skates, making the team at eighteen. At twenty-six, he was killing it, and his opinion meant everything to me. His mentorship and guidance were why hanging with his sister was a bad idea. It had been torture sitting next to her on the couch earlier today while we scrolled through photos. God, she had been so cute how she got excited about helping me. But Maddie Kennedy needed to be safely in the friendzone. My career and my nuts counted on it.

"Mads did alright today?" he asked.

"Huh?"

"With the ad you needed help with. She said you ran into each other last night."

I inclined my head in recognition. "Right. My buddy goes to Franklin, and he just got dumped. Ran into her at the bar."

He frowned. "I don't like her going out by herself."

"She wasn't by herself, but...I made sure she got to her dorm safely."

Noah sighed in relief. "Thanks, bro. Appreciate you looking out for her."

"Of course."

Not gonna mention her friend ditched her, and that's why I walked her to her dorm. Or that she wanted me to help her find a guy to deflower her. Still needed to iron out those details, but I was hoping she'd forget about it. Why she wanted me to help and not one of her girl friends was a mystery to me.

"She doesn't make the best choices," he admitted, the frown still etched across his face.

I couldn't ask him to elaborate because he parked his car and cut the engine.

And after that sobering thought, I needed several drinks.

When we entered the bar, Noah's face lit up at seeing Dinah at the bar talking to a tall brunette. It took me a second of staring at the stranger's ass to figure out it was Maddie.

Dinah practically jumped into Noah's arms, and I made a face at spying her tongue down his throat. I'd give them a pass since they were newlyweds. D might say I wasn't cramping their style, but there was definitely a reason I preferred living in their basement.

I went to the bar and ordered a beer. I shot a smile at Maddie. "I thought you weren't coming to the game?"

"I didn't," she shot back. "Came here after my night class. I didn't even watch the game and barely caught the post-game presser."

I grabbed my drink from the bartender and threw a tip on the bar. "Hey, it impressed my agent with the work today."

I had texted her earlier about it, but I wanted to make sure she knew she did a good job.

Her blue eyes brightened. "Really?"

"Thanks to you."

She beamed, and it was cute watching her chest puff out in pride. She should be proud of her hard work. I glanced across the bar and noticed Dinah had led Noah over toward Rox and Benny, distracting him.

Was Dinah trying to set up Maddie and me?

Maddie took a pull off her beer and scanned the bar. "When will you uphold your end of the bargain?"

"Not with any of these assholes."

She frowned. "Why not?"

"Too old for you."

"Come on! The guy at the other end of the bar's cute."

I glanced over and saw a guy with greying hair nursing a beer. "He looks like he's forty."

"Ageist!" she teased.

I shrugged and took another sip of my beer.

"What if I like an older man?" she asked with a cheeky grin across her face.

"Okay...but not your dad's age."

"Why not? Maybe I have a daddy kink."

I groaned. This girl was gonna be the death of me. My dick wanted to yell, 'pick me,' but yeah, no, I wasn't going there.

I scanned the bar. There were a lot of attractive women hanging off the words of my teammates and South Philly bros trying to get lucky with them when my teammates weren't interested. None of those guys were good enough for Maddie.

"Tell you what," I began and pulled out my phone to check my schedule. "We find you a guy closer to your age. How about some night I have off, okay?"

Her face lit up. "Really?"

"Sure," I lied.

Did I want another guy to be with her? To feel her soft lips on theirs? Absolutely not. But I owed her for helping me out earlier, and there was no way I could be that guy. Not if I valued my friendship with her brother.

She grabbed my arm. "Matt, that would be amazing. I've got zero game. I need a wingman."

I cocked my head at her, processing what she said. How could this gorgeous girl have zero game? All she had to do to get a man to fall in love with her was to flash those pearly whites. Maddie was a smokeshow, and she didn't need my help. I was pretty sure that old guy at the bar was ready to propose. But fuck him. He wasn't worthy of her greatness.

"I travel tomorrow, but what about next Wednesday?" I suggested.

She opened her phone and checked something, her cute

nose wrinkling as she thought. "Okay. I'm free, and it's university. There's usually a party going on."

Ah, college parties. That wasn't something I had experienced. After getting drafted at eighteen, I never did the college route. Some guys played college hockey until they got sent to the minors, but I went straight to our minor team in Reading. Played there a few years until last year when I got called up. My life had been nothing but hockey since I could skate. College had never been something I considered, but...a college party could be fun at least.

"Okay, it's a date," I relented.

"YAY! Thank you, thank you, thank you," she gushed.

I knew it was good I was helping her, but it didn't help the rock that lodged itself in my gut.

Christ, this guy was a douche, and Maddie was hanging onto his every word. This was the third guy she'd shown an interest in since she dragged me to a house party on campus. I regretted coming as soon as we entered the house. I was beat from a shitty game in Toronto last night, and this guy had done nothing but talk about himself and stare at Maddie's tits.

Sweet pea had a type—douchey hockey players. Not that I was a saint, but man, was this guy a fucking pylon. Didn't need to get on the ice with him to know that. Guys who talked about their success on the ice this much were full of shit. Even TJ didn't talk up his game this much.

"Right, babe?" he asked her.

She smiled up at him. "Right."

I pulled myself away from my thoughts. Maddie gave me a look to ask what I thought, and I raised my eyebrow back at her. I didn't know why she needed a wingman. If this was the kind of guy she was interested in, she didn't need my help. To him, Maddie was just another pair of tits for him to stare at.

"You know who needs to get cut from the Bulldogs?" he asked, staring at the Bulldogs v-neck Maddie wore.

"Who?" I demanded.

I don't think he recognized me. In my backward Bulldogs cap and plain black t-shirt, I blended in with the college athletes.

"Kennedy," he sneered. "What a useless waste of money."

I watched Maddie clench her fists, and her features hardened.

"Bro, are you for real?" I asked.

But Maddie didn't need me to stand up for her brother. "You don't know what you're talking about. My brother works harder than you ever have in your entire life. He has more talent in his pinky than your whole body."

Dude-bro's face morphed into an 'oh shit' expression, and I shook my head with a laugh as he looked to me for guidance. "Come on, sweet pea, let's get out of here."

"Fine by me," she huffed. She muttered under her breath, and I led her outside of the party, guiding her with my hand on the small of her back.

"What an asshole," I said.

She dipped her head down in a silent agreement. "Thanks for having my back. That guy was hot but not too bright and had zero hockey sense."

I walked beside her, not sure what direction we were heading, but she was definitely done with the party. It was still early enough that I was down to hang with her if she wanted.

"Is that important to you? A guy who knows his hockey?" I asked.

She shrugged. "Not entirely, but if you're going to talk shit on my brother, you better back it up."

"No criticism from me. I learn so much from him."

"I know I complain about Noah, but I love him. I really do. He just..."

"Can be too overprotective?"

She nodded.

"Is there a reason he's like that?"

Her mouth sank into a sad smile as we walked side by side back to her dorm room. "Yes."

"You don't have to tell me."

"There's a reason I transferred to Franklin," she muttered.

"We don't have to talk about it."

She released a tight breath. "Do you know what revenge porn is?"

Oh no. That would explain why Noah looked like he wanted to kill me at his wedding when I danced with Maddie. Holy shit, what an asshole.

"What happened?" I asked.

"Was dating a guy last year. I told him I was still a virgin, and he said he wanted to work up to sex. We did a lot of oral and sexted, so I felt like we were almost there...then I went to a party and found his tongue down another girl's throat."

"Oh, Maddie, that guy was a douche."

The pain in her voice made me want to find the guy and punch him.

"That's not the worst part. I broke up with him, and next thing I knew, I was getting DMs from literally every douche-canoe on the men's hockey team. Apparently, my private photos to him got blasted out to everyone."

White-hot rage bubbled up inside me. Because what the actual fuck? That guy did her dirty, and she got the worst of it. If anyone did that to my sister, I'd probably be protective like Noah.

"Maddie, that guy was an asshole, and you didn't deserve that."

"I know that, and I'm not ashamed that I sent nudes to my boyfriend!"

I held up a hand. "I'm not judging you. At all."

She looked down at her feet. "Noah does. The first thing he asked was why I didn't cut my face out of the photos."

"He was just looking out for you."

"Judging me," she argued in a harsh whisper.

I wasn't sure I believed that. Noah was such a great guy. If he hadn't taken me under his wing last year and mentored me, who knew if I'd even be in the league. He didn't strike me as the kind of guy who judged anyone for what they did. Although, he did say Maddie didn't make the best choices. Maybe this was what he meant.

"He wants to protect you. That never should have happened to you. You know it's not your fault, right?"

She nodded. "It sucked because I felt like the girls on the hockey team judged me too. I wanted to drop out, but Mom told me I needed to hold my head high and move on. Since then, Noah's gotten worse about being overprotective. That's why I don't want to move in with them."

"They want you to move in?"

She rolled her eyes. "Noah does. D said it's my choice, but she'll gladly have me." She yawned and checked her watch. "Anyway, thanks for coming with me. Let's do it again."

"Maybe not another house party?" I offered.

"Where else am I supposed to meet a guy who wants to fuck me and never talk to me again?"

Literally anywhere. The guy who just passed us on the street would fuck her if she asked. I really didn't understand why she needed my help to be her wingman.

"Maddie..."

"You promised to help me."

I held up my hand. "Okay, okay. I did. Let me look at my schedule, and I'll wingman for you again. I'll help you find someone decent."

She beamed, but the thought of someone else being with her left a sour taste in my mouth. I had no right to be jealous, but it didn't help my feelings raging inside me.

CHAPTER NINE

MADDIE

I frowned at a text from Matt that only depicted the puke emoji and nothing more. That was odd.

We had been texting back and forth for the past couple of weeks. He went out with me last weekend but shot down every single guy I pretended to be interested in. Here was the thing: I was picking douchebags I had no interest in on purpose because I wanted to make him jealous. I hoped Matt would see that he was the man for the job, but so far, he was resisting hard.

I set my phone down and went back to working on the paper I needed to complete for my communications class. This class was easy for me since it was a prerequisite I already did back home, but Franklin didn't accept my credits, so I was taking it again. I thought it was great to hone my writing skills, but the class was cake compared to my major classes.

My phone vibrated again, but I ignored it as I tried to

finish this last thought. It kept buzzing, and when I flipped it over, I saw Matt was trying to video call me.

Panic coursed through me as I looked down at my ratty Franklin U hoodie. It was fine for going to classes, but not great when the guy you were crushing on wanted to video chat. My hair was in a messy bun, and I didn't have makeup on. I was so not presentable for a video call.

Why was he trying to video chat with me?

I saw another text come through.

MATT: My eyes! I'm pretty sure I walked in on Noah and Dinah!

I laughed out loud, and my worries about my appearance went out the window because I was nosy and immediately called him.

Matt answered the call right away, his handsome face showing up on my phone screen as I placed it on the stand on my desk. He gave me a pained look. He wore a hoodie from the company we did the ad spot for, but he looked comfy, and I liked that casual look in men.

Before he said anything, I started laughing.

"It's not funny!" he fumed.

"It's kinda funny."

He glared at me.

"How did that even happen?" I asked because I wanted to avoid that, too. I loved that Noah was happy with Dinah, but ew, I didn't want to walk in on that.

"I came home from training with Benny, and all I saw was Dinah's head pop up from the couch as I walked in. While your brother looked a little too comfortable with his head resting back against the couch."

A laugh bubbled up inside me.

"Not funny!"

"I wouldn't want to see it either, but it *is* their house."

"Is this why you don't want to move in with them?"

I shook my head. "I told you, Noah's way too overprotective. It would be like living in prison. I'm sorry you had to deal with that, but it might not have been what you thought."

He vigorously shook his head from side to side. "Yeah, no, it was. Noah jumped up at my footsteps, and his face was beet red."

I couldn't contain another giggle. Okay, it definitely was what he thought. My brother couldn't control the way his pale face reddened when he was embarrassed.

"You poor baby," I cooed, giving him a sympathetic look.

"I need to get out of the house."

"You wanna come over?"

If I got to hang out with Matt again, one on one, maybe he'd give in. I heavily put on the flirt when we were together, but he resisted. He was still scared of my brother, but what Noah didn't know wouldn't hurt him. I knew for a fact Matt didn't confess what happened the night of my brother's wedding. Why couldn't he get behind a sneaky one-night stand? Isn't that what hockey players like him wanted?

Matt looked uneasy at my suggestion.

"Aren't we friends?" I asked.

"Yeah."

"And friends hang out, so come over. We could go to the bar and grab dinner. Or chill and watch a movie."

"Okay, sure. Let's do dinner in a couple of hours."

"Don't walk in on Noah and D again," I teased.

He shot me an annoyed look and then hung up.

I jumped up and searched through my closet. I needed

something cute to wear, even if this was a casual hang. Something that would make Matt forget I was Noah's little sister and remind him what he was missing.

Ari walked by my room a couple of minutes later on her way to the bathroom, but then she backtracked and arched an eyebrow at me. She gestured to the clothes strewn across my bed. "What's going on?"

I put my hands on my head in frustration. "I need something cute to wear to impress Matt."

"Show a lot of cleavage or wear skin-tight leggings. It's kryptonite to men."

I laughed. "Okay, true, but we're going to Local Hangout for dinner."

"Like a date?"

I shrugged. "Just as friends."

She crossed her arms over her chest. "So...is he still trying to be your wingman? Or has he caught on yet?"

I groaned. "No. He's too scared of my brother."

"Explain it to me again."

I pulled out a pair of my nicest jeans and a black tank top. I paired that with a long-sleeved white and blue plaid shirt. It would look comfy left open, like I hadn't thought too hard about what to wear.

Ari nodded when I held it up for her opinion.

"I want it to be him," I explained.

"But why? If you want to get laid, there are thousands of guys on campus who would do it and never call you again. That's what you want, right?"

That was what I wanted, but truth be told, I'd rather it be someone I trusted. I didn't trust any of the guys I'd met so far. They all screamed douchebags. Plus, Matt and I already had great chemistry, and I knew he'd be gentle. Also, he'd make me come. That was the most important part. Someone who would make my first time having sex not as awful as everyone said it would be.

"Matt and I already hooked up, so I know he'll make it good. I already know he can satisfy me."

"Ooh. Okay. I guess I get that."

"We have great sexual chemistry. We already did oral, so why is he being so weird about it?"

She pinned me with a look. "He's probably worried about it being awkward between you afterward."

"But it won't!" I protested.

Ari shook out her colorful mane. "I guess it depends. It wasn't awkward after Ty and I hooked up. I'm actually surprised he knew where to find my..." Her face reddened. "Never mind, that's too much info. We agreed it was a one-night stand, and I told him to take a hike the next day."

"Really?" I asked. That surprised me about Ari because she seemed like the kind of girl who looked for forever. "You didn't give him a shot?"

"Do you remember meeting Ty? He's not a serious guy. Plus, I met someone else."

"Ooh, tell me! Is it someone I know?"

She bit her lip. "Maybe...I don't want to jinx it yet. I'll tell you later. The outfit's fine. Why don't you tell Matt how you feel? Because, to be honest, that boy looks at you like he wants you too, but he's trying to control himself."

I squinted at her. "He does?"

She nodded. "Yeah, girl! He's trying to hold back. It's so obvious to everyone else. It's probably why the other guys backed off because it looks like you're together."

"Then maybe my plan's working. I want to make him jealous so he'll see he's the guy for the job and no one else."

She stared me down like she could see through my motives. "Are you sure you want sex and nothing more?"

"Yes. I just want to sleep with him," I lied.

She shrugged and walked off toward the bathroom. I wasn't sure she believed me either.

I put away my discarded clothes. The outfit I picked was perfect because it didn't scream date and make him run away. It looked casual, like I didn't put that much effort into it.

The thing was, I really liked Matt, and if he wasn't so scared of my brother, maybe I'd want something real with him. It was true I was crushing hard on him, but university was all about exploring your sexuality, and I was fine with doing that. I just needed to convince the man in question.

I took a shower and painstakingly did my hair and makeup, making sure it was perfect. I had awesome beachy waves, and my lip gloss looked painted on. I knew we weren't going anywhere fancy, but I wanted to show Matt what he was missing.

I was putting the finishing touches on my mascara when my phone buzzed.

MATT: Come downstairs when you're ready.

I rolled my eyes. I texted him after I got out of the shower to meet me at the bar.

ME: I told you we could meet at the bar!

MATT: No way in hell I'm letting you walk by yourself, sweet pea.

I rolled my eyes again, but a smile played on my lips. While it infuriated me, it was also sweet that he wanted to make sure I was safe. Another reason I wanted him to take my virginity and no one else. Matt was so kind, and he'd be gentle through it all. If I slept with any of those hockey boys, I had doubts about that.

"Have fun tonight," Ari called after me.

"I hope so," I said with a wink as I walked out of our suite.

I went down the elevator and found Matt waiting for me outside my dorm. His gorgeous dark hair was styled tousled like always, and he wore a red-plaid button-down and jeans. I was glad he went casual, too.

I skipped over to him and slung my arm through his.

"Don't even say it," he warned.

I grinned as we made our way to the bar. "Are you traumatized?"

He shuddered. "Yes."

I tried not to laugh, but I couldn't help myself.

"I need a drink," he muttered, but he didn't remove our linked arms and kept pace with me.

"I'll buy you one for your troubles," I offered and flashed him a bright smile.

I almost saw the corner of his lip upturn. He was being grumpy, but I didn't blame him. Noah and D were very much in the honeymoon phase, and it was probably hard to remember someone else lived with them. I'd be traumatized like Matt if I walked in on that.

We walked in step to the door of the bar, and he unraveled himself from me to open it and let me inside first. For a Tuesday night, it wasn't that crowded, and a host sat us at a booth immediately. Matt helped me out of my jacket, and I felt all gooey inside at how he was a gentleman. He took our jackets and set them on his side of the booth while I slid in across from him.

A server came over, and we ordered local beers while we scanned the menu.

"I saw you scored a goal last night," I told him and closed my menu. I was going to be boring and get the grilled chicken Greek salad, but in my defense, it was really good.

His lips twitched into a ghost of a smile. "You did?"

"Totally. I watched the game with Dinah when she was supposed to be working."

"You cracking the whip working for her?" he joked.

"Trying!"

The server came back to drop off our beers, and we put our food order in. Matt rubbed a hand over his freshly shaven jaw and took a sip of his beer. God, I wanted so badly to rub my hand over his face or feel the stubble of it across my own as he kissed me.

"How's your team doing?" he asked.

I shrugged, taking a sip of my beer and thinking about how to answer that.

Kiira was the only person on the team who actually liked me. Elsa was so hardcore, while I just wanted to have fun. Last practice, she accused me of not being serious about the team. It wasn't like any of us were going to go pro after college, so I didn't understand what her problem was. My linemates seemed nice, but they kept to themselves.

"It's okay. It's only club hockey."

He shook his head. "Don't sell yourself short. Just because it's not pro doesn't mean it's not serious."

Okay, he had a point, but that was the issue.

I sighed. "I want it to be fun, but the captain has a stick up her butt about us buckling down and winning the championship. It's like chill, it's not that serious. I'm so stressed about everything else, I need hockey to be fun again."

"Again?" he asked.

"My old university was intense. I've got a lot on my plate this year, and I need something to relieve my stress."

He nodded in understanding but said nothing as our food came, and we chowed down.

"Thanks for offering to get me out of the house," he said after a few minutes of us silently chewing had passed.

I shot him a flirtatious smile. "I needed to get out of my dorm, anyway. I had a bunch of classes today and have been doing assignments since I got out of them."

He leaned back and winced. "I'm glad I never went the college route."

"Why? Because of classes?"

"I wasn't the most studious. I want hockey to work out for me."

I reached out a hand toward him. "It will. You looked like a beaut out on the ice last night. You're still making your way. Plus, with you under my brother's wing, you'll do great."

"Thanks, sweet pea. I really needed to hear that."

I rolled my eyes. "Again with the sweet pea."

His eyes twinkled. "You love it. It's our thing. I tease you by calling you sweet pea, and you call me..."

"A douche," I joked.

He cracked a smile because we knew he was the furthest thing from that.

But he was right. I loved that he called me sweet pea, even if it was in a teasing way. I wanted to hear him moan it in my ear while he was on top of me. But a girl could only dream because this man took the code to heart. Kinda wished he was an asshole playboy so I could get what I wanted. That was the problem with liking the nice guy – they never wanted to be bad with you.

CHAPTER TEN

MATT

Damn, she was so pretty. When she gave me that sunny smile, it was like her whole face lit up despite the dim lights of the bar. Her hair was in those loose waves chicks always put it in, and I wanted to slide my hands through her dark locks while I kissed her senseless.

Get it together, Callahan! Off-limits!

"Matt?" Maddie's voice came from far away, and I looked up at her in question. She stared at me with her cute little nose scrunched up like when she was thinking too hard. "Did you hear anything I said?"

I rubbed my jaw. "Sorry. A lot on my mind."

"Tell me," she urged.

I huffed out a frustrated breath.

I was still worried about fighting for my spot on the team. Getting benched was a wake-up call. I'd been training with my teammates, watching video, and studying our plays as much as I could. The goal last night was my first of the season, and it felt like I wasn't playing to my potential.

"You don't want to hear about it," I told her.

"Yes, I do."

I pinned her with a disbelieving look. "No, you don't. You won't get it."

She crossed her arms over her chest, but that made me notice her lacy bra peeking out beneath her cleavage. Good God, hanging with her made it harder to resist temptation. "I'm also a hockey player. Talk to me. What's going on?"

"Normal worries that I'm not good enough."

"You play in the big leagues. You scored that awesome goal last night. Matt..." She bit her lip and paused for a moment.

"What?"

"It was hot."

I furrowed my brow. "What?"

"Watching you make that backdoor goal!" she exclaimed a little too loudly, and some people looked at us with curious glances. Hockey lingo was so weird to those not in the community. "It was such a beauty of a goal. So yes, I was partly jealous of the goal, but also kinda horny about it."

My throat felt thick at her words. She was not saying watching me score a goal made her horny. Nope, definitely not what she was saying at all.

"Maddie," I warned.

She gave me an innocent grin and took another sip of her beer. Innocent my ass, this girl was trouble for me, and she knew it.

I cleared my throat. "So anyway...do you still need your wingman?"

Her smile faltered so slightly, I barely would have noticed it had I not been staring intently at her glossy lips. "Yeah."

I glanced around the room for a suitable guy. Not the guys in backwards hats making a lot of noise at the dartboard. Not the frat bros having a chugging competition either. There was a guy a few tables away with a bushy beard and glasses. He looked nice.

I nodded my head to the guy in question. "What about him?"

She wrinkled her nose. "Pass."

"What's wrong with him?"

"I don't like beards. Or nerds."

"Glasses don't mean he's a nerd."

She lifted one shoulder apathetically. "It would be like kissing my brother. Gross."

"So what's your ideal guy, then?"

She set down her beer and chewed on her lip in thought. "I love the clean-cut look. Maybe tall with dark hair that looks like he rolled out of bed, but he actually spent a long time styling it. Maybe he's great at hockey."

I gulped and tried to ignore that she was describing me. From the naughty smile playing across her pretty lips, I couldn't tell if she meant it or if she was messing with me.

She put a hand on her cheek and sighed. "I'm not interested in any of these guys."

"Okay. Want to hit up a different bar? Or find another party?"

"I want to head back to my dorm."

I nodded. The server came back around to ask if we wanted a refill on our beers, but I asked her for the check. She brought it back a couple minutes later, and I snatched it before Maddie could. I hid my grin at her pout.

"I said I'd buy you a drink," she argued.

"No way, sweet pea. I got this."

She groaned. "Fine. Do you want to hang out? Watch a movie?"

There was a hopeful look in her eye that should have made me suspicious.

"Do *you* want to hang out?" I slid my credit card onto the table and left it waiting for the server to come grab it while we finished our beers.

"Sure. Aren't we friends?" Maddie asked, that bright smile of hers returning.

"Are we?"

I wouldn't say we were friends, especially when I found out she moved to Philly and she looked like she wanted nothing to do with me. Although we had been chatting since I promised to help her with 'operation lose it' as she called it.

She frowned. "I thought we were."

"We're getting there," I teased.

She slapped my arm. "Then come hang out with me! It'll be fun. Then you don't have to go back to the awkwardness at my brother's."

I shuddered. It was pretty obvious what had been going on when I came home. Noah had looked embarrassed, but Dinah laughed her ass off. That lady did not give a single fuck about anything.

I was sure my unease was painted across my face because Maddie's laughter rang out through the bar again.

I couldn't help the way her bubbly laughter made my lips upturn in a smile. Or how the way she looked at me made me want to forget the fact I lived with her brother.

"You're not gonna make me watch a chick flick?" I teased after I finished my beer.

"First of all, sexist! Second of all, no. I prefer cheesy action flicks."

I raised an eyebrow. "Really?"

"If The Rock's in it, I'm in!"

"Really?"

"Yes. He can get it."

I laughed again, and she gave me a teasing smile. God, that smile. I needed to stop feeling like it was for me. Our server dropped off my credit card. I hadn't noticed she picked it up, having gotten lost in the conversation with Maddie.

I picked up my card and signed my name. I gave the server a nice tip. She had been good, and I always tipped well.

"Okay Action Queen, let's roll."

I grabbed our jackets and helped her into hers. I untucked her hair out of the collar once she had it on, and she gave me a shy smile in thanks. I pulled my jacket on, and we walked out of the bar together. She didn't link our arms together like she had on the walk in, and part of me was bummed about that.

I was so screwed when it came to Maddie Kennedy. She had me wrapped around her little finger. I had no business going back to her dorm room with her. Red flashing lights were shining in my head, but I didn't want to stop hanging out with her or talking to her.

We walked toward her dorm, and she scanned her ID to unlock the door. I held it open for her and let her go inside first. I followed her through the lobby and onto the elevator, where we went up to her floor.

It was a bad idea to come upstairs with her, but the truth was, I liked Maddie. A lot. I hadn't stopped thinking about her since our hookup at Noah's wedding. When she helped me with the ad spot, it shone a different light on her. Maddie was smart and kind, and the more I hung out with her, the more I wanted to get to know her better. We had been texting a lot, and I'd gone with her to parties twice already, but none of the guys she told me she was interested in could measure up. They weren't worthy of this beacon of sunshine.

She unlocked the door to her suite and led me through a small hallway, then through another door where a small room held a twin bed and a desk across from it. She toed off her shoes, and I repeated the action.

"You can sit on the bed. Sorry, I know my room's small," she said with an apologetic smile.

"I'm surprised you don't have to share a room. I thought that's what all colleges were like."

"It surprised me too. I think the first-year dorms are like that, but I'm in the four-year house since I'm an international student."

"I always forget you're Canadian," I said as I climbed onto her loft-style bed.

"Why? Because I'm not a Canadian stereotype like my brother, who says 'eh' like every other word?"

I grinned at her.

"Ass." She shed the outer white and blue plaid shirt she was wearing and grabbed something from her dresser. "I'll be right back."

I sat on her bed, leaned against the wall, and scanned the room. It was neatly organized, but it had little touches of Maddie all over it. Above her desk was a Winnipeg Whitecaps calendar—interesting that it wasn't a Bulldogs one. Next to it was one of those corkboard things with a spattering of photos pinned up. On her desk was a stack of books, but none of which looked like textbooks. They looked like the books that made up her social media profile.

There was one such book lying next to me on the bed. I

picked it up and scanned the cover. An oily, muscular man stood behind a woman with his hand wrapped around her throat as he kissed her neck.

Jesus, what was she reading?

"Gimme that!" she shrieked as she came back into the room, now wearing a thin tank top and a pair of leggings that hugged the curves of her thighs. I couldn't see her ass, but I bet it looked fantastic. I had to tell my dick to settle down at the sight of her comfy attire.

"What kind of books are you reading?" I asked. I turned it over and read the summary on the back. I was sure my eyebrows were at the ceiling at what I read.

She took the book from me and placed it on her desk. "The kinky kind. Don't judge!"

She walked back to her bedroom door and shut it behind her. Then she found the remote for the small TV that sat on her dresser, and she turned it on. She flipped through until she put on a cheesy action film that she no doubt loved. She climbed up on the bed beside me, her thighs pressed against mine.

"So, are those books like your guilty pleasures?" I asked.

"Nope."

"No?"

She turned toward me with a fiery fight in her eyes. "No, because I don't have guilty pleasures. I'm not ashamed of what I read. You can try to shame me for liking books that explore love and sexuality, but you won't make me feel bad for wanting to read steamy romance novels that give me a happy ending."

I held up my hands in surrender.

"The world's such a mess. I like that I have one thing that can comfort me," she continued.

Damn, she really told me off about that.

"Okay, I get that. Sorry if you thought I was judging you. My mom read a lot of bodice rippers growing up."

"Nothing wrong with that. Your dad probably got laid a lot. Probably still does."

"EW! Maddie, what the fuck!"

She belted out her laughter. "You totally walked into that one."

"I don't want to be traumatized twice in one day."

She leaned against me, and as if on instinct, I wrapped my arm around her and let her lean into my chest. "Sorry, that was too easy."

"And I thought Canadians were nice," I teased.

"Um, that's a stereotype. Only my brother's that way," she chirped back at me.

This girl. She really could dish it out, and I loved that about her.

"Now, shush, this is the best part!"

She pressed up against me, and I realized I was cuddling her like this was a date. Like we weren't strictly friends. The feeling of her thighs pressed up against mine was making my hormones work into overdrive. I needed to get a grip.

I wasn't paying attention to the movie, and I barely registered the not-subtle way she slid her hand into mine.

I was so totally fucked. You never slept with your teammate's sister, but I was pretty sure that was exactly what I was going to do.

Fuck me.

CHAPTER ELEVEN

MADDIE

"Maddie," Matt whispered in the dark of my dorm room.

I slid my eyes open and found myself pressed against his muscular form as we lay together in my bed. I didn't remember that happening. The last thing I remembered was subtly sliding my hand into his as we sat against the wall watching one of my favorite action films. Now we lay side-by-side in my twin bed.

"What's up?" I asked, my voice still thick with sleep.

He laughed. "Not you. I'm gonna head out."

I was too tired to school my features and pouted instead.

He studied me and reached a hand out to brush my hair out of my face. "I gotta go."

"Why?"

He shifted and I pressed my face into his T-shirt, breathing in that woodsy scent of his cologne. My bed was small, but friends shouldn't cuddle. Not that I wanted to be his friend. Not one bit.

He sighed, his breath coming out ragged. "Sweet pea, please."

I moved and stared up into his face, placing my hand against his chest and feeling his heart beat loud against my hand. "Please, what?" I purred seductively.

"Christ. I'm so fucked," he muttered as he squeezed his eyes shut.

I opened my mouth to ask what that meant, but in a flash, he had me on my back and his lips were on mine.

I moaned into his mouth as I opened to him and shifted to let him settle between my thighs. I slid my hands to the back of his neck and caressed the short hair there while he attacked my mouth. His cock pressed against the thin material of my leggings and I ground up against him in anticipation.

He cradled my face and kissed me like he was gonna swallow me whole. I clung to him as his kisses got deeper and rougher. His lips felt like fire as he traveled down to my neck.

"Madison," he whispered against my skin.

I moaned at hearing him say my full name.

"Sweet pea, you make me do bad things."

"I want you to do bad things to me."

God, if he knew all the fantasies I had he might run away. I saw how his eyebrows shot up to his hairline when he found the daddy kink book I had been reading earlier. As much as hockey players talked a big game, I got the feeling Matt wasn't that adventurous in the bedroom. Which was fine. Maybe my fantasies were all in my head. I didn't know what I liked yet. Oral and hand stuff hadn't allowed me to explore the side of myself that was waiting to be unlocked.

He groaned but didn't stop kissing my neck. He made

his way to my chest and slipped the strap of my tank top down over my shoulder. "We shouldn't do this."

He kept saying that we couldn't and shouldn't, but his lips still marked a path across my skin. I wanted to scream, 'go lower.'

"Sure we can," I reassured him, arching up and trying to give him the green light to take my top off and play with me already. God, couldn't he take a hint? I had been throwing myself at him for weeks.

He kissed and licked at my skin, teasing me by staying at the swell of my breasts.

I reached down and rubbed his dick through his jeans. He was hard and thick, and now I wasn't sure this was a good idea. Matt was well endowed. I had that thing in my mouth already and I hadn't forgotten the lockjaw after our disastrous night together.

Shit, how was that gonna fit inside me?

"We should stop," he whispered against my skin, but it didn't seem like he wanted to.

"It wasn't a religious thing or because I wasn't ready," I blurted out.

"What?"

"Me being a virgin."

He lifted his head up from my chest and caressed my face with the back of his hand. "Then why?"

I shrugged. "I poured my energy into hockey, and then anytime I met a guy I liked...he got intimidated by Noah."

Noah never liked any of my boyfriends, and now because of the revenge porn thing, he was a thousand times more protective.

"That's why we can't do this."

"Why's everyone so afraid of my brother? It's my fucking body!"

He grimaced. "I'm sorry."

"No, you're not. If you were sorry you'd have your dick balls deep inside me, and you'd be giving me exactly what I want. But everyone cares so much about pissing off my brother that I don't get laid. I want to have sex! I want to be held down and pressed into the mattress by a guy who tells me to be a good girl and to come for him."

His only response was to kiss me again. I wrapped my legs around his waist and pulled him into me, pressing his dick closer to my center. The feel of him against me almost made me come right then and there.

I rocked against him and clawed at his t-shirt while he kissed the air out of me.

He pulled back to take his shirt off, and I ran a hand down his muscular chest. I might go for the douchey hockey players, but they had their perks. Like the wall of muscle that was in front of me. Holy hell, did Matt have an amazing body.

"You sure?" he asked.

I nodded.

"Sweet pea, your first time should be with—"

I pulled him back down for a kiss and rolled him onto his back. I stripped myself of my top and unclipped my bra. Matt's eyes widened with his desire, and I sighed in relief when he finally reached up and touched me. He thumbed across my nipple with one hand and leaned his head up to take the other in his mouth. I tipped back my head in pleasure when he did the same with the other one.

"I want it to be you," I admitted.

He pulled away from my chest and had so many questions in his eyes. "Why me?"

I reached down and framed that handsome square jaw. "Because I trust you. And you already know how to make me come. I want my first time to be good. I could have a sloppy, uncomfortable experience with a frat bro, but I'd have a better time with you."

Anguish crossed his face. "This is such a bad idea."

"I don't care."

"Maddie," he groaned.

I pulled away, self-conscious thoughts filling my head. "Unless you don't want to. I—"

He gripped my hips and rocked me against his cock. I moaned as I felt his hardness press against my clit. "Does it feel like I don't want to do this?"

I slowly slid my head side to side.

"Are you absolutely sure it should be me? You don't want to wait for someone special?"

"Matt, I know you'll make it special. You'll take care of me."

He blew out a shaky breath. "Do you have condoms?"

I nodded and reached down underneath my bed. Like most dorm rooms, I had my bed up high for maximum storage underneath. I reached into the storage container below and opened the top drawer where I kept all my sexy items. I pulled out a condom and handed it to him.

"You want to be on top?" he asked.

I shrugged.

"It might be better for you. You can control the pace, okay?"

"Okay..." I whispered, nerves suddenly taking flight in my stomach.

"But first...I want a taste of that pussy again."

I yelped as he flipped me over and yanked my leggings, thong and all, down my legs. He spread my legs while he teased me with soft, tiny kisses on the inside of my thighs.

"Please," I begged.

"I'm getting there. Be a good girl and be patient."

I pouted, and he nipped at my thigh. He looked up at me with a wicked grin. "Or are you a bad girl, hmm? Do you need to be punished?"

"If I say yes, will you finally lick me?"

His laughter vibrated across my body until I was gasping because he had sucked my clit into his mouth with no fanfare.

"Matt," I moaned as the pressure built inside me.

"Mmmhmm, so good," he moaned. He licked and sucked his way into my deepest parts, and I clutched at his hair while he drew out my pleasure.

"Matt," I panted out, letting my body relax into his ministrations.

He slid two fingers inside my tight entrance, and I shifted uncomfortably, thinking of how I was gonna fit his huge cock inside there.

"Relax. It'll fit."

I felt heat burn my face.

"It's cute when you blush even though we both know you can take my big dick all the way down your throat."

"Uh-huh." I felt myself soaring above on the edge of ultimate pleasure. He was drawing it out of me, pulling me apart in the best ways possible.

He pressed a third finger inside, and I relaxed my body, letting myself get used to the fullness. He was stretching me out on purpose, trying to make sure it wouldn't hurt as much when I had penetrative sex for the first time. I appreciated that, and it was why I wanted him to be the one to do this with me.

He curled his fingers up and sucked on my clit, and then I was off like a rocket. I gripped his hair as I ground against his mouth, letting him take me over the edge as the waves of my orgasm washed over me.

"Good girl," he purred.

I wanted to hear him say that over and over again. I wanted to be his plaything. I'd be his good girl who did whatever he wanted. I wanted him to use my body for his own. To tell me my pussy belonged to him and him alone.

Hmm. I might read too many romances with domineering alpha men, but I wanted that with Matt. For him to be the first man to claim me.

I released his hair and smoothed it down while he gave me a devious grin. "Good?"

The pleasure he pulled out of me had rendered me speechless, and all I could do was nod.

He kissed my thigh and made his way back up to my face. He cradled it in his hands. "We can stop anytime."

I shook my head. "No, I want this. Please, Matt? I want to ride that big cock of yours."

"Christ," he groaned.

He got up from the bed, and I watched him remove his jeans and boxers. I bit my lip when I saw his cock was hard and ready for me. He slid back into the bed beside me, so I reached down to wrap my hands around his length. He groaned as I stroked him nice and slow, feeling the steely weight of him in my hand.

"Matt?" I asked, my voice shaky with nerves.

"Hmm?"

"What if you're too big?"

He dropped his head back and laughed. "Then I'll just give you the tip."

"Matt!" I laughed.

"If you ride me, you can control how fast we go. You set the rules. Okay?"

I thought about it for a second. I wanted to see the look on his face as I rode him to satisfaction, but my fantasies had me picturing him holding me down or chaining me to the bed. Okay, there were a lot of things I wanted to explore, but maybe not tonight. Definitely not with him, even if I wanted to.

He cupped my cheeks. "We don't have to do this, sweet pea."

"I want to be good enough for you," I said in a hushed whisper.

"You're naked with your hand on my dick. You're more than good enough. So you gonna be a good girl and ride it?"

The smug grin on his face sent a spark of excitement through me.

"I want to be your good girl," I whispered.

He handed me the condom. "Then put this on and get on top of me."

"Oh...o-okay," I stuttered out.

I fumbled with the package so much that he took it out of my hands. He guided me through it, rolling it down his cock. I felt like such an inexperienced virgin, having never put a condom on before.

"C'mere," he ordered in a husky whisper.

I straddled his thick thighs, and he helped position me with the head of his cock at my entrance.

He lifted to kiss me, all the while teasing my clit with the head of his cock. "Set the pace. I can wait."

"Okay," I said with a shaky breath.

"Wait, do you have any lube?" he asked.

"Right under the bed. Top drawer."

He reached down underneath the bed, fumbled around, and then pulled out the small bottle of lube. He spread some across his sheathed cock and then between my legs.

"I don't want to hurt you. This should make it better for you," he said after tossing the bottle onto my floor without a care.

"Thank you," I whispered.

"We can always use more. I want this to be good for you. You ready?"

I didn't answer. Instead, I repositioned myself and slowly began to slide down onto his cock. I gritted my teeth at the pressure of his cock entering me. He stretched me more than I'd ever been before, and it hurt a little, but I knew once he was seated fully inside me, the pain would turn to pleasure.

"Am I hurting you?" he asked.

I shook my head as I got my bearings and slid all the way down until he filled me up.

"Look at you," he cooed as he ran his hands down my sides and gripped my hips. "Such a good girl."

"Matt..."

"You okay?"

My breath came out in ragged pants. "I'm nervous. I don't know what I'm supposed to do."

His thumb slid across my clit, and I bucked against him.

"Ohhh," I moaned while I met him in his slow thrusts.

"Do what feels good to you."

"I don't know!" I cried.

He cupped my face with his free hand. "Aw, sweet pea. Just ride my dick and enjoy it."

"Maybe this was a bad idea. I don't think I'm good at this."

"Mads, relax. I want you to feel good."

"Okay..."

"Kiss me," he demanded.

I bent down to kiss him. His lips on mine relaxed me

while he moved beneath me, sliding his cock in and out in shallow thrusts.

I moaned into his mouth and moved against him, getting into a rhythm as I felt myself squeeze around his cock. I pulled away from him and leaned back, riding him slowly as my orgasm climbed up inside me.

"That's it, sweet pea, just like that," he said, his voice thick with desire. It turned me on and made me want to do a good job. To be as good as the other women he'd had in his bed.

"Good?" I asked and leaned back further.

"Fuuuck yes."

I moaned as pleasure coursed through me, and our bodies moved together in sync, like we were made for each other. My thighs were on fire, like I had been skating lines, but instead, I was gliding my pussy up and down Matt's cock. And it felt so good. Even better than any of my toys or my hands.

He pressed his thumb against my clit again, playing with me while I rode him, and then I was off once more. My body tingled, and I cried out, not even thinking to muffle my screams while I came better than I ever had before.

I collapsed onto his chest, and he took over. He played my body like he knew every song to it until he growled out his release in a long, guttural grunt. It was a sexy sound that I wanted to hear in my ear again and again.

He pressed a small kiss to my temple and ran a hand through my sweaty sex-hair. I practically purred at his gentle touch."You okay?" he whispered.

I peered up at him through heavy-lidded eyes. "So good," I slurred, as if drunk off the pleasure he drew out of me. Drunk off *him*.

He shifted me off his chest and got up to get rid of the condom.

Everyone talked about their first time being awful, but Matt made it good for me. It hurt a little, but once the pleasure took over, it was easy to ignore the pain. Practice was gonna suck tomorrow when I skated with sore thighs, but it was worth it. Matt had been gentle and let me set the pace; he even thought to add lube into the mix so it wouldn't hurt as much. None of those hockey dudebros would have offered that.

It made me want to climb on top of him again. Or lay back and offer myself to him, letting him drive into me as hard as he wanted while I wrapped my legs around his powerful hips. I wanted him to bind my hands behind my back and press me into the bed while he fucked me from behind. But I couldn't explore my desires with him, no matter how much the horny girl inside me wanted to. If my overprotective brother didn't scare Matt so much, maybe I could have shown him my deepest wants over time. But this wasn't the start of something real. It was just for tonight and never again. I steeled my heart to remind myself of that reality.

I slid out of my bed and put my clothes back on, then walked out into the hall bathroom to pee. When I walked back into my room, I shut the door behind me and found Matt lying in my bed with one arm behind his head, scrolling through his phone. It was late, so I figured he'd want to take off, but he was in my bed like he didn't want to leave. My uncomfortable twin bed that was too small for him.

I slid in beside him, pressing against his side so we'd fit together in the small space. Dorm beds were not ideal unless you loved cuddling. He brought the comforter up over us and put his phone away.

He turned and nosed across my neck, making me giggle as his kisses tickled me. "We good?" he asked.

I stiffened against him."Yes."

"I—"

"Matt, it was just sex," I lied to both of us. I wanted to enjoy being in his arms, and the lie would let me do that without thinking about the heartache that would come later.

"Right," he said, but in the dark of my bedroom, I saw the way his jaw ticked.

"It doesn't have to be weird," I tried to convince myself more than him.

I couldn't make it weird with him. We were just becoming friends, and I didn't want to ruin it because we had sex. But my heart was already whispering feelings at me.

"Right. Yeah," he muttered.

I eyed him. "It doesn't."

"Okay, sweet pea. It was good for you, right?"

"Definitely. I'm glad it was you."

Instead of answering, he kissed me again, cradling my face in his hands like I was something to be treasured. This was all we could have, so I savored the feeling of his lips on mine. When he pulled away, he wrapped his big arms around me, and we fell asleep in my cramped twin bed together, pretending we could have more than this one night together.

CHAPTER TWELVE

MATT

I stared up at the ceiling in Maddie's dorm room and tried to think of my next move. My neck had a crick in it from sleeping on her tiny twin bed, but as uncomfortable as it was, I didn't want to leave. Not with how she curled around my neck like that spot was where she belonged.

But I had to go, and I was about to leave without saying goodbye. Because I wasn't supposed to sleep with her, and now I had to pretend like this didn't change anything.

I carefully untangled her from around my chest and slid her head back onto her pillow. I crawled out of bed as quietly as I could.

I had zero regrets about our night together, but taking her virginity made me feel like it shouldn't have been me. She was my teammate's baby sister. Not just any teammate but my mentor's sister. The guy who invited me into his home and gave me pointers on my game. The one guy on the team that I trusted with anything. And what did I do to repay him? Snuck out and slept with his sister. If Noah found out, my body would be at the bottom of the Schuylkill River.

I found my phone, changed back into my clothes from last night, and walked out of her suite. I pulled out my phone and brought up a rideshare app. I had to be at morning skate, and I was on the opposite side of the city, so SEPTA was not a choice.

I ordered a car and groaned at the rate. Panic coursed through me when I saw a text from Noah.

NOAH: Yo dude. You riding with me?

NOAH: ??

NOAH: Did you come home last night?

Fuck me.

ME: Sorry. Crashed at a friend's last night. See you at morning skate.

I waited for the car to arrive, and once inside, I let my thoughts marinate inside my brain. I shouldn't have left without saying anything, but I couldn't be late for morning skate. I didn't want to get benched again. It was still a dick move, though, and she didn't deserve that.

I liked Maddie. I really did. I liked how she helped me do that ad, even though she had still been pissed at me for what happened at the wedding. She was honest about her joys and passionate about her work with Dinah. It was refreshing when she pushed back at me when she thought I'd shame her for her reading choices. I especially loved that she knew more about hockey than those douchey pylons she wanted to hook up with.

But as much as I liked all those things about her, or

loved her pretty smile and how it lit up the room, she was still my teammate's sister. And we could never ever have a repeat of last night, no matter how much we both wanted it.

When I got to the arena, I rushed into the locker room and shed my clothes for my equipment. There were only a couple of guys still milling around the locker room. Some teams got rid of morning skate, but LaVoie kept it, making it optional. If you were a rookie like me who wanted to make sure you stayed on the team, you knew that meant it was mandatory.

Benny was lacing up his skates when I pulled on my jersey.

"You okay, Cally?" he asked, a dark eyebrow raised at me.

"Yeah," I muttered.

Huge lie.

"You sure? Because you look like you got a lot on your mind."

I swallowed.

And then it hit me. Holy shit. Benny was the one guy on the team I could talk to about my situation since he had been in the same one when he and Rox got together. If anyone could guide me on how to handle Noah, it was Benny. I couldn't believe I hadn't thought of it before.

"Can we talk?" I asked him.

He tilted his head at me, curiosity materializing across his face. "Sure, bud. Now?"

"After? Can you give me a ride home? I didn't sleep at Noah's last night."

That got me another raised eyebrow look. "Girl problems?"

I laced up my skates. "Partly. Can we talk privately?"

His eyebrow rose even higher. "Okay, kid. Let's do lunch at my place, and we can talk."

I nodded, and we walked out of the locker room and onto the ice together. Most of the guys were already on the ice warming up. I skated across it, trying to shake away my conflicted thoughts. I hadn't checked the lines this morning, so I wasn't sure I was getting ice time tonight to begin with.

I did a couple of laps before Coach blew the whistle, and we did a few drills to get ourselves loose for the game tonight. Morning skate wasn't as taxing as practice, and that was why Coach made them optional, but I needed to show up to prove how important they were to my game.

After morning skate was over, a few of the guys met with the media. Then I sat through a couple of meetings going over video review of our opponent. We were playing Columbus, but we were the stronger team, even though our past few seasons we'd been struggling.

I had been avoiding Noah all morning, but when lunch came around, he came up to me. "Hey, man, you doing lunch with us?"

I shook my head. "I'm going elsewhere today."

Noah narrowed his eyes at me. That was out of the ordinary for me. I always did lunch with the boys in the player's lounge, and hockey players rarely changed their routine. We were superstitious like that.

"You okay?" he asked.

"Just need to switch it up. "

"Right."

"I'll see you at home," I told him and then high-tailed it out of there.

I had no idea where Benny was, but I figured I'd wait at his car for him. This situation with Maddie was a mess.

Normally, Noah would have been the guy I asked for advice, but I couldn't ask him for advice about himself.

When I walked out to the player's parking lot, Benny was standing outside of his SUV, twirling his keys in his hand and waiting for me.

I gave him a wave and got into the passenger seat. Once we were settled, he drove off to his place in Old City.

"What's on your mind, kid?" he asked.

"I fucked up," I admitted.

"Okay..."

"How badly did TJ take it when he found out about you and Rox?"

Benny groaned. "It was colossally bad! But that hadn't been my intention. Rox and I had a plan. We were gonna sit him down with a few drinks and tell him we were together. That I loved her and nothing, not even him, would stand in my way."

That sounded like a good plan, and it could work with Noah. If I came to him upfront about my intentions with Maddie, he'd respect that.

"But what happened?" I asked.

Benny frowned. "He came home and heard us fucking."

My eyebrows rose all the way to the ceiling. That was worse than I had imagined.

Benny ran a hand through his beard. "Yeah, it was bad. His dad and him got me drunk and then had me doing lines on the ice the next morning until I wanted to puke. Alain only accepted me because I got up into his face about Rox. What does that have to do with your lady problems..." he trailed off before he could complete his question, the answer already hitting him. "Oh, fuck. Who?"

"Maddie."

"Who?"

"Noah's little sister."

Benny cringed. "Oof. And you live with him. But that shouldn't be too bad. Noah's a level-headed guy."

Yeah, he was, but not with Maddie. It looked like he wanted to murder me at his wedding.

"It gets worse," I revealed.

"What did you do?"

"I took her virginity, and then I left this morning without a goodbye."

Benny rubbed his temples and breathed out an annoyed sigh. "One, virginity's a social construct, and Rox told me you two already did oral, so technically, you already had sex. And two, what the fuck is wrong with you?"

Rox told him? What the fuck?

"I told you I fucked up. And why does your girlfriend know that?"

Benny laughed. "She only told me because she thought it was funny we had similar stories. But again, what's wrong with you?"

I groaned. "I was going to be late for morning skate. To be honest, I think she just wanted to have sex. I've been her wingman."

His eyes were on the road, but I saw the way his face scrunched up in confusion. "Her what?"

"She helped me with a sponsor thing I needed to do, and I was supposed to help her find a guy who could deflower her."

"Are you sure she wasn't trying to get you to be that guy?"

Wait a second. He was onto something. Maddie had picked out the douchiest guys she could find when we went out. Had she done that on purpose? Last night, she said she wanted it to be me. Was her dragging me to all those parties just an elaborate ruse? Did sweet pea really play me like that?

"I'm not sure," I admitted.

"You like her?"

"Yes."

"Do you want to be her boyfriend?"

Yes. I did. I wanted to resist her, to keep her in the friendzone, but I wasn't sure I could. Maddie, with her sweet smile and her passion, made me want to listen to her forever. I loved being near her and talking to her, even if it was just a couple of texts. That's why I knew going to her dorm last night was a bad idea. But I did it anyway because she made me want to be bad with her.

"I really like her," I admitted.

Benny turned down on his street and drove into the parking garage of his building. "Okay, tell you what. First, you apologize. Second, you need to tell her what you want. Rox and I weren't on the same page when we got together. If she wants a casual thing, no point ruffling feathers by talking to Noah."

I nodded. Right. If she wanted to use me for sex, we could go back to the friendzone, and I didn't have to tell Noah anything. We could pretend it never happened.

Benny parked his SUV. "Gotta admit, kid, it surprised me you asked for my advice, but you can't ask Noah about fucking his sister."

"Benny!"

The dick laughed at me. "Come on, rookie, let's eat. Focus on the game tonight, and then you can go talk to your lady about whatever's going on. You need to work that shit out with her before you go to Noah."

I nodded and followed him up to his condo. He was right. I knew he was right, but it didn't dislodge the rock in the pit of my stomach.

CHAPTER THIRTEEN

MADDIE

The hurt cut deep when I woke up naked and alone in my bed. I wasn't stupid; I knew he'd still keep me at arm's length after our night together. But I hadn't expected him to run out on me without a goodbye.

I told him it was 'just sex.' So why should he have treated me differently from any other one-night stand? I had no right to be upset. And yet, I couldn't help the way my heart felt gutted at his absence.

Last night, he made me feel like we could have something more than a strained friendship riddled with sexual tension. In my wildest dreams, I knew it wasn't possible. No matter how much I liked him or how Dinah buttered up my brother. Noah would never accept me dating one of his teammates.

I climbed out of my bed at the sound of my alarm ringing, and I moaned in pain from the soreness between my thighs. Practice was going to kick my ass today. But it had been so worth it. Playing club was a breeze compared to the level of competition at my old university, but it didn't mean I didn't hustle on the ice. Not sure I could slack off today with the Ice Queen nipping at my heels. Elsa was far too serious about her hockey. I might have appreciated that intensity last year or if I was trying to make the national team, but not when I was playing club hockey to an audience of hockey moms.

I dressed and ate breakfast in my room while I checked my email and made notes in my planner for my to-do list. I had stuff I needed to do for Dinah, and she kept nagging me to come to the game tonight, but I couldn't do that after I slept with Matt. I needed some distance. Or else my heart might get more ideas than it already had.

I went to class, but my mind kept wandering, running over the way Matt held me tight last night and how his kisses made me feel that spark of electricity. All I could think about was how much I wanted to do it again, but that was an impossibility.

I went through the rest of my day in a daze, and I didn't even flinch when Elsa snapped at me for being late to practice.

"Dude, chill!" Kiira came to my rescue. "She's five minutes early."

"If you're five minutes early, you're on time," Elsa snipped and then took off in the direction of the ice, her blonde braid whipping around behind her.

"What's her problem?" my linemate, Karen, asked me.

"No clue," I said as I got dressed.

"She needs to get laid," Kiira joked.

"Maybe," I conceded.

The conversation forced my thoughts back to last night again. I was supposed to feel better now that I finally got laid, but I felt so blah. Not that it wasn't good—it was—I just wasn't sure how to process the confusing thoughts in my brain. God, maybe I should have fucked one of those douchey hockey bros instead of the sweet gentlemanly one I was crushing on.

I tied my skates, and when I got up, my inner thighs screamed. "Fuck me."

"What's with you?" Karen asked.

"Nothing. Sore from last practice?" I lied but said it like a question because I couldn't believe my own lie.

She raised an eyebrow at me. "Is that so?"

"Uh-huh."

A smirk worked its way up her mouth. "No way. You got it in last night, didn't you?"

I felt heat rise to my face. "Uhhh…"

Karen gave me a smile. "Holy shit, good for you."

"Hell yeah. No more pesky virginity for this one," Kiira cheered and danced in her goalie gear.

"Kiira!" I hissed.

I had told her that in confidence. She gave me shit for virginity being a social construct, and when I told her I wasn't completely innocent, she said oral sex was still sex, so I wasn't a virgin.

Kiira pulled her goalie mask down before making her dramatic exit out of the locker room.

I sighed when I found my teammates still sitting around grinning at me.

"Was it good?" one teased.

"Yes, nosy."

Karen bumped me with her arm. "So you're sore from riding that dick, huh?" She stood up and humped the air.

Well, yes, exactly. It *was* from riding Matt's dick. Which I thoroughly enjoyed.

I rolled my eyes. "Ridiculous, all of you."

"Good for you, Mads. But maybe find someone for Ice Queen out there to give us all some peace."

I shook my head. "I'll try!"

I headed out onto the ice and stretched out on it. My muscles were so tight that I should have stretched this morning to work out the kinks.

I skated over to a pile of pucks and did stick work as I got warmed up. The rest of the girls piled in, and Coach began practice, having us run through drills and hammering into us what to watch out for in our upcoming game.

I wanted to die by the time it was over. My legs were on fire, and all I wanted to do was take a nice bath, but we only had a stand-up shower in my dorm. That was one thing I missed about home. I could always go to my brother's and use the one in his house, but I'd rather not.

I showered in the locker room after practice and was surprised to find Kiira and Karen hanging around waiting for me.

"Hey, let's get dinner," Kiira said.

"Okay..."

This was the first time they invited me to anything. I wondered if they were hazing me and trying to get me to crack. I didn't feel that close with my new teammates, but we'd only been playing together for a couple of months. Kiira was my favorite of the bunch. Even if she was a bit of a wild card. But she was a goalie, so that was to be expected.

"Come on, Kennedy! Be our friend," Kiira joked.

I paused and stared at them. "Wait...did you think I didn't want to hang out with you? I thought none of you liked me."

Karen shook her head. "No way! We thought you were shy. It seems like you're too busy."

Okay, fair. I was busy with taking an extra class, working for Dinah, and 'operation lose it.' That last one was over with now and would free up my time for my other responsibilities. I didn't want my teammates to think I didn't like them. Maybe I hadn't been putting in enough of an effort either.

"Let's go!" Kiira said.

"You like Local Hangout?" Karen asked.

I wanted to laugh. Of course I did. Everyone at Franklin did. It was nice we could all drink too. It was so weird to see the age restrictions in this country. If I didn't take a gap year after high school, I'd be stuck underage drinking like the rest of the kids in my year.

"Yeah, but I was literally there last night," I told them.

Karen shrugged. "Me too! Who cares?"

We must have just missed each other because I was sure I would have noticed her. Although, I was preoccupied by flirting with Matt.

I grabbed my bag and threw my coat on. It was close to the end of October, so it was getting chilly, and Halloween was almost upon us.

"I love fall," Karen said as we walked outside.

"You're just a pumpkin spice latte basic bitch," Kiira teased.

"Yeah, no shame in that," Karen joked back. "But I love Halloween, and then it's Thanksgiving, which is my favorite."

I wrinkled my nose. "I'm not sure how I can get used to Thanksgiving in November. That's weird."

"What do you mean?" Karen asked.

"We have it in October in Canada."

"No, that's weird. You have to have Halloween first!" Kiira exclaimed.

I shook my head at her while the two of them razzed me about being a weird Canadian.

It was a hike to the bar from the skating rink. Since Franklin was Ivy and smack in the middle of Philadelphia, there was actually a rink. That had surprised me in a good way. I was worried about having to find transportation to the rink. It wasn't an easy walk, but it was manageable.

On the way over, we chatted about our upcoming game and commiserated over Elsa being way too serious about hockey when it was just club. I was glad they felt the same way. It was nice that they wanted to include me and hang out. So far, finding friends at school had been hard. I had friends back in Winnipeg, but I was so far away, it felt like I was all alone here. That was one reason I was grateful for Matt. There might be some awkwardness the next time we saw each other, but I valued our friendship before anything else. My heart would get over it.

When we got to the bar, it was wall-to-wall drunk college kids. I'd never understand why Thursday night was the biggest drinking night here. We grabbed drinks at the bar, squeezing in between frat bros while we waited for a booth to open up. Karen shamelessly flirted with the bearded bartender, who grinned like he was going to get lucky later. With the way Karen eyed him up, he might.

On the TV above the bar, warmups for the game had started, and the between-the-glass reporter was interviewing Aaron Riley. I spied Matt in the background, and unease spread through my chest.

"Riley's so hot," Karen sighed dreamily.

I laughed. "He's happily married."

"How do you know?" Karen asked.

Oh, boy. I knew because I got drunk with his firecracker wife at my brother's wedding. But I hadn't been forthcoming about my relation to one of the biggest hockey stars in the city. Back home in Winnipeg, people treated my brother like a God, and it was nice being at Franklin without that hanging over my head.

Kiira snorted. "I read his wife's romance book. Dude's definitely not going anywhere."

I swiveled my head at her. "You read Fi's book?"

"Yeah! It was pretty good."

Karen narrowed her eyes at me. "Wait, do you know his wife? You're always posting about books on your Insta."

I blew out a breath. Yeah, I knew her, but I wasn't sure if I should tell them the truth.

"What's wrong with you?" Kiira asked.

I sighed. "Do you know who my brother is?"

Karen's eyes got wide. "No way!"

Kiira raised an eyebrow, but before she could ask, the host came over to us and told us our table was ready. She walked us over to our booth, and I was hoping they'd forget about the conversation, but they stared at me with comical looks of excitement on their faces.

"What?" I asked and buried my face in the menu.

Kiira slapped it away. "No one comes here and reads the menu. Spill."

"Fine. My brother plays for the Bulldogs."

"No shit!" she exclaimed, then she frowned. "Wait... who?"

"Noah Kennedy. Duh," Karen explained.

Kiira's mouth formed an 'o'.

"He's hot," Karen said with a grin.

I blanched. "Gross, no. But also happily married. I love my sister-in-law. I actually work for her now."

"Oh yeah. What's that like?" Karen asked.

Before I could answer, our server came over and

dropped coasters on the table. She cocked her head when she saw me. "Weren't you just here?"

I gave her a small smile. "Yeah. Last night."

"Let me guess, girl's night where you tell them all the juicy details about your hot date last night? He was cute. Hope you nabbed a good one. Now, what can I start you ladies off with?"

I felt my face burning red, especially with the way Kiira was snickering into her hands. I muttered something to our server and tried to sink into my seat, but Kiira and Karen wouldn't let it go.

"Hot dude, huh?" Karen teased.

"Give us the deets!" Kiira urged.

I frowned at her. "Why do you want to know?"

"Because we know nothing about you, and this is juicy."

I frowned. "That's not on purpose. I didn't think any of you liked me."

Karen shot Kiira a sideways glance. "Honestly? We thought you were kinda stuck up."

"Me?" I squeaked out. That was the last thing I wanted someone to think.

Karen shrugged. "Sorry. We didn't know you, but Kiira likes everyone, so she's not a good judge."

Kiira scowled. "I don't like everyone."

"Yes, you do," Karen and I said in unison and then laughed.

They were still bugging me by the time we got our beers.

"It's complicated," I explained.

"How?" Karen asked.

"He lives and works with my brother. He didn't want to break the code."

"He works..." Kiira trailed off, and her eyes lit up. "Oh, he plays for the team, too."

I dipped my head down in silent confirmation.

Karen was immediately on her phone. "Who?"

"Cally."

"Oh. Lucky you, he's a dreamboat."

I gave her a funny look. "I guess? He's really sweet. And a gentleman. But I'm pissed at him."

"Why?" Kiira asked.

"When I woke up this morning, he was gone. I told him it was just sex and it wouldn't change our friendship, but I didn't expect that."

She peered at me and then shared a look with Karen. "Do you...want it to change?"

"I don't know. I really like him, but...my brother would get his meathead brothers-in-law to help put his body in the Schuylkill River."

They bursted out laughing.

"That's a bit...much," Karen said.

"So?" Kiira asked.

"So?" I repeated.

"Yeah. Do you like this guy?"

I nodded. So much, and I felt silly over my schoolgirl crush.

"Then get it in!" Karen cheered, and she and Kiira high-fived. "Who gives a shit what your brother thinks?"

"Hey, you could always have fun sneaking around," Kiira suggested.

I shook my head at them. I was glad for their support, but it wasn't that simple.

CHAPTER FOURTEEN

MATT

"That's holding!" I yelled from the bench, trying to support my teammates on the ice.

The Columbus Assassins had been getting away with every dirty play in the book tonight, and it was pissing me off. Hallsy shook his head at my antics since he was used to me being vocal during games. Sometimes that got me in trouble. Riley told me to work on that so refs didn't call me for a bullshit penalty like they did last period. Those assholes seemed to remember who made their job a little harder. Maybe if they actually did their job, I wouldn't have to speak up so much.

Hallsy nudged me—it was go time. While he used the door, I hopped over the bench and skated onto the ice into play. Benny took the face-off while Hallsy and I studied our opponents, looking for our in to get possession of the puck. We needed Benny to win the face-off first.

But he didn't, and we raced off down the ice, trying to get the puck away from the Assassins while Riley and

Logan tried to be our wall of defense in front of the net. There were five minutes left in the period, and we were winning, but nothing was ever over that quickly in hockey. I'd learned that lesson the hard way. Every second in hockey mattered, and any second could be the difference in a tide-turning game.

After getting benched, I was ready to prove to my coaches, my teammates, and even this city that I was here to win it all. That meant showing up on the ice every night and skating my balls off if I had to. Tonight was no different.

I hustled down the ice, my heart wanting to explode as I skated from zone to zone, trying to get the puck into the net, but to no avail. The Assassins D-men were on my ass all shift while Riley and Logan were killing it, and Metzy was a brick wall in front of the net. I needed to find that opening if I wanted to put up another point and help my team toward another win.

But that point eluded me. We got shots on goal, but nothing connected. After skating back to the bench when my shift was over, I watched as we won the game by merely running out the clock. I hated winning games that way. It was still a win, but I couldn't help but feel disappointed in my performance tonight.

Part of it was because I was distracted by my conflicted thoughts about Maddie.

"You did fine tonight," Benny said as we shuffled back to the locker room.

"I need another point," I argued.

"We won the game. That's what matters."

I tried not to argue with him. Benny had been in the league for a while and knew what he was talking about, but it didn't assuage my worries about my standing with the team.

"He's worried about getting benched again," Hallsy piped up.

Benny waved me off. "That was to give TJ more ice time. Don't take it personally."

Kinda hard not to, but Riley had reassured me of the same thing. I trusted both veterans not to steer me wrong.

The locker room was bumping with our victory song when we walked in. I stripped off my gear while we waited for Riley to announce who got the Silver Bucket we gave to the MVP of the game. It was pretty obvious who the star player of the night was. It wasn't a team win. Tonight was a goaltender game. Fucking chess match.

Riley turned down the stereo. "Alright, boys, no surprise, it's that beauty, Metzy!"

"METZY! METZY! METZY!" my teammates cheered. It was contagious, especially with TJ standing on top of the bench and lifting his hands in the air, urging us to get louder.

Metzy pale face reddened. He was a quiet guy, kinda serious like Noah, but for a goaltender, it made more sense. He had a lot riding on his shoulders, and sometimes he took the blame for a loss when he didn't have good skaters in front of him. Goalie seemed like the worst yet most important position on the team. I wasn't sure I could handle that pressure. Metzy carried the weight in stride, never letting the pressure get to him. He had shone brighter than the rest of us tonight with his aerobatic moves in net. Proof once again why the young kid was our superstar goalie.

Metzy took the helmet and put it on his head. He said a few words, and then we all finished taking our showers. Noah had to meet with the media since he scored the lone goal in the game, but I planned to take off without him anyway.

"You need a ride home?" he asked before heading into the media room.

"Nah, I'm gonna meet a friend tonight. I'll see you later."

He eyed me suspiciously. "Don't be late for the jet tomorrow."

"I won't."

He walked off, and I got dressed. Benny gave me a nod in confidence as I walked out. I called a car and headed to West Philly. I needed to set things right with Maddie. I had to lay out all my cards for her. If she only wanted me so she could lose her virginity, we could go back to being friends. That would be totally fine. Even if I didn't like it.

I cringed at the rates for the rideshare app but did it anyway because she was worth it. When I got out of the car and walked up to her dorm, I wasn't sure what I was going to say. I should have called her—I didn't even know if she was home. She could be out with another guy. Jealousy clawed up inside me at that thought.

Turned out I didn't have to worry about any of that because as I approached the high-rise building she lived in, I saw her with a tall blonde and petite brunette. The three of them laughed as they stumbled down the sidewalk.

Her pretty mouth slid down into a frown when she saw me. "Matt?"

"Hey, sweet pea."

"Oh, it's the guy!" the blonde exclaimed. She had her arm around the other brunette, and they looked a little tipsy. That explained the stumbling.

"We'll be going now," the brunette said. "Good luck, Mads."

"Hope you get it in!" the blonde cackled.

Maddie clenched her jaw and glared at her friends. The

two girls waved goodbye and then took off, drunkenly stumbling along together. Maybe tonight wasn't such a good night to say all this to Maddie.

She crossed her arms over her chest. "I'm mad at you."

I sighed. "Can we talk?"

"Fine," she snapped and spun on her heel toward her dorm.

I followed as she scanned her ID and opened the door to her building. Tension as thick as fog wrapped around us while we stood in the elevator, waiting to go up to her floor. She made big strides once we were on her floor, and if my legs weren't so long, I might not have been able to keep up with her.

She kicked off her boots in her room, and I shut the door behind us.

"I know I said it was just sex and nothing would change, but it hurt when you left without saying anything," she said.

I crossed the room to her and framed her face in my hands. She looked up at me, her eyes searching my own, but the words weren't coming out. I had so many things I wanted to say to her, but I felt frozen. So I did the only thing I could think of—I slanted my mouth on hers.

She flinched at first, but then she slid her hands around my neck and leaned into me. I angled her head and kissed her deeper, sliding my hands down her sides until they rested on her hips.

Kissing her made me forget all the reasons I came here tonight. All the things I wanted to say melted out of my brain when her lips were on mine again. It was like I forgot all my worries when she was in my arms.

I slid my tongue across the seams of her lips, and she opened to me. Our tongues battled, and she moaned into my mouth as the kiss got heated. Until I hiked her up into my arms and deposited her on the bed.

The sight of her on her back brought the memories of last night rushing back into my brain. "Maddie..."

"C'mere," she purred, crooking her finger at me.

"I... We need to talk first."

She frowned. "Why?"

"Sweet pea. I..."

Her eyes blazed at me. "You're the one who kissed me. If you didn't want to lead me on, you shouldn't have done that."

I crawled onto the bed beside her and kissed her again, softening her resolve. I pulled away and rubbed a thumb across her cheek. "I need to know we both want this."

"Of course I do."

I pointed between the two of us. "No. I need to... I really like you."

She nodded slowly, processing the words. "I like you too."

"I want to be with you."

Her mouth dropped open. "Oh."

"Oh?"

Dammit. Did she not want that? Had she only used me for sex?

"What are you saying?" she asked.

"I don't want to be in the friendzone."

"I don't want that either."

"But I don't want to be a casual fuck buddy, either."

Her eyes widened. "Oh. Like you want to date me?"

I nodded, tipping her head up to look me in the eye. "I want to take you on a proper date. Not just to Local Hangout. I want to hold your hand and say you're my girl."

"Really?" she whispered.

"Yes."

Her smile lit up the room, but then it immediately slid off her face. "Oh. But...my brother."

"I'm gonna sit him down and talk to him."

She shook her head. "Matt...we still don't really know each other all that well. I don't want to say anything until we know for sure that this—us—is something we want."

I furrowed my brow. "I don't understand."

"Can we...keep this on the down-low? Not forever. I want to figure us out before getting my brother involved."

Unease spread across my chest, telling me this was a bad idea. I needed to be upfront with Noah. I couldn't date his sister behind his back.

"Are you sure?" I asked.

She ran a hand down my chest. "Come on, it'll be fun. We get to sneak around and be naughty together. Don't you want that, babe?"

I wanted to date her, but I didn't like this plan one bit. Going behind Noah's back was a bad idea, but when she looked up at me with that naughty twinkle in her eyes, the rational part of my brain lost. Horny Matt won out, and he didn't give a fuck about the right thing to do.

"If that's what you want," I said.

"You know what I want?" she purred.

I grinned as she slid her hands through my hair. "What's that?"

"You."

My lips upturned into a grin. "Yeah?"

She nodded. "Out of these clothes and making me come again."

The grin on my face got bigger. "You're a horny little thing, huh?"

She groaned. "You have no idea. Now that I've had you, I want you again and again."

I pulled away from her, shedding my suit jacket and undoing my tie. She ran a perfectly manicured hand up my dress shirt, her touch sending a shock through me. She pulled me down for another kiss, and I settled myself between her legs.

We kissed with a hunger we hadn't expressed last night. This wasn't going to be a slow and gentle exploration. Not judging by the way she undid my shirt and pulled it off my shoulders. Or by the speed at which I pulled her shirt over her head and peeled her jeans off.

I kissed my way down her body, taking in the sweet floral scent of her body wash and perfume. She was a vision in her mismatched underwear. Chicks only matched if they thought guys would see. Not like we cared—we'd rather it be off.

She groaned.

"What's wrong?" I purred between kisses along her thighs.

"You're taking too long," she whined.

I hooked a finger into her underwear. "I want to savor you."

"Well, do it faster."

I traveled back up to her lips and kissed her again, silencing her needy demands. She writhed against me, trying to feel me against her.

"Such a horny little girl," I growled into her ear and kissed her neck. "What am I going to do with you?"

"Please, Matt."

I wanted to bite my fist at the sound of her voice when she begged. God, she was sexy, and she didn't even know it.

Didn't know how I was about to explode if I didn't have her soon, but I wanted this to be good for her again.

My lips marked a path down her chest, and I pulled the cups of her bra down to expose those gorgeous breasts. Maddie was lean and athletic with a small chest, but everything about her was perfection. I rubbed a thumb against one nipple while I sucked the other into my mouth. She ran her hand through my hair while I did, encouraging me to continue. I rotated to her other breast until she was arching her back and begging for me.

When I pulled back, she leaned up and unhooked her bra, tossing it to the floor. I pushed her back down against the bed and made my way toward her center. I peeled her panties off, tossing them to the floor, and dipped my head down for that first taste.

"Fuuuuck," she cried out, making me grin as I feasted on her.

I sucked on her clit and pumped two thick fingers inside. Within seconds, she was moaning my name and thrusting up into my face. Until I felt like she was about to pull out my hair.

When I lifted my head up, her eyes were closed, and she looked like an angel in her post-orgasm bliss.

"Good, sweet pea?"

"Mmmhmm." She opened her eyes and stared at my undressed attire. "Now get those pants off so I can return the favor."

I wish, but I would blow my load and not be able to perform if she wrapped those pretty lips around my cock. "Later. I want to be inside you. Condoms?"

She pointed under her bed, and I got up, kicked off my pants and boxers, and opened the drawer where she kept her condoms. The condoms and lube were in there, but I also noticed three different cloth bags in the drawer.

"How many toys do you have?" I asked as I opened a condom package and slid it down my length. I squeezed some lube on it and rubbed it down my shaft.

Maddie's face got beet red. "A few."

I climbed back into the bed and kneed her legs apart. "Such a horny girl."

"I was a horny little virgin."

I laughed. "Not anymore."

"Matt, stop stalling. I want you so badly."

I rubbed the head of my cock against her clit, teasing her but not giving her what she wanted. She arched up against me, begging me with her body to give her what she wanted. I leaned down to kiss her again before finally pressing inside her. We groaned in relief at the sensation of me filling her up.

I slid all the way out and then back in, giving her what she wanted while she wrapped her legs around me so I could feel her deeper.

"Fuck," I groaned into her hair. "You feel incredible."

"Don't stop," she moaned. "Use me. Take what you want from me."

I leaned up on my knees to get a better angle and pressed her hands above her head. I interlaced our hands, giving me leverage, and took her harder. She was pliable beneath me, and we moved in unison, like our bodies were made to be locked together. Like we fit.

"Matt," she cried out.

I kept going as the waves of her orgasms washed over her. Her eyes closed, and she sank back on the bed. Then I couldn't stop myself. I took her roughly, rocking her bed against the wall until my eyes rolled back into my head, and I growled out my release.

When I opened my eyes, she was still pinned beneath me but looking up at me like I hung the moon. I unclenched our interlocked hands and gave her a quick kiss before pulling out and getting up to get rid of the condom.

I came back to the bed and pulled the comforter over us as we lay together, trying to catch our breath.

She swirled a hand over my chest and kissed my neck sweetly. "I was so mad at you this morning when you were gone, but I think you made up for it."

I kissed the top of her head. "I'm sorry. I wasn't sure what to do, and I had to get to morning skate. Are you sure you're okay with us not telling your brother?"

She nodded. "He doesn't need to know. Not yet."

"Okay. If that's what you want."

"I want to figure out what we are first."

I looked down at her and tilted her chin up to look at me. "You're my girl, right?"

The smile cracked her face. "You want me to be?"

"I wouldn't be here laying all my cards out if I didn't."

"I want to be your girl."

"Good."

She laid her head on my chest, and I knew I should head home so I wasn't late for the jet tomorrow, but I didn't want to leave the comfort of her arms.

"Matt?" she asked after a few minutes of silence had passed.

"Hmm?"

She put a finger to her lips. "I like when you restrained my hands tonight."

I quirked up an eyebrow. "Oh?"

A pink tinge spread across her cheeks. "I know I'm inexperienced, but being restrained is one of my fantasies."

"Like being tied to the bed?"

"Maybe..." she said with a sly smile. "I like the idea of my hands being above my head in leather cuffs while you have your way with me."

"Okay," I breathed out.

That was not something I thought she was going to say. Or something I'd ever done with a chick. My high school girlfriend and I never explored that, and none of the hookups I had on the road said they wanted me to tie them up. I'd only ever had vanilla sex.

She put her hand over her face. "Sorry. I made it weird. If that's not something you want—"

"I'm willing to try it to figure out what you like. What position did you like better?"

"I liked both. But my thighs are on fire from last night and practice today."

I grinned. "Next time we'll try something different, okay?"

She smiled up at me. "Really?"

"Yeah, girl. I'm all yours. What you want, you get."

Then she kissed me again, and I definitely wasn't going home tonight. I could get up early to catch the jet tomorrow. Tonight, I'd stay in my girl's arms.

CHAPTER FIFTEEN

MADDIE

Sharing my twin bed wasn't ideal, but sleeping in my brother's basement with Matt was not an option either. Especially since I asked Matt to keep us a secret. Not forever, just until I figured out the best way to break the news to Noah. He'd flip out, and I wanted to be sure about Matt before we had that awkward conversation. No reason to tell Noah if we ended up breaking up.

I moaned at the feeling of Matt's lips on my neck. "I gotta go, sweet pea," he whispered.

It was early, like dawn early, but my internal clock was permanently set to hockey practice time. The Bulldogs were on the road this weekend, and I felt selfish keeping Matt in my bed last night. He needed to be well rested for his road trip ahead.

"I know," I sighed but craned my neck to give him more access.

Last night had been so great, but I couldn't believe I told

him I wanted to be restrained. I'd blame that on the post-orgasm bliss.

He pulled away from my neck and turned me so we were side-by-side, looking into each other's eyes. "When I get back, let's go out."

"You don't have to. You already took me out when you didn't let me pay for dinner."

He squinted at me. "That didn't count."

"Yeah, it did. We went out and enjoyed each other's company, then we banged."

He laughed. "Geez, Maddie."

I grinned. "What? I had a great time."

"Me too. So let's go somewhere else and do it again."

"Okay, if you insist."

He gave me a quick kiss. "I do. But I gotta go. I get to do the walk of shame and need a clean suit for the jet."

He got out of the bed, and I watched the muscles in his back and butt as he bent over and got dressed. He gave me a wink when he noticed me staring. I felt heat course through me. How did I nab this hockey hottie?

He put his tie back on and cleared his throat. "So...last night you mentioned wanting to be restrained. Was that heat of the moment talk or something you really want to explore?"

I pulled the comforter over my head. "Oh, my God! I can't believe I told you that."

I heard him laugh, and then he lifted the comforter off my head. "Hey, I'm willing to do it if that's what you want. Let's research it."

"Really?" I asked. I peered up at him, waiting for the sarcastic smirk, but Matt looked at me with those kind eyes he always gave me. He was always sincere.

"Sure. I've never done that before, but if it's something you want, let's look into it."

"Maybe some leather cuffs?" I offered and bit my lip. I was sure my face was as red as a tomato. "I'm not sure I want to be tied up with rope. If we do that, we should use proper equipment, not a tie or scarves. That can be dangerous."

He cocked his head. "Dangerous how?"

"I've done research already. If you use ties or scarves, the knots can fall in, and you want to make sure it's safe."

His lips curled up. "You've already done research?"

"We don't have to... It's a fantasy. I might not actually like it."

I wanted to pull the comforter back over my head and stop having this conversation.

I read a lot of romance books. I didn't want him to be my Dom or anything, but the idea of being chained to the bed or held down by him while he fucked me appealed to me. I didn't want to scare him off, though, especially if he wasn't comfortable with it.

He climbed back into the bed with me and cradled my face. "I'm game if you want to do it. You say no, and we don't do it, okay?"

"Okay."

He stroked a thumb across my cheek. "I'll text you when I land and get situated."

"You don't have to."

"Let me. But I really gotta go."

He kissed me one last time, and I savored the feeling of his lips on mine. It disappointed me when he let go and left, but I knew he was running late if he was going to run back to my brother's house and then catch the jet with the team.

I got dressed and started my day, bummed that he was already gone. Was it too early for me to miss him? Well, too bad. I already did.

With a sigh, I made coffee and sat down at my computer to get work done before I had to head to my first class.

I was on cloud nine the rest of the day and only half-paid attention to my classes. I hadn't been expecting Matt to come over and announce his feelings like that last night. It surprised me in the best possible way. He didn't like that I wanted to keep us a secret, but I needed time to figure us out and to warm my brother up to the idea of me dating one of his teammates.

I was knocked out of my daze when I got to practice and Kiira threw a towel at my head. "Ow! What the fuck?"

She snickered. "Did you get it in last night after you ditched us, you bitch?"

I felt my face heat. "Maybe..."

Karen laughed. "Good for you. He's cute."

"I guess," Kiira agreed with a shrug. "If you like men."

I grinned. "He is. And very sweet. It's just complicated with my brother."

"LADIES!" Elsa walked in with a stern look on her face. "Enough chit-chatting. Get on the ice."

She zipped out to the rink, leaving us all staring at each other in confusion.

"What's up her ass?" Karen muttered.

I shrugged. "I don't know. She hates me."

"It's because you're a better player," Karen said.

"No, I'm not."

Karen nodded. "Hell yeah you are. It makes sense now knowing who your brother is."

I pulled on my practice jersey. "Oh, yeah, keep that on

the down-low. It's much easier for no one to know I'm Noah Kennedy's baby sister."

I checked my phone, and a small smile played on my lips when I saw a text from Matt.

MATT: Going to dinner with the boys.
Miss you.

My heart fluttered.

He missed me, too.

ME: Have fun. Miss you too. Good luck
tomorrow.

I set my phone down and got out on the ice. We ran through drills, and I felt like my thighs were on fire as Coach had us doing laps at one point. We had a game tomorrow against Maryland, and they were our fiercest rival. I was feeling good about it, but it might have explained why Elsa was being so hard on us.

I wasn't worried about the game because we beat Maryland the last time we played them. Kiira would be a brick wall in front of the net again, and I'd skate circles around their players. I was confident in at least that.

"We're gonna kill them tomorrow, right?" Karen asked.

"Hell yeah!" I agreed. "We're gonna bring it to them."

"Atta girl, Kennedy!" she cheered.

I was so ready to kick ass in this game. Maryland had to bring the heat, or else they'd be eating my pucks.

Elsa was screaming at us from the bench as I made my way with the puck up past the neutral zone. Karen and Casey were on my wings, but I was fighting Maryland's defenseman. I deked a shot and passed it to Casey, and she took the opening. It bounced off the post, and then I scrambled in front of the net.

It was a sloppy goal, but it went in, and my teammates rounded on me in a goal celly. I hugged it out with them, glad to make the game 2-1 us, with only a few minutes left in the final period. It was the much needed goal to edge Maryland out.

I skated back to the bench, high-fiving my teammates and getting back on the pine for the change up.

"Good job, Kennedy," Elsa said to me, and then whipped her head back to study the ice.

Karen nudged me. "Look at you, getting approval from the captain."

I laughed her off and watched as the minutes ticked by at the end of the game. We ended up winning, and we were all in high spirits. Even the Ice Queen.

We went into the locker room, all of us laughing and dancing at the much needed victory.

"Party at my house, bitches!" Kiira yelled from the center of the room.

I laughed.

"You better be there, Kennedy! We all know your boyfriend's on the road, so no excuses."

"Boyfriend?" Elsa asked.

"It's...new," I explained as I shrugged off my gear.

"He's on the road?" she asked, curiosity marking her face.

I sighed. "He plays for the Bulldogs...with my brother."

"Oh!" she exclaimed. "I went to highschool with a guy on the team. Matt Callahan."

Matt never mentioned he knew her, even after I bitched about her. Not that I mentioned her by name. But Ty was his best friend so they must have known each other.

"Matt's a good guy, great hockey sense," she continued.

"I know. But he's not putting enough power into his shot."

She laughed. "You're right. Well, good luck with that."

I felt like she meant it sincerely, but I never could tell with her.

I got off my gear and headed for the showers. If I didn't feel so disgusting, I would have waited to get back to my dorm; the showers at the rink were terrible. After a cold shower because my teammates took all the hot water, I shrugged on clothes and headed out.

My phone buzzed in my hand as I was sliding it into my hockey bag. Seeing Matt's name on my screen made me answer it and put it against my ear. "Hey!"

"Hey, sweet pea. How'd the game go?"

I beamed at his question. We had texted last night about it while we bonded over our worries about our upcoming games. "Good. I scored the game-winning goal."

"That's great!"

"How was your game?"

The Bulldogs had an afternoon game today against the Carolina Thrashers, and then they were headed to Nashville for another game tomorrow. I hadn't checked the score before I went to the rink for my own game.

"Good. We won, but I didn't put up any points. Where are you now?"

"Walking home and then I have to go to a victory party."

"By yourself?" he asked, and I heard the protectiveness

in his voice. It was sweet, but at the same time, it annoyed me.

"Babe, I'm fine!" I walked up to my dorm building and scanned my ID card to open the door. I got on the elevator and rode it while we kept on chatting.

"I don't like you walking alone at night by yourself," he said.

"Babe, I know, and it's so sweet you worry, but I'm okay."

He grumbled on the other line, and I was glad he couldn't see me roll my eyes. I got out of the elevator and walked down the hall toward my door. I unlocked it and dropped my bag down on the floor in my room.

"What are you doing?" I asked him.

"Waiting for the jet to go to Nashville."

"Oh!"

"He's talking with TJ like twenty feet away," he said, answering my unasked question. "Are you sure we shouldn't..."

"Not yet. You still need to take me on that date."

He chuckled into my ear. "Okay. Is it bad that I miss you already?"

I grinned to myself. "I miss you, too."

"I better go. Just wanted to hear your voice. I'll see you in a couple of days."

"Okay, I'll see you then."

I hung up with him, and I felt giddy.

He was mine. He was my boyfriend, and he called me tonight because he missed me. I couldn't wait for him to be back home again. To be in his arms and kiss him like he'd never left.

My feelings for Matt were already so deep. But that

little voice kept reminding me that we needed to keep this a secret. Just for now. If Noah found out now, his freakout would break us. Like it had with every other guy before Matt. I needed to figure out if this was going to work before my brother threw that wrench into our relationship. I wished Matt understood that.

CHAPTER SIXTEEN

MATT

Noah was agitated. We got off the jet, and he rushed toward his SUV like there was a fire.

"Are you okay?" I asked.

He grimaced. "Sorry. I miss my wife."

"Why are you rushing?" TJ asked as he walked beside us. "She's still at work."

Noah groaned. "I forgot it was a weekday. I wish she'd quit her day job."

I held my tongue. Maddie told me last night when we were on the phone why Dinah didn't want to quit her day job yet. I got that. D was a very independent lady, and she didn't want to rely on Noah's income, even if it was far greater than hers.

I understood now why Noah was so antsy. I couldn't wait to see Maddie later. I didn't like that she didn't want to tell her brother about us, but she had a point about us figuring things out first. Still, I felt like a boulder was lodged in my gut every time I talked to Noah. He took me in, gave me guidance, and how did I repay him? By sleeping with his sister behind his back. I felt like such an asshole, but if that's what sweet pea wanted, that's what I'd give her.

This road trip had been draining. When you got the call up to the big leagues, one thing you didn't realize was how exhausting all the travel could be. It was fun to bond with your teammates on the road, but it could weigh down on you. Cully and I bonded a lot since, as rookies, we still shared a room, unlike guys like Noah or TJ on bigger contracts who didn't have to share anymore. The trip had been a good one since we won two more games, and I was feeling more confident about my place on the team.

I got into Noah's SUV, and we drove back to his townhome. He went up to his room, and I went into the basement. I dropped my bag on the floor and shed my jacket. Halloween was next week, but it was already getting chilly outside.

I cocked my head as I noticed someone left a package on my bed. My eyebrows shot up when I realized what it was. I may have swiped one of Maddie's books off her desk before I left. Cully howled with laughter when he saw what I was reading. Until I reminded him I heard Lily call him her 'warrior' when they did video calls. That shut him right up.

I read one of Maddie's BDSM romance books while I was on the road, and then I did research. If she wanted to experiment in the bedroom, we'd do it safely. I bought a pair of leather cuffs with velcro fasteners and faux fur on the inside. Everything I read said they'd be good for beginners. I'd figure we start with binding her hands together first. The cuffs had a metal ring around each one where they hooked together, or I could hook on a strap that I could tie to the bed. We needed to warm up to that first. Baby steps.

I checked the label and breathed a sigh of relief that,

true to the company's word, the packaging was discreet. Thank God, since Dinah clearly saw my name on the front and set it on my bed.

I was nervous but excited to try these out with Maddie. I wanted her to be comfortable, and if she decided she didn't want to do it, we'd stop. I'd already had a speech in my head to talk to her about safety, safe words, and comfort. But based on the book I read, she might have a better handle on this.

I shoved the package into my backpack, giving it no chance of being seen by Noah or Dinah by accident.

I lay back on my bed, pulled out my phone, and shot off a text to Maddie.

ME: Hey, sweet pea, I just got home. Call me later?

A grin spread across my face when she immediately texted me back.

SWEET PEA: Eeeee!!! I missed you. But I have class [frowny face]

ME: Dinner? I still need to take you on that date.

SWEET PEA: Okay! Gimme the deets later.

I did some research on where to take her. She wanted nothing too fancy. She loved pub food like at Local Hangout, but I wanted to take her somewhere a little nicer. There was an Italian place in Rittenhouse Square Dinah said was good, and I trusted her judgment on that. Based on the photos online, it looked low-key.

I was looking through my closet, trying to find an outfit, when I saw my baby sister wanted to video chat with me.

"Hey, pipsqueak!" I said.

Luna rolled her eyes at me. "Ugh. Please, not that nickname."

I grinned. "What's up, kiddo?"

"Do you know anyone who goes to Franklin?"

I arched an eyebrow.

"Other than Ty. He doesn't count."

"Why doesn't Ty count?"

She rolled her eyes again. "Because he's Ty. Or Elsa. I heard they broke up for good this time."

"Actually...I do."

Her face lit up. "Really? They only have club hockey but...I'm thinking of applying, and I want to do a tour."

I broke out into a smile. "Lu, that's great!"

She frowned. "Mom and Dad are fretting about the cost."

"Let me take care of it."

"No!"

"Lu, Mom and Dad sunk all their money into having us. Let me do this."

She frowned.

Lu and I were IVF babies. My parents thought they'd only get lucky to have me, but when they tried one last time, Luna showed up. We were their miracle babies, and IVF was expensive. It was one reason I worked so hard at hockey. My parents had sacrificed everything for me to make it to the league. Helping my sister achieve her own dreams was something I'd do in a heartbeat.

Huh. I guess I understood Noah's need to help his sister. We were cut from the same cloth.

I flipped through my closet and held up a black sweater. "Is this too weird to wear for a date?"

She shook her head. "Wear a white dress shirt underneath. Wait, is it casual or more upscale?"

I rocked my head back and forth. "Not too casual, but not fine dining."

"Okay, wear jeans with it, and you're fine. Tell me about the girl!"

I laughed. That was Luna, so demanding.

"It's a little complicated, but you'd like her."

"Is that who you know at Franklin?"

"She plays on the hockey team."

"Wait!" she cried. "You're dating a female hockey player? I can't believe it. Oh my God, it's not Elsa, right?"

I blanched. "Hell no. She's way too serious. Plus, you think I'm gonna date my buddy's ex?"

My sister shook her head. "Hell no, that's why I wanted to check. Well, I'd love to meet her. I want to come out for a visit and see the school."

I nodded a little uneasily. "Okay, we can do that sometime soon."

She squinted at me. "Matt, what's wrong?"

I rubbed the back of my neck. "Nothing. Nervous about my date."

Luna beamed. "It's gonna be great. Everyone knows you're a great catch. Good luck on the date. And thank you, big bro. I might still get into Minnesota."

"If you don't, we'll figure it out."

She hung up with me, and I reminded myself to give my mom a call later. I needed to talk to her about the finances. Sure, I was still on a rookie salary, but I wanted to help with Luna's school.

I took a shower and got dressed, then I walked upstairs.

Dinah and Noah were in the kitchen making dinner together. I felt weird watching as he wrapped his arms around her and kissed her neck.

"I'm going out," I said.

Dinah laughed and turned around. "Matt, we're not your parents. You don't have to tell us."

I shrugged. "Just letting you know, probably not gonna be home."

She peered at me, and then her face lit up. "Oh! You have a date."

I nodded.

"First date?" Noah asked.

"Sorta. We went out before, but I thought it was just as friends."

"Ooh, so that's where you were before your road trip," Dinah said. She walked over to the key ring at the front door and handed me her car keys. "Take my car."

"D, I can't do that," I protested.

She waved me off and went back to the counter where she and Noah were preparing dinner. "I barely use it. Go for it. Have fun."

"Yeah, man, take D's car. We have mine. And remember, we have morning skate tomorrow," Noah said.

"Okay, thanks."

"Use protection!" Dinah called after me as I walked out the door. I heard Noah chastise her, but I shook my head. I was used to her ridiculousness by now.

I went into the garage and got into her car. Before driving off, I shot a text to Maddie.

ME: D lent me her car, so I'm picking you up.

SWEET PEA: Okay! See you soon.

I drove over to Franklin and somehow found a free spot in front of her dorm. I sent her a text that I was waiting for her, and within minutes, she sprinted out of the building. She wore a black dress with thigh-high boots, and her dark hair looked so pretty in those loose waves she put them in. I couldn't help the smile spreading across my face when I saw her. She moved faster when she saw me.

I got out of the car and caught her in my arms as she wrapped her long legs around my waist.

"Oof. Hey, sweet pea."

She slanted her lips on mine, and I gripped her ass as I kissed her again for the first time in an entire week. God, that was such a long road trip. I had missed her every single day. That should alarm me, but it didn't.

We only pulled away at the sound of douchey frat bros yelling obscenities at us. She tipped back her head and laughed.

"Hey, baby," she greeted with that cheeky smile of hers.

I put her down and walked her over to the car. I watched for cars and then opened the passenger door for her. She jumped in, and I shut the door behind her before getting in on the driver's side.

I pulled out of the parking spot and sped off.

"Where are we going?" she asked.

"That Italian place D loves."

"That place is great, and I trust the Italian girl's opinion on that."

I laughed. "Me too."

On the ride over, I asked her about her day, and she lamented her worries about a pop quiz she had in her math class. I found a garage to park in, and we walked over to the restaurant together.

It was a quaint little place with dim lights and an open-concept kitchen. There was a brief wait for a table, but we didn't mind. Maddie told me more about her week as we waited. I could watch her get excited about anything.

After we were seated, we ordered wine and perused the menu.

"Did D ask who you were going out with?" she asked.

"Nope."

"Okay, good."

I scowled.

She frowned. "I want time for us to figure this out before...I need to warm Noah up to the idea of us."

"Or we can be adults and tell him," I grumbled under my breath.

"Matt...can you just trust me on this?"

I nodded, but it didn't dislodge the guilt that sat like an ulcer in my stomach. Our server came back with the wine, and we put our orders in. Maddie got gnocchi while I ordered the bolognese.

"This place is cute," she said after taking a sip of her wine.

"D likes it because it's not too upscale."

Maddie nodded. "That sounds like her. How do you feel after the road trip?"

"Tired. And we have another game tomorrow."

"Right. D's been nagging me to come, and I don't have a game."

I perked up. "You're going to come?"

"Yup. I haven't been to any this season. Still figuring everything out with school, hockey, and working for Dinah."

And having a secret boyfriend. But I didn't say that out

loud. I liked this girl a lot, but I couldn't help but think hiding our relationship from her brother was going to backfire badly.

"You've got a lot on your plate," I said instead.

She smiled at me from over her wine glass. "Not enough to not make time for you."

I smiled back at her, and we clinked glasses. When our food came, I laughed at how she moaned. It was great food, and I wanted to have her moaning like that later while she was underneath me.

I brought up my sister Luna while we ate dessert. "Hey, so I have a weird request."

She rested her cheek against her hand, tilting her head in curiosity.

"My sister's applying to Franklin, and she'd love to talk to someone here."

"Oh!" The surprise was written across her face. "I didn't know you had a sister."

"Yeah, you'd like her. She plays hockey, too."

Maddie smiled. "I'd love to meet her. Tell me about her."

I grinned. "Well...she's nineteen. She took a year off because she didn't know what she wanted to do, but also because she was worried about wasting my parents' money if she didn't like it. I told her I'd take care of it."

Her eyes softened. "You said you'd pay for her school? Franklin's really expensive."

I nodded. "My parents sunk their life savings in IVF to have me and Luna. If I'm making more money than my sister ever will in her lifetime, I want to help her."

She put her hand over mine. "Matt, that's so... Wow, I admire you so much. I didn't know that about you or that you had a sister."

I pulled out my phone and showed her a picture of me and my sister on draft day. Luna was so sure I was going to get drafted, and when the Bulldogs drafted me, she immediately denounced the Minnesota Tundra and started rooting for my new team.

"Oh wow, I see the resemblance. She's cute."

"I guess? That's my sister."

She laughed. "Her grades must have been good, though, if she's thinking of applying."

They were. We were all shocked she took a year off because Lu took a bunch of AP courses and had college credits already. She was so smart she questioned my agent about stuff in my contract before I signed with the Bulldogs.

"Well, I would be happy to tour her around and talk to her about the hockey team whenever she comes in," Maddie said with a smile.

"That would be great. If I asked Ty, she wouldn't take him seriously."

She laughed. "Ty seems...fun."

"Yeah, he is, but he fools everyone. That dude's serious about his studies. If he wasn't, he'd be going to Minnesota for hockey. But Franklin has great opportunities in the medical field."

"Interesting."

I grinned and sipped on my water. "Ty's my best friend since preschool, but Luna only sees him as an annoying brother she didn't ask for."

"I can see that." She finished the last of her wine. "Wanna get out of here?"

"I thought you'd never ask."

CHAPTER SEVENTEEN

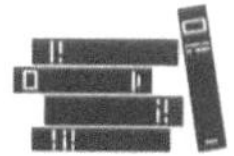

MADDIE

I jiggled my knees excitedly as Matt drove us back to my dorm. Dinner had been awesome, and spending time with him made my heart do that little fluttering thing inside my chest.

He grabbed my hand and kissed the back of it, sending a warm, giddy sensation through my whole body.

Anticipation had me bouncing in the passenger seat while Matt tried to find a parking spot. We ended up having to use one of the garages. After getting out of the car, he slipped his hand into mine, and we walked toward my dorm.

I swung our hands back and forth, and Matt pretended he wasn't smiling about it. I eyed the backpack he had swung over one of his shoulders. "Are you going to stay over tonight?"

"Maybe..." he said slyly.

"Maybe?"

"If you're a good girl."

I gulped at that phrase, and he knew it. I wanted to be a good girl for him. While he was gone, I had to placate my horniness with toys and the memories of us together. I'd never admit that to him, but now I was desperate to be skin-to-skin with him again.

"Do you want to be a good girl tonight?" he asked, his voice low and husky.

"Y-yes..." I whispered.

We walked up to my building, and I scanned my ID to get inside. He held the door open for me, like the gentleman he was, and we walked inside. On the elevator, he rubbed his thumb against the back of my palm, and I felt heat course through me. If I didn't get this man into my bed soon, I was going to explode.

I nearly leapt out of the elevator when we got to my floor. I rushed us down to my door, and by the time I slammed my bedroom door shut, I was on him. He hiked me up against him, letting me wrap my legs and arms around him as I deepened the kiss.

I leaned my head back to let him take my neck while his hands slid up the bottom of my dress. "Maddie," he moaned.

"Mmm," I moaned back. "Please, bed now."

He carried me over to the bed and set me down gently. I grabbed for his sweater, but he pushed my hand away. "Wait."

"Mattttt," I whined.

He grinned despite how bratty I was being. "We need to talk first."

"About what?"

"I got you something."

"You got me a present?"

He nodded. "But we don't have to use it if you decide you don't want to."

I arched an eyebrow at him. What sort of present did he get me that made him say that?

He walked over to the door where he had dropped his bag and pulled out a package. He came over to the bed and sat down beside me. He handed me the package. "Open it."

I tore the cardboard box away, and my mouth dropped open at what was inside. I trailed a manicured finger across the leather-bound handcuffs. Excitement coursed through me that he wanted to explore my fantasies.

"We don't have to use them if you don't want to, but I figured we could try cuffing your hands above your head. These are velcro, so if you're uncomfortable, you can get yourself out." He took the package out of my hands and pulled out two pieces of thick cloth that had a hook on the end. "I bought the straps too. We can use them later if you want to be tied to the bed."

"Matt..." I breathed.

He set the restraints on the bed and cupped my face. "Sweet pea, we don't need to use any of this if you don't want to. But you said you wanted to test out your fantasies, and I'll do what you want. So let's talk about safe words and hard limits."

My words were a tangled web in my throat. "I...wow. Matt, Um."

He looked into my eyes. "We can set this aside for another time."

"I want to use them."

His eyebrows rose high, and I felt embarrassment heat my face. "You sure, sweet pea?"

I nodded.

"Safe word?"

I chewed my lip. I hadn't thought that far ahead. "Do we need one?"

He nodded. "This is all about safety and consent. Pick a safe word, any word, you say it, and we stop."

"Muffin," I said.

"Muffin?" he asked with a laugh.

I shrugged. "I don't know! It was the first thing I thought of. You need one, too."

"Cupcake."

I laughed. "Okay, so hard limits...You can slap my ass, but I don't think I want to be whipped or have anything but a hand used on me. I want to be restrained, but I don't think I want anything further than that. Like we don't need to be doing a 'scene' or anything like that."

"Okay, I can work with that."

"What about you?"

He shrugged. "Whatever you want, I'm game."

I leaned up and kissed him. "Thank you."

"I didn't do anything yet."

"For being so cool about this and wanting to experiment with me. You did research..." I trailed off as a realization dawned on me. "Oh my God! You took one of my books."

A sly smile crossed his face. "Guilty."

"Ass! You could have asked."

"Next time. What say we get you out of these clothes, huh?"

"Yes, please!"

He leaned down and took my mouth. He didn't just kiss me; he took control of my mouth, branding me with his lips. And I let him because it was what I wanted most. I slid my hand down his sweater as we kissed, feeling the tight muscles of his chest. His hands roamed down my sides until he slid one up my dress.

He pulled back when he came across my bare flesh. "Maddie," he hissed.

"What's wrong?" I asked as I pushed his sweater over his head.

"I thought you were a good girl?" he asked.

"I am. I'm your good girl."

"Good girls don't forget their panties."

The protest died on my lips when he pumped two thick fingers inside my pussy and stroked. Oh God, he was so good at that. His fingers were like magic, and I wanted more and more.

I tried to undo the button-down he wore underneath his sweater, but he slapped my hands away. Instead, he held them down on my bed with his free hand while he continued to stroke me toward an orgasm.

"Matt," I whined, but I arched my hips up to meet the movements of his fingers. His long digits slid in and out, the wet, slick sounds echoing in the room.

"Come for me," he purred.

I felt the pressure building up inside. I was burning up, and I needed that release. I'd been fingered a lot in my quest to get someone to take my virginity, but Matt seemed to have memorized the song of my body. He knew what strokes to press until I moaned his name and rocked against his hand.

"Good girl. Now strip for me," he ordered after taking his fingers out. I moaned as I watched him put them in his mouth and taste me. So hot.

I got off the bed and slid the slinky black dress off. I let the material fall to the floor and then took off my bra. Matt undid the buttons of his shirt and pulled it off, all the while staring at my naked form.

He shed his jeans, shoving his boxers down his legs in a

swift motion. I reached out to stroke his cock, smirking at him being hard and ready for me. I slid down onto my knees before he could stop me. I licked him from root to tip and slid my lips down his cock. The sound of his groan and the pull on my scalp told me he liked it. I stroked with my hand, sliding him in and out, loving the sounds that came out of his mouth.

"Fuuuck," he groaned as he fisted my hair.

I moaned around his cock, taking him further down my throat.

"Maddie," he whispered.

I looked up at him and pulled off for a second. "What's wrong, baby?"

"Get that sweet ass in the bed. I'm only coming in your pussy tonight."

I gulped at the commanding tone of his voice, but I loved it. I got into the bed, and before I knew it, he was on me again, boxing my head in between his arms as we kissed. He ground his hips against me, tormenting me with the feeling of his hardened cock against my thigh.

He put my hands above my head, pressing me down on the mattress, and took my mouth again. I moaned into it and struggled against his grasp. That was the fun of it, struggling and knowing I couldn't get out. My body buzzed with the prospect that he was going to put handcuffs on me to keep me in line. I loved that he did so much research and sat me down to talk about limits. I never thought he'd be game for what I desired.

I whined when he pulled away, but excitement spread through me when he held the cuffs up for me to see. "Okay?"

I gave him a silent nod and raised my hands above my head, palms up. He undid the velcro of one cuff, slid it around one of my wrists, and then repeated the action with the other one. There was a chain that linked the cuffs, binding my hands close together. We could unhook the chain and add the straps if I wanted him to tie me to the bed, but I wanted to try this first. He was right that we should warm up to it before testing out my limits further.

He got out of bed and reached down into my storage drawer for the condoms. He took one out, opened the package quickly, and put it on. He hopped back into bed, kneeing my legs apart.

I lifted my hips up, desperate to get him inside me, and struggled against the cuffs. Instead of giving me what I wanted, Matt kissed his way down my body. He made a tortuous path of kisses from down my jaw to the side of my neck until he pulled one of my breasts into his mouth. I moaned and arched up, using my strong core muscles to get what I wanted, but he pressed me back down against the bed and continued his descent down my body.

"Matt, please," I moaned.

He gave me a naughty grin from between my legs, and then he parted me with his tongue. The sensation of being pleasured when I couldn't touch him sent a thrill through me. I wasn't sure I would like this, but I loved being in his control, letting him set the rules, as I lay helpless beneath him. My orgasm ripped through my body, and before I could recover, he lifted and found my entrance, sliding all the way inside.

I clenched my hands into fists as the pleasure coursed through me, and I wrapped my legs around his waist, letting him take all of me. He drove deeper, finding that perfect spot that sent sparks down my spine.

"Good girl," he whispered into my ear. "That's my good girl. Come for me."

"Mmm," I moaned in agreement. I would have done anything he asked at this point.

He slid inside me faster and faster, taking me deeper and rougher as my vision blurred, and I came in a fury of screams. He silenced me with his mouth, but I felt his own release pulse inside me seconds later.

I opened my eyes and found him staring back at me. They were soft and concerned while he cupped my face. "Okay, sweet pea?"

"So good..." I slurred, slumping my head back against my pillow.

"Yeah?" he asked. He pulled out of me and threw the used condom in the trash can underneath my bed.

Words failed me, and I could only dip my head down into a solemn nod.

Matt undid the cuffs above my head and pressed a kiss to the back of one wrist and then the other. "What do you need for aftercare? I forgot to ask you."

I beamed. He was so sweet. He wanted to try out my fantasies in the bedroom, and he knew about aftercare. It was clear he had done more research than just swiping that book off my desk. Books were great for inspiration and introducing you to kink, but they weren't a blueprint. The little effort to make me comfortable had my heart singing.

"I want cuddles and a movie," I told him.

He grinned. "Anything with The Rock?"

"Yes!" I exclaimed. My love of The Rock knew no bounds. Seriously, I would watch him read the phone book. "But what do you need? That was intense."

His eyebrow shot up, alarm setting in across his face. "Intense?"

"In a good way. Thanks for trying that with me. We never talked about your fantasies, just mine."

He cupped my face and gave me a quick kiss. "My fantasy's making you come."

I beamed again and wrapped my arms around him as I kissed him. My heart was doing cartwheels. I was already in deep with this kind, gentlemanly hockey player.

I pulled away and got up to change into a pair of pajamas. He hopped off the bed and searched through his bag, pulling out the book he stole and handing it back to me.

"Ask next time!" I said with a grin and put it back on my desk.

"Oh, I bought the rest of the series on my e-reader. They're fantastic."

I beamed. "I've converted you."

He gave me a sheepish grin and then pulled out a pair of pajama pants to change into. "I'm all yours for the night. But I need to get up early for morning skate."

My heart did a happy dance. I missed him so much, and I was glad he was staying over to spend more time with me. "Are you sure? My bed's so small."

"It's not like we can chill in my room."

I frowned. We definitely couldn't do that.

"I don't mind," he reassured me. "I want to spend time with my girlfriend."

I felt so happy I could burst, and because I had no shame, I did a little dance in place, which made him laugh. I loved the way he smiled at my excitement, like I wasn't a complete weirdo.

After hitting up the bathroom, we crawled into my bed with him behind me. He wrapped an arm around my waist and pulled the covers over us. I turned on my TV and put on one of my favorite action movies.

"Hey, do you have plans for Halloween next weekend?" I asked.

"I'm in New York for a game."

"Oh. Right. I forgot."

"Why?"

"The girls on my team are having a party. I wanted you to come."

"Sorry. But you should go have fun."

I would have loved him to go with me, but I understood. He was so busy with hockey, he couldn't help that he was away a lot. I never realized how hard it was when the boys were away. Now I understood why Dinah worked a lot when my brother was gone.

He ran his fingers through my hair and kissed my temple. "I'm excited you're coming to my game tomorrow."

"I can't wait. I haven't been to one this season yet."

"Guess I gotta play well, huh?"

"Mmmhmm. Score a goal for me."

He laughed. "Just for you, sweet pea."

I grinned and snuggled down into him as we watched the movie together. I tried not to let the guilt of sneaking around behind my brother get to me as I enjoyed the feeling of being in Matt's arms. Future Maddie could deal with that later.

CHAPTER EIGHTEEN

MATT

Waking up to a crick in my neck sucked, but I'd sacrifice my body if I got to keep waking up with her in my arms.

The sex last night was intense, and I had been afraid of hurting her, but she loved being under my control. When she asked about my fantasies, I wasn't lying, but now, I'd warmed up to the idea of trying different things in the bedroom. With *her*. I couldn't wait to find out what other positions she loved or when I could tie her to the bed.

It wasn't just the sex I loved. Spending the rest of the night watching her favorite cheesy action movie while we cuddled in bed had been perfect. I didn't need to go to nightclubs or frat parties. I just needed to be with her.

I nuzzled into her neck, breathing in the floral scent of her shampoo while I procrastinated getting up. I could skip morning skate since it was optional, but I needed to give Dinah her car back. I wondered if it had been smart to take her up on the offer of borrowing it.

Maddie made a little noise in her sleep, and I couldn't help breaking out into a smile. She was so adorable. I kissed her neck. "Sweet pea," I whispered.

"Hmm."

"I gotta go."

Her eyes fluttered open, and she got that crease in her brow when she was thinking. "Oh. You have morning skate."

"I'll see you later?"

She chewed on her lip. "After the game? I feel like D and my brother are gonna corner me."

"Tell them you have to study, and I'll come over."

She laughed. "I *do* have to study."

"Then I won't come over."

She turned in my arms. "No. I want to spend time with you. You dropped all your feelings on me, and then you went on the road for an entire week. I missed you."

"That's why we texted non-stop while I was gone. I had to tell you before I went on the road and changed my mind."

Her mouth turned down into a sad frown. "You were gonna change your mind?"

I ran a hand across the scuff forming on my face. "I don't like lying to Noah."

"I'm not ready to tell him. Let me work on it."

She said that last night, too. I still didn't like that. Sure, it was fun being naughty together, but I wasn't good at hiding my feelings. How was I supposed to act around her when her brother was there? Was I supposed to pretend she didn't exist?

She pushed me onto my back and climbed on top of me. "Let me worry about it."

I slid my hands up her sides. "Okay."

She grinned. "I love what we did last night."

"Yeah?"

She nodded. "Maybe next time we can try a different position? Or you can tie me to the bed."

I looked her in the eye, searching her face to make sure she was ready for that. "You sure? We can work up to it. We don't have to always do bondage either."

"I want to."

"Okay...next time, we'll test something else out."

She grinned and bent down, pressing her lips to mine. I wanted to give into the kiss, to let her rock against me until I was buried deep inside her again, but I really had to leave.

She pouted when I pulled away.

"Sorry. I gotta go."

She rolled off of me, the sadness on her face killing me.

Reluctantly, I slid off her bed and got dressed, even though I'd rather be cuddled up with her. I gave her a quick kiss and then left.

I walked over to the parking garage and got into Dinah's car. I didn't have a car right now because it seemed foolish to have one when I lived in the city and could rely on public transportation or getting a rideshare. Dinah had been thinking of getting rid of hers, but Noah didn't like her being without one when we took his to the airport. I'd feel differently about a car once I felt better about my career in Philly. Or had my own place.

I drove to the townhouse and parked in the garage just as Noah was coming out to his SUV.

"Just in time," he said. "Hop in, and I'll drive you over."

"Gimme a sec," I told him. I went inside and hung up Dinah's keys on the hook, then I dropped my bag in my room. I walked back out to the garage and hopped into the passenger seat.

"So...date went well?" Noah asked as he backed out of the garage and drove off to the arena.

Sweat dripped down my forehead. Yes, it went well, but how was I supposed to talk to him like normal when I was dating his sister behind his back?

"Yeah," I managed to squeak out.

"I'd love to meet her. You should bring her over for dinner one night."

I rubbed the back of my neck.

Oh my God, this was why I wanted to tell him. Lying to Noah had not been part of it. I was never supposed to even look at his sister. Now she was my secret girlfriend who was into bondage, loved action movies, and told me my shot wasn't powerful enough. She would be the perfect girl if she wasn't my freaking mentor's baby sister.

"Cally, you okay?"

"Huh?" I asked, realizing I hadn't said anything for a couple of minutes. "Yeah. Running through plays in my head."

"So, girlfriend? Or is it still too new?"

It was still new, but she was definitely my girlfriend. One hundred percent.

"It's fairly new...I don't want to jinx it yet."

"Well, good for you, man. You seemed a little off when you and Kylie broke up again."

I grimaced. Kylie was my high school girlfriend. We briefly got back together last year, but then she remembered the distance was too much. We ended on okay terms. It sucked when it didn't work out, but I wasn't hung up on her or anything.

I got Noah to focus on preparing for the game ahead, which put my mind at ease. I didn't realize how hard it was going to be talking to him and pretending like I hadn't been kissing his sister an hour ago.

Fuck, all of this was turning out to be way more complicated than I imagined.

Once we arrived at the arena, we got our gear on and onto the ice. My worries about my relationship melted away as I hit the ice, my focus centered on the game. Morning skate was good to shake off the nerves. We were a little jet lagged from traveling yesterday, so Coach didn't have us doing any intense drills. He wanted us well rested for tonight.

After a quick lunch in the player's lounge, I went with Noah back to his house for our pregame naps. Some guys were cutting out the naps, but it was standard for me now, and if I didn't do it, it messed up my game. Hockey players were very superstitious. Riley taped his stick at least fifteen times before a game, Noah had to put his gear on in a certain order, TJ insisted on yelling everyone's nicknames, but I only needed my pregame nap.

Down in my room, I stripped to my boxers and set my alarm. I saw a text from Maddie.

> SWEET PEA: Miss you already! Good luck. I'll be the one screaming my head off when you have the puck.

> ME: About to take my nap. Can't wait to see you later.

She sent me a heart emoji, and I felt the warmth of her smile on me, even though she wasn't in the room. Then I shut my eyes and fell asleep.

❄

When I woke from my nap, I grinned at a few more texts from Maddie, offering me encouragement. Not having had a girlfriend in a while, I forgot how nice it could be to have someone in your corner.

I got out of bed and took a quick shower. That was one reason I moved down here. With the full bath, I could have my own space downstairs, while Dinah and Noah had theirs upstairs.

I rubbed a towel over my head and tried to figure out which suit to wear. I tossed two of them on my bed and sent a text to Maddie for an opinion. I grinned when she texted me back right away.

SWEET PEA: The blue one! You look so hot in it.

That was my favorite one, too. It was the one I had worn to the wedding the night I met her and on the night I told her I didn't want to be in the friendzone anymore. I was glad she loved it, too.

I dressed in it and snapped a selfie. My face hurt from smiling too much at the heart eyes and fire emojis she texted back.

SWEET PEA: Good luck, baby! Score a goal for me. Remember, more power in your shot.

ME: Okay, coach!

SWEET PEA: [grimace emoji] Sorry, can't help it.

ME: Your place after the game?

SWEET PEA: Yes, please. You can tie me to the bed this time.

ME: Can't wait.

I put my phone in the pocket of my suit and walked upstairs. Noah and Dinah were sitting at the kitchen table while Noah had his pregame meal. Dinah had her laptop, and her hair was in a bun, which meant she needed to get shit done. Those were her words, not mine.

"Hey," I greeted them.

I walked toward the fridge and pulled out my pregame meal. I got pretty serious about nutrition during the season and was hardcore about meal prepping. I had to do extra laps on the ice today to work off dinner last night. I sat across from the couple and ate while my thoughts turned to tonight's game.

"You ready for the game?" Dinah asked me.

"Think so."

Noah nodded. "Good."

"How was your date?" Dinah asked, her lips curving up into a mischievous grin.

I felt a lump in my throat. Was she fishing for information? "Good. Thanks for letting me use your car."

"Anytime. When do we get to meet her?"

I sighed.

Noah nudged her. "He said it's too early."

"Oh. Well...hopefully, it works out. We'd love to meet this girl that makes you almost miss the jet," Dinah teased.

Noah gave his wife a warning look, but I shook my head with a smile. That was D. She always busted my balls, and I wouldn't have her any other way.

We cleaned up after eating and got ready to head out.

Noah lifted Dinah up onto the kitchen counter so he could give her a kiss goodbye. I couldn't help but smile at that. Dinah was so tiny beside him, but the love radiated off of them. I felt weird watching them while I pulled on my coat, but I couldn't help but admire their love.

"Alright, rookie, let's get to the arena," Noah said and met me at the door.

"You ready for tonight?" I asked.

"Yup. We got this."

I hoped he was right. I had been working hard both in the weight room and during practice, trying to prove myself. I had to make that all count when I got on the ice tonight. I wanted to fight hard for a win, and part of that was because my girl would be watching. I had to play my best game for her.

CHAPTER NINETEEN

MADDIE

"Hey, you came!" Dinah cheered and raised a beer when I found all the wives and girlfriends in their section in front of the glass.

In some cities, a lot of the families used a box, but in Philly, all the WAGS liked being down right behind the glass.

I stopped in my tracks when I saw a baby in her lap. "Umm..."

Dinah laughed and bounced the cute little redheaded girl while I took a seat next to her. "This is Scarlet. Fiona and Riley's daughter and my goddaughter. Fi asked me to hold her because she went to go vom."

I laughed and waved at the baby. "You look pretty good with a baby."

She wrinkled her nose. "Now that Fi's pregnant again and after watching Max go through hell with the twins...I think I'm good."

"But you could adopt," I said. "Or foster."

"Noah and I talked about it. We like adopting the rookies instead. Plus, Fi said it's almost like being a single parent at times, and I barely remember to eat dinner if Noah doesn't text me reminders."

"Are you going to take in more rookies?" I asked with a laugh.

She shrugged. "We'll see next summer at training camp."

"Mama!" Scarlet cried.

I turned and saw Fi coming back over to our seats. She looked sick, but she smiled at her baby. She took Scarlet into her arms and sat on the other side of Dinah. "I know, baby, you missed Mama, huh? Thanks, D."

"How do you feel?" Dinah asked.

Fi blanched. "Like I'm never doing this again. Two's enough."

I hid my grin behind my hand and looked down at the ice where the players were coming out for warmups. I saw Matt skating around one zone. He looked so focused that I didn't think he saw me.

Riley skated over to the glass, and Fi held Scarlet up for her to wave. "Look, it's Daddy, Scar."

Riley's face broke out into a huge grin, and he waved to his baby. It was so adorable. Fi blew him a kiss, and he pretended to catch it before he skated off to the other side of the ice.

"They're so cute," Dinah said.

My brother skated over and slapped the glass while Dinah raised her beer at him.

I found my eyes glued to the ice, watching Matt as he weaved the puck up through Metzy's five-hole while he warmed up. Then he got down on the ice and stretched next to Benny. Was I thinking about how his body moved on top of mine last night? Definitely. I couldn't wait to let him torture me with impatience as he tied me to my bed and had his way with me later.

"Maddie," Dinah's voice cut through my horny thoughts.

I felt the blush creep up my neck. I thought, having finally lost my virginity, I'd be less of a horny mess, but nope, Matt brought out the horndog.

I turned back to my sister-in-law. "Hmm?"

She gave an amused look. "How's school going? You're not holing yourself up, right?"

I shook my head. "No, it's great. Hard, but good. I like to be busy."

Fi bounced Scarlet onto her other hip. "D said you're doing work for her. Are you looking for any other authors?"

I stared at her for a second. It hadn't occurred to me to take on more than Dinah's admin work. I did quite a bit for her, but it wasn't uncommon to have more than one client. I had some book blogger friends who assisted for more than one author, so it was doable.

"I haven't thought about it, but I'm open to it," I told Fi. "What do you need?"

"I have a signing in a couple of months. I could use a second set of hands."

"I'd love to help."

Fi smiled. "Great. I need help, especially since I'm probably gonna have pregnancy brain."

I laughed. "I'm down for more experience. I'd love to work for a PR company for authors."

Dinah nudged me. "You're so organized, you could start your own."

The thought had crossed my mind. I had a big presence

on social media, and it could be something I made a career out of, but I wanted to finish my degree first.

We watched the players go back down the tunnel for a couple of minutes, and then the starting lineup was announced on the PA. Pride swelled in my chest when I saw my brother taking the face-off at puck drop.

Noah was so good at what he did, and he deserved all the money on his contract. The Bulldogs have been a struggling team for years, but they had so much potential. The past couple of games had been good, but there was still a lot of hockey left to be played. I was confident they could at least make the first round of the playoffs this year.

"Come on, come on," I muttered under my breath as I watched the New Jersey captain bat the puck away from Noah.

"Dammit," Dinah muttered next to me.

If Riley and Blaise did their job and got it out of our zone, we could still get possession back. But I watched in agony as the team spent way too much time in the Bulldogs' zone trying to play keep away. I felt the air release out of my chest when Jersey went in for the kill, and then our Metzy made an aerobic save.

"Metzy, you beauty!" I cheered.

Dinah laughed. "Yeah, I mean, he's the only one showing up today."

I belted out a cackle. Most WAGs would not say that, but Dinah didn't give a fuck. She had been a desperate Philly fan way before she and my brother ever got together. Her marrying him didn't change that, and I loved that about her.

Nothing happened on that first shift, but I noticed Matt out on the second line, and that made me happy. He was so worried about whether he was good enough and would stay on the team, but Coach LaVoie wouldn't put him on the second line if he didn't see his potential. Matt was far too hard on himself. I watched every single game while they were on the road, and I saw how he was pushing himself. He was hungry to keep wearing the red and black, and I admired that about him.

Dinah gripped my arm as we watched the Bulldogs set up a play. Hallsy had the puck, and he was trying to find an opening, but a Jersey defenseman screened him. Matt was wide open. He could do this. Hallsy deked the shot and passed to Matt, who took the chance.

In a split second, the puck flew into the back of the net, and the crowd around us let out a relieved cheer. The red light lit up behind the Jersey goaltender, and Benny and Hallsy were grabbing Matt into hugs. The arena was buzzing, and I felt it all throughout my body, excitement for Matt coursing through me. I was giddy as I watched him skate down the bench, high-fiving all his teammates before play restarted.

"That was such a sick goal," Dinah said.

I grinned. "He's too hard on himself. That was a beauty."

She and Fi pinned me with raised eyebrows.

"How do you know that?" Fi asked.

"We're friends," I explained.

"Does my husband know that?" Dinah asked but with mirth in her eyes.

Shit. I couldn't let her think there was something more than friendship between me and Matt. If Noah found out... we'd be screwed. I wasn't ready to tell him yet, and he and Dinah didn't keep secrets from each other, so I couldn't confide in her. It wasn't time to open that can of worms yet.

I lifted one shoulder weakly. "We're just friends."

She gave me a hard look. "So you know nothing about his new girlfriend?"

I played dumb. "What new girlfriend?"

"Maddie," Dinah said with an edge to her voice. "I know all about overprotective brothers, okay?"

Fi nodded in agreement.

Dinah lovingly called her brothers the meatheads, and they kinda were. I loved them all, but yes, overprotective and scary, they certainly were. They tried to scare Noah off with their protectiveness, but Dinah told them to fuck right off with that bullshit. She didn't let anyone intimidate her. I wished I could stand up to my brother like she did to hers, but I wasn't as blunt as her.

If I told her about me and Matt, I was afraid of what my brother would do. She didn't know what it was like to be constantly compared to your more talented and famous brother. That was par for the course with women's hockey. We couldn't have the media talk about us without bringing up our famous brothers or dads or cousins. Like our own merits didn't matter unless they were tied to a man. Matt and I were still so new that I wanted us to enjoy this happy little bubble before all hell broke loose. Before he realized what a mistake I had been.

"Maddie," Dinah said again.

"I told you. We're just friends," I lied again.

Dinah didn't look convinced. She put a hand over mine. "Tell me if that changes. I have pull with that brother of yours, okay? If you want to date Cally, go for it. Don't let your meddlesome brother control that. He loves you and wants the best for you. He'll deal."

"It's your life," Fi agreed. "Cally's a cutie. So if you want to date him, it's none of Noah's business."

Their words were heartfelt, but I still didn't feel like I

could tell them the truth. Matt breaking the code was a big no-no, and I wasn't sure how my brother would handle it. Definitely not well. Noah Kennedy was a force to be reckoned with on the ice and when it came to guys wanting to date me.

I shook off the feeling of dread and guilt and watched the team fight hard in the first twenty minutes of play. And then I watched with a giddy grin on my face when my secret boyfriend scored a second goal of the game.

I sat back and enjoyed what I knew was going to be a superb game while trying to forget my worries.

CHAPTER TWENTY

MATT

"CALLY! CALLY! CALLY!"

I walked into the locker room with a shit-eating grin and the glorious sounds of cheering from my teammates. That was probably my best game of the season. I set it up early, sinking two goals in the back of New Jersey's net in the first period and then getting an assist on Benny's game-winning goal.

The energy in the room was on fire, all of us in high spirits after a much-needed win. I was buzzing with excitement at the fact Maddie saw me play tonight. I couldn't wait to see her later and celebrate.

I stripped off my jersey and undid my pads, leaving me in my undershirt, when Riley came over and handed me the silver bucket. I'd never received that before.

"Good job," Riley told me, and I knew he meant it.

My teammates got riled up, cheering me on, and I shook my head at their antics before putting the helmet on my head.

"Alright, boys," I said. "We played a good game. Let's make sure we do it again!"

"LET'S GET FUCKING LIT!" TJ yelled out into the locker room, screaming like a hyena.

I kept the helmet on long enough for our PR team to take photos. TJ's fiancée, Max, worked for the social media team, and she shook her head at him while she snapped photos. Max was so quiet and mild-mannered, I didn't understand how they worked.

"Your husband's out of control," I teased.

She laughed. "Not my husband yet. I still have time to give him back."

"Nuh uh, baby girl. You're not giving me back!" TJ protested.

"Behave," she told him, and he gave her that lopsided grin like he would do nothing of the sort.

I took the helmet off once PR let me, and I went to get a shower. I had to do the post-game presser since I had the most goals in the game. I was nervous, but I had media training so I didn't say the wrong thing. There was a reason hockey players were so conservative in their answers to media questions.

I sat down at the press table in the media room and waited for the reporters to hammer me with questions.

"LaVoie has been shuffling your line this season. What's it like playing next to Bennett and Halls the past couple of games?" the first reporter asked.

"Benny and Hallsy are great. I'm trying to learn from them. Pick up any little thing that they do to make us a better team. Fix little mistakes. Trying to do my best every night," I rattled off.

"What was your thought process going into tonight's game?" a different reporter asked.

"Getting pucks deep, trying to find that opening."

They asked me a couple more prodding questions before the head of PR signaled I could head out.

I went back into the locker room to grab my stuff.

"You're coming with us to the bar," TJ told me.

He didn't ask, he commanded, and since I was a rookie, I didn't have a choice.

"I have plans," I tried to argue.

He shook his head. "Nope! Drinks with the team, rookie."

I scowled. "Doesn't your girl need to drag you back home to the kids?"

"Max said I'm allowed to come out and play tonight."

I gnashed my teeth. I wanted to see Maddie tonight, but I couldn't invite her out to drink with the team. She didn't want Noah to know about us yet, so I was stuck in a hard place.

"Just invite your girl," Noah said as he pulled on his coat.

Benny peered at me from where he was fixing his hair at his cubby. He gave me a hard look, and based on our last heart-to-heart, he knew what my problem was. I stared back at him with a 'help me' look.

Benny playfully punched TJ in the arm. "He doesn't want you to scare her off."

"Me? But I'm so nice," TJ protested, but with that mischievous grin across his face.

"More like a pain in my ass," I muttered under my breath.

Team camaraderie was important, but I'd rather spend time with my girlfriend than these assholes.

Resigned, I grabbed my phone from the shelf in my cubby and texted Maddie.

ME: TJ's forcing me out for drinks. I feel like I'm not gonna be able to get away...

It crushed me when she sent back a frowny face emoji. Then a second message appeared.

SWEET PEA: Dinah's making me come out too.

Dammit.

ME: I'm sorry.

SWEET PEA: It's okay. Time with your team's important.

I was about to argue, but then I felt a presence beside me. I glanced up and saw Benny standing in front of me, giving me a knowing look.

"Ride with me, rookie," he said.

I grabbed my coat and followed him to his SUV outside. I climbed into the passenger seat, and Benny gave me an annoyed look before starting his engine.

"You're sneaking around behind Noah's back, aren't you?"

I blew out a long, frustrated breath.

"Bro!"

"It wasn't my choice."

He pulled his SUV out of the parking lot and drove toward Eileen's Tavern. "How so?"

"She thinks it's too soon to tell him. She wants to warm him up to the idea."

Benny ran a hand through his hair. "Alright. I get that. But it's better if you tell him sooner rather than later."

"I don't disagree. She's scared of his reaction."

"I'm in your corner, ya know? I've been there. Noah's not like TJ; he'll probably handle it better."

I wasn't so sure. Not with what Maddie said about how he handled what happened to her last year. I wanted to pound that guy to a pulp if I ever found out who he was. I could only imagine Noah wanted to bury him in his backyard.

"She's the boss," I said.

Benny laughed. "Yeah...I got one of those too. Just be careful."

"I'm working on it."

He parked his car, and we hopped out. When we entered the bar, he went over to Rox, who was at the bar with her brother doing shots. That was a sign I was in for a world of hurt tonight. I noticed Max next to them, shaking her head at the twins. Maybe Max could reel them in, but I highly doubted it.

I spotted Maddie at the bar with Dinah and Noah. When our eyes met, she gave me a sad smile. I rubbed my chest. I hated that look of disappointment on her face. We wouldn't have to deal with this bullshit if she told her brother we were dating. Better yet, if she let me sit him down and talk to him one-on-one.

"Hey," I greeted.

"Hey, nice goals," Dinah said.

Noah nudged me. "You did good."

"I don't know...you could have scored a hat trick," Maddie teased.

I laughed. "Maybe next time."

I ordered a beer and rolled my eyes when TJ came over with a bunch of shots. "You're doing a shot. To our rookie, Cally, for being a straight-up beautician!"

I shook my head at him but downed the shot like

everyone else. If anyone thought Max or their babies would tame TJ's wild ways...they didn't. Not by a long shot.

"T's so extra," Dinah laughed as he sauntered back over to Max with that lopsided grin on his face.

"That's our TJ," Noah agreed.

I sipped on my beer and nodded.

Noah bumped his sister's shoulder. "Hey, stranger."

"I've been busy," she explained.

"How's school going?" he asked.

"Good. Like I said, busy. Working for your wife, class, hockey, and —" She clamped her mouth shut and took a sip of her beer.

"And what?" Noah asked. He crossed his arms over his chest and gave her a suspicious look.

She dipped her head down and nervously pushed a strand of hair behind her ear. "I didn't want to tell you because it's new."

I felt my heart in my throat. Was she going to tell him about us?

A scowl formed across Noah's face and he narrowed his eyes, the action matching his already pissed off stance. "What's new?"

Maddie lifted her head and straightened her shoulders, like she was squaring up against him. "I'm seeing someone new. Not that it's any of your business."

Dinah raised an eyebrow, and her gaze pierced into me like she had already detected who the new guy in Maddie's life was. Shit. Dinah was scarily perceptive.

"Oh, really? Who is he?" Dinah asked with keen interest.

Me. Obviously. I kept my gaze on Maddie, gauging if she was ready to reveal that information, but her pinched expression was on her brother, ignoring my presence completely.

"It's too new. I didn't want to tell either of you about him yet," she explained.

"Who, Maddie?" Noah asked, ice lacing through his tone.

"It's none of your business, Noah," she seethed through gritted teeth. "It never is."

The siblings sent matching death glares to each other, while Dinah sighed and took a swig of her drink. I clenched my hand around my bottle of beer, trying to hold my tongue from saying something that would've gotten my face punched in.

"I'd like to meet him. Make sure he's not like the last one," Noah bit back at his sister.

Christ. I wasn't like that last asshole. Rage built in my chest that Noah would think that about me. Would he feel differently if he knew I was Maddie's new boyfriend and not some stranger he didn't know?

"This is exactly why I didn't want to tell you. I'm not subjecting him to your overprotective shit," Maddie told him, the annoyance at her brother written on her face.

Too late, sweet pea.

This was why I wanted to be upfront with Noah. The longer we waited the worse his reaction would be when he found out she was talking about me.

"It's not my fault you pick losers who end up hurting you. I'm just looking out for you," he argued.

That did nothing to assuage her anger. "Who I date isn't your fucking concern."

Noah dragged out an annoyed sigh. "None of the guys you date are good enough for you. You pick the biggest fucking douchebags you can find. I swear it's like a game for you to pick one worse than the last!"

"I don't need your approval on who I fucking date," she screeched.

"Maddie..."

She held up her hand to him and set her unfinished beer on the bar. "You know what? I'm out of here. I'm not dealing with this with you tonight. Fuck off, Noah."

Then she spun on her heel and stormed out.

Now it made a hell of a lot of sense why she didn't want to tell her brother about us. It wasn't just about me being his teammate. Noah didn't approve of *anyone* dating her. I wanted to get up in his face and tell him tough shit, that I'd never hurt his sister, and I was good enough. But I was more chicken shit than I realized.

I wanted to comfort my girl, but since no one was supposed to know about us, I couldn't go after her.

Dinah gave Noah a sharp look. "You remember how annoying it was to deal with my brothers?"

"Lovey, I know," he sighed.

"Stop sizing up her boyfriends. You gotta stop with that overprotective shit. I don't like that side of you."

"She's my baby sister."

"I have a little sister, and I don't do that bullshit," I blurted out.

I didn't mean to say that, but it was true. Luna had dated some losers, but that was her business, not mine.

"You have a sister?" Dinah asked. "I thought you said you were a miracle baby?"

"Luna was the bonus miracle."

Dinah looked back at Noah. "See! Matt's not that way. Be like Matt. You need to apologize to Maddie. You're treating her like a child, and that's not okay."

Noah looked down at the ground, guilt marring his face. I could tell this protectiveness came from love, not a way to control Maddie or anything like that, but it didn't make it cool. It was why she wanted to keep quiet about us, and I hated that.

I needed to go see my girl and cheer her up.

"How long do I have to stay to appease TJ?" I asked Noah.

The three of us looked over to see TJ on top of the bar, holding up a bottle of whiskey and yelling out into the crowd. The fact none of us thought this was weird or that the bartender just rolled his eyes should have been concerning.

Dinah belted out a laugh. "He's preoccupied. You're itching to see your girl, huh?"

"Yeah."

The way she studied me unnerved me, like she saw through me. Almost like she knew without a shadow of a doubt who my girl was and why I was being so coy.

"Great game tonight," Noah said. "You keep doing that, and you'll be here to stay."

I nodded in thanks.

I didn't care about finishing my beer; I just needed to go see my girl. I got a rideshare over to the townhome and packed a bag to stay over at Maddie's. I had off tomorrow, and I didn't know Maddie's plans yet, but I wanted to make it up to her. She deserved a fun date, and I had the perfect plan for my little bookworm.

CHAPTER TWENTY-ONE

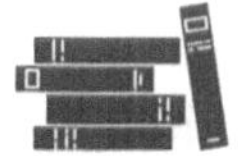

MADDIE

I was a ball of rage when I got back to my building. Matt had to understand why I was scared to tell my brother about us. Noah was too overprotective to the point it was irritating. Even my dad wasn't like that. I couldn't tell Noah I was with Matt tonight, but I had been testing the waters. Pretty sure Dinah knew, and she was letting me tell her on my own terms. I had to be extra careful around her.

I took a shower to calm down, but I was annoyed and cold when I got out. I sat on my bed with my hair up in my towel while I stewed. I was brushing out my hair, ready for a late night of cuddling up in bed with my e-reader, when I heard Ari come in from the hallway. There was someone with her, as I heard another voice, and then Matt stood in the doorway of my bedroom. He had changed out of his suit and was in comfy sweatpants and a hoodie. That casual combination shouldn't be hot, but it was.

Ari popped her head in. "Hey, look who I found outside like a lost puppy?"

I checked my phone and saw I had several missed calls from Matt. "Sorry."

Ari smiled at me and then walked back to her room. Matt shut my bedroom door and set his bag down.

"Maddie."

"I'm sorry. I'm in a bad mood."

His eyes softened, and he kicked off his shoes and got into bed with me. I pulled the comforter over him and felt warmth envelop me as he squeezed into my twin bed. He hugged me to his chest, and it felt so nice, like he knew this was what I needed. He didn't speak but instead stroked my hair and held me close. Exactly what any good boyfriend would do.

"I'm sorry, sweet pea," he said into my hair.

I couldn't help but grin. I loved that cheesy nickname and the way his voice purred like it was honey off his lips.

"It's not your fault."

He turned me in his arms and cupped my face. "I don't want to be a wedge between you and Noah."

"It was already there. Do you understand why I said we can't tell him yet?"

He nodded. "I hate it. I want to hold your hand in public and tell everyone you're my girl. I hate that we're lying."

"I know, baby, but...until my brother gets more comfortable..."

"Were you trying to tell him about us tonight?"

"Feeling him out," I admitted weakly. Just the thought of me having a boyfriend set my brother off. I couldn't imagine what he'd do after I told him that boyfriend was his teammate. Who lived with him. Noah would blow a gasket, and it could put Matt's career in jeopardy.

"Okay. Whatever you want. I just want you," Matt admitted.

Butterflies fluttered around my stomach at the sincerity in Matt's voice. When I stared back into his eyes, I saw all his feelings pouring out at me. Matt was a people pleaser, and it killed him not to tell my brother about us. I loved that about him. He wanted to do the right thing, but right now, we had to keep this from my brother for a while longer.

"Okay..." I whispered back.

"What do you need tonight?" he asked.

"Cuddles," I said meekly, snuggling back down into his chest and laying my head there.

He kissed the top of my head. "I can do that."

"Sorry. I'm not in the mood for sex."

"That's okay. I want to be here with you. "

If I wasn't already horizontal, I would have melted into a puddle of swoon. This man. Oh boy, he was so good with his words. It wasn't that he was a smooth talker, either. Matt was sincere in everything he said. If I read him in a book, he would be the perfect book boyfriend. But he wasn't fictional. He was real, and he was mine.

"Movie?" I asked. "I might fall asleep, though."

He kissed my temple. "Sure."

I turned on my TV and snuggled down into him again, loving the warmth of his body beside me.

"Hey, what do you have going on tomorrow?" he asked.

"Nothing much. Studying. Why?"

"I have plans for us."

I peered at him curiously. "What plans?"

"I want to spend the day together. I'm back and forth

traveling next week, so I want to take the day to enjoy it with you. If you'll let me."

"I'd love that."

"Yeah?"

I felt my mouth twitch at the start of a smile. "I love spending time with you."

"Good. So it's a date."

I broke out into a full grin then, giddy that this man was putting in all the effort.

First, he came over after a fight with my brother to see if I was okay. Most guys would expect sex, and even though I felt Matt's arousal against my back, he wasn't acting on it. Instead, he wanted to hold me and tell me it was going to be okay. Then he planned a date for us tomorrow.

How did I get so lucky?

"Really?" I asked Matt and put another book on the stack he was holding for me.

"Really, sweet pea. I want to spend the day with you, and I know how much you love your books."

I wanted to do a little dance, but that would be weird, and I didn't want to embarrass him. The way his lips curved up into a shy smile told me he was sincere.

This morning, Matt woke me up and told me to dress cute. He took me to the local brunch place I loved, where we drank coffee and ate delicious French toast. Then he said let's go to the bookstore. He was perfectly content with watching me walk around the local bookstore, scouring the shelves for romance books. He already had a stack of four, and I was going to add more.

"This is a perfect date," I told him as I walked down the aisles, finding another book to add to the pile.

"I knew you'd like it."

"I do."

I picked up another book, read the back, and then put it back on the shelf. I peered at the stack Matt was holding and put a finger to my lips. Did I really need all those books? Maybe I could get the ebooks instead?

"Whatever you want," Matt said.

"Huh?"

"I'm buying."

Oh, no. He wasn't supposed to do that. I was content with him being my human cart, but I didn't need him to buy all these books, too.

"That's not necessary," I told him.

"Let me."

"But you paid for brunch."

He grinned. "Then you can pay for dinner."

I grinned back at him. "Deal!"

I browsed for a little while longer, placing one more book in my pile. I preferred my e-reader because it was more portable, but sometimes having paperbacks was great.

Matt graciously purchased all my books for me, even though I felt bad. He made a lot of money as a hockey player, but after he told me he was going to pay for his sister's school, I didn't want him to spend money on me or think I was taking advantage of his kindness.

"Oh, I loved this one," the clerk at the bookstore said as she scanned our purchases.

I beamed. "I love that author. So good."

"Do you want a bag?" she asked.

"I can carry it," Matt said.

"A bag would be great, thank you."

Matt pulled out his credit card and handed it over. He didn't even flinch at the cost. The clerk gave us a smile when she handed over the bag to Matt. He took it and slid his hand into mine as we walked out of the store.

I loved to hold his hand and walk beside him. If we weren't in West Philly, I'm not sure I'd be that brazen. We couldn't do that if we were out and about near my brother's.

I was still so afraid of what Noah would think. He made it clear last night he didn't think I had good judgment. He called me this morning and texted an apology, but I sent his call to voicemail and left him on read. I was still mad at him for being an overprotective brother. He obviously already liked Matt, but he'd be furious when he found out. Matt felt guilty, and he already pushed me on it, but I needed time to figure this out. Noah didn't like any guy I dated. How much would he freak out when he found out I was dating one of his teammates?

"You travel tomorrow, right?" I asked as we walked back to my building.

This upcoming weekend was the Halloween party at Kiira's. I was bummed he couldn't come, but I was still gonna go.

Matt nodded. "In Buffalo tomorrow, game's on Tuesday, then home for practice, then back out to take on New York."

"The traveling's a lot, huh?" I asked.

He shrugged. "You get used to it."

I wasn't sure I would. Rox played in one of the fledgling pro women's leagues, and I couldn't imagine how she dealt with her schedule, Benny traveling, and having a full-time job. Granted, her league only had a handful of teams, so it wasn't as intense. Everyone thought since I was so good at hockey, I wanted that too, but that wasn't my goal in life.

We made it back to my dorm, and as soon as we got

inside my room, I kicked off my shoes and took my books out of the bag. I arranged them on the desk and grabbed my camera from underneath my bed.

Matt cocked his head at me with interest. "What are you doing?"

"I'm behind on my reviews, and I need to take pictures for my account. Book haul is the perfect thing to post."

He lay back on my bed and took his phone out. "Do your thing. I have to watch game tape anyway."

"You don't mind?" I asked. "I have to write some reviews. And Dinah's newsletter."

"I don't mind. I feel bad keeping you from your work."

I shook my head. "I want to spend time with you, and then you'll be traveling a lot this week."

"True," he conceded.

I took a couple of photos and scheduled posts for my feed, and then I sat at my desk and wrote Dinah's newsletter. She hated doing it, and it was one of the biggest things I took off her plate.

"What's book boyfriend material?" Matt asked.

I laughed and checked my phone to see he saw my book haul post because he liked it. I had shot off a caption that read, "*The boyfriend took me on a fun date to the bookstore today. He didn't even mind when I spent hours picking new books or making him carry them. He's like a total book boyfriend!*"

The comments were rolling in, some asking about the boyfriend because I'd never mentioned him before, and others talking about how much they loved or hated the books I posted. Readers could be so opinionated, but I loved it.

"It's a good thing," I told Matt.

A text came through from Dinah.

D: Newsletter looks great, thank you so much! Be proud of me. I wrote three chapters today.

ME: Yay! Now finish the draft.

D: Okay, boss! Also...when do I get to meet the boyfriend?

ME: When your husband learns to behave himself.

D: I'll talk to him. I'm mad at him for the way he's acting.

ME: D!!! It's between me and him.

D: I'll talk to him.

I wrote a couple of reviews, and then I crawled into my bed with Matt. He put his arm around me, and I lay on his chest while he watched video, preparing for his next game.

"Thanks for today. It was fun."

He kissed the top of my head. He turned off his video and set his phone down. "I enjoy spending time with you. I'll hold your books whenever you want."

I couldn't help the smile that broke out on my face. Oh boy, this man was so sweet. The more time we spent together, the more my heart did that little pitter-patter. My feelings for him were growing so strong.

"Are you worried about the game?" I asked.

He shook his head. "No. I feel more confident, but Noah said I had to watch out for Chester when we play New York. He just got called up."

I stiffened beside him. "Jaime Chester?"

"You know him?"

It felt like there was a brick in my stomach. I didn't

know Jaime got called up. When we were dating, New York had drafted him, but he was still in the prospect system while he played at university.

Oh no. Noah was going to go after him during the game.

"You need to worry about my brother losing his shit," I warned Matt.

"Why?"

I stared at Matt, hoping he wouldn't make me say it.

He frowned. "Maddie, what's going on?"

The brick sank further, anxiety snarling itself inside me. "He's my ex."

A scowl darkened across Matt's face. "The one who did the revenge porn?"

I nodded.

Matt folded me into his big arms. "Oh, sweet pea, I'm sorry."

"Please promise you won't fight him?"

His jaw was set into a hard line.

"Matt..."

"Okay, I won't. But he's gonna try to rile up Noah."

"I know!" I exclaimed. "Try to tell him to keep a cool head, okay?"

He tilted my head down and looked deep into my eyes. "I promise. No fighting. But how does New York not know that?"

I shrugged. "They probably don't care. A lot of white men in hockey get away with anything."

That was the unfortunate part about the sport I love. There were a lot of shitty people in it who did terrible things and got away with it all because they could score a goal. I didn't want to talk to my brother, but I pulled out my phone and gave him a warning.

ME: DO NOT GO AFTER THAT ASSHOLE CHESTER!

NOAH: I thought you were mad at me?

ME: I still am, but don't jeopardize your career by going after some rookie that's probably not going to stay in the big league.

NOAH: I'm not making any promises.

I groaned. Big brothers were the worst.

Matt seemed to know I needed a distraction because he rolled me over so I was straddling him and took my mouth. I melted into his touch, letting him slide his tongue into my mouth. It didn't take long for our clothes to fall off.

Matt grabbed a condom when I stopped him. "Wait."

He stared into my eyes. "What's wrong?"

I raised my hands over my head. "You didn't get to tie me to the bed last night."

He gave me a wolfish grin. "Oh, is that what you want?"

"Mmmhmm."

He set the condom down and reached into the drawer for the cuffs. He unhooked the chain in between the cuffs and hooked straps onto each one. He got back into bed and straddled me. He lifted one of my hands above my head and put the cuff around my wrist, and then he tied the strap to the headboard. He took my other hand and repeated the action so I was spread out like his plaything.

He cupped my face. "Okay?"

I tried to move my hands to escape and struggled. "Good."

"Not too tight?"

I shook my head. "It's perfect. Now get inside me."

That naughty grin spread across his face. "Oh, I don't think so."

"Please?" I begged, putting on a playful pout. We both knew it was all for play, and I was begging him to torment me.

He kissed his way down my body, making a slow descent as he savored every inch of my skin, and I couldn't stop him. I couldn't push his head down so he'd eat me out or grab him and make him get inside me faster. I was a horny mess, and he wasn't letting me have him.

I fucking loved it.

I loved that he was being a tease by slowly circling my nipple with the tip of his tongue and then doing it to the other one. He danced his fingers down between my legs, but he stroked my thighs instead of going where I wanted him to.

I tried to arch my hips up to meet his fingers, and he nipped at my thigh. "If you're not a good girl, I'm gonna end up having to get you ankle restraints too."

Well, I wasn't going to say it, but I wanted to try that out eventually.

He pressed a thumb against my clit and plunged his thick fingers inside my entrance. "You want to be a good girl, right, sweet pea?"

"Y-yyes," I moaned out as his fingers stroked me deep, finding my g-spot and setting me off.

His voice was like honey. "That's a good girl. Come for me."

Matt taking charge in the bedroom was a surprise. He was so mild-mannered and gentlemanly that watching him transform into this growly tormentor made play all the better. It made me obey his every word.

He barely gave me time to recover until he was sliding inside me, and then the pleasure coursed through me again.

He took me hard, pressing me into the mattress as I was bound and laid out for him. I couldn't dig my nails down his back or hold onto him, but the inability to touch him made it hotter. It made me cry out harder.

He didn't stop until I came at least two more times until I was begging him for that final release. Then he roared out his own climax in that beautiful guttural sound I loved.

He pulled out and took care of the condom. Then he came back to the bed and untied me. He cradled me in his arms as he kissed my wrists one by one. I giggled at the sensation. He hadn't hurt me with the restraints, and he had been so good at making me comfortable. I loved the care he gave me afterward.

He cupped my face. "You okay?"

"So okay," I breathed out.

We lay together for a little while, cuddling in my too-small dorm bed, as we basked in the afterglow. In that moment, I knew I was in big trouble. I had fallen hard for Matt Callahan, but it was far too early to express those words. So I just kissed him instead.

CHAPTER TWENTY-TWO

MATT

This game was getting chippy.

We were tired from back-to-back games on the road, and New York was fighting hard tonight. Especially Chester. He was getting in Noah's head so much he fucked up on the face-off in his last shift, and that was unlike him.

If Chester knew I was dating Maddie, he'd probably be going after me. He didn't expect it when I got away with slashing him. I told Maddie I wouldn't go after him, but this guy sucked. Fuck him for making her feel bad about herself. She had no reason to be ashamed of anything.

"What's Chester's problem with Kennedy?" Benny asked.

I chewed on my mouthguard. It wasn't my place to tell him what happened to Maddie.

"I've never seen him like that," he said, confusion marking his face.

"He's Maddie's ex," I muttered.

"Oooh. That's why *you* keep going after him."

"Fuck that guy."

He couldn't press me on that because the arena started getting loud, and I looked back on the ice and saw Noah had dropped his gloves.

Oh, shit! I specifically promised Maddie this wouldn't happen.

Fuck. Fuckity. Fuck.

My teammates banged on the boards like the dicks they were, egging Noah and Chester on. Chester dropped his gloves down, and they danced around each other for a bit. Noah struck first, getting in a few blows, but Chester fought back. They fought long enough for the refs to pull them away and send them both to the box for a five-minute penalty.

"Fuck! What the fuck was that shit?" Riley swore.

It was 2-1 us, with only a few minutes left to spare in the last period, and we needed to be on the offensive. Noah getting into an uncharacteristic fight was the last thing we needed.

I watched my teammates on the ice as they tried to set up a play. If we could wait out the clock, we'd still get the W. The shift changed, and then, out of nowhere, McCarthy found an opening, and the boos poured in. The lamp behind the Gladiators' goalie lit up and our bench cheered.

The clock ticked down, and Noah was let out of the box. Pretty sure Coach would have words with him later. I hopped over the bench for the last shift of the game, but I didn't put up any points. We unfortunately couldn't make another play, but a win was a win.

In the locker room, TJ had our victory song going while we stripped off our gear. McCarthy got the silver bucket this time, and he said a few words before we all headed to the showers. I got an assist off one goal, so I talked to the media with Noah briefly. He was prodded about the fight since it was unusual for him, but he tried to brush them off.

"He knows what he did," Noah said with a hint of finality, and then our PR handler signaled we could leave.

"Dude, you shouldn't have lost your head," I told him afterward while headed toward the bus where we'd ride back to Philly as a team.

Noah stared at me. "Do you know why I did that?"

"Maddie asked me to make sure you didn't lose your cool," I snapped at him.

He gave me a hard look. "She told you?"

"Yes! Because she's my friend, and she was venting about how the overprotective shit has gotten worse and that you blame her for what happened."

Noah stopped as he was about to get on the bus. "She told you all that?"

I nodded.

He narrowed his eyes at me. "I didn't realize you were so close."

"We're friends," I reiterated.

Maybe I let that slip so he'd realize how much his overprotectiveness was driving her away. Last week, she had been working for Dinah at the house when we got home from practice, and she barely said anything to either of us before she left. When we talked that night, she said she was still mad at him.

"I don't blame her. But that guy's a piece of shit," Noah snarled.

"She doesn't know that. She thinks you're ashamed of her. And you need to stop treating her like a child."

He wanted to say something else, but Hallsy yelled at him to get on the bus already, and he turned back around. I needed space away from Noah, so I found a seat in the back next to Cully. He didn't mention my bad mood, but he had his phone to his ear, and his voice was soft. He was either talking to his girl or saying goodnight to their kids. I tried to be quiet so I didn't interrupt him.

I took out my phone and saw a frowny face and then an angry face emoji text from Maddie.

ME: I'm sorry, sweet pea.

SWEET PEA: You promised!

ME: I know.

SWEET PEA: [angry face emoji]

She stopped texting me after that, and I sat on the bus for the next two hours, stewing in my thoughts. Guilt wrapped itself around my chest. I couldn't fulfill my promise. I wanted to rock that douche's shit like Noah had, but I had no reason to do so. I even tried to goad him into a fight, and he brushed me off.

I let out a long sigh.

"You alright, man?" Cully asked.

"Girl trouble."

He nodded and ran a hand through his shock of red hair. Cully gathered I had a girlfriend by now since we had to share a room when we were on the road. That was also why I knew what songs got his kids to sleep.

"You wanna talk about it?" he asked.

"Nah, it's okay."

He peered at me for a second. "Alright. What was up with Kennedy tonight?"

I sighed. "Don't worry about it. That was a one-off."

I couldn't help but wonder if that was what Noah was

gonna do to me when he found out I had been fucking his sister behind his back. I sat back and watched the skyline go by and tried not to think about it too much. Maddie wasn't ready to tell him, and I wanted to respect her wishes, but this weight on my chest kept getting heavier.

It was late by the time we got home. I changed out of my suit and slumped down on my bed. The futon bed was so much more comfortable than Maddie's twin bed, but I missed her pressed up against my side.

As if she knew I was thinking about her, my phone vibrated, and I saw she was trying to video chat with me.

I answered immediately. Her cute face greeted me, along with her dark makeup and a witch hat. But she was pouting. "Aw, sweet pea. What's wrong?"

"You promised...y-you...said you would reel him innn," she cried, slurring her words.

It was loud wherever she was, and I didn't like that because it was so late already. "I'm sorry. I tried. Where are you?"

"Hockey house," she muttered, and she wiped her eyes.

Panic coursed through me. "What's wrong?" I asked again.

"I miss you. Did you get home okay?"

I stared at her image on the screen, sensing something wasn't right. Her makeup was a little smudged now that I was paying attention. "Where are you?" I asked again.

"Hockey house."

"Give me the address."

"Why? You're tired from the game."

"Doesn't matter. I'm coming to get you."

"Okay," she muttered and then ended the call.

I shoved clothes into my bag and headed upstairs. Faint sounds of voices floated down from the second level. Dinah was a night owl, so it wasn't unusual that she was still up working when we got in late. I didn't say a word to either of the Kennedys as I left the house.

Maddie texted me an address so I could order my rideshare, and I waited a while before it got here. Something was wrong with my girl, and I might not know how to fix it, but I was gonna try.

Plus, I missed her. Traveling could be rough on the body. I loved playing hockey, don't get me wrong, but since Maddie and I started dating, I realized how the travel schedule got to some of the guys. I understood now why Noah was always antsy to see Dinah. Or why a lot of the coupled-up guys ditched us to see their partners. That's what I was doing. McCarthy even called me out on it for bailing on him a couple of nights ago. Ty, too. I hadn't told him about me and Maddie yet.

After my rideshare picked me up and dropped me off at the hockey house, I heard the party bumping from outside. Spooky music played on the stereo, and I didn't need to knock because a sexy nurse walked out, letting me inside. I moved through the crowd, searching for my girl in vain.

I wasn't familiar with this house. When she said 'hockey house,' I thought she meant the one we went to last time, but realizing the amount of women in the room, I think she meant the women's team.

"Yo, Cally!" a familiar male voice called out to me.

I weaved through the crowd into the kitchen, where I found my best friend doing shots with my girlfriend. Maddie's face lit up when she saw me, and I had to gulp when I saw her outfit. Her video call did not do that slinky black dress justice. Or the fishnet stockings she wore underneath. Or the stilettos. Good God, I wanted to see her in nothing but those.

"Baby!" she cried and jumped into my arms. I stumbled back at her immediate action, but then I wrapped my arms around her as she planted a big kiss on me.

I brushed her hair behind her ear. "I thought you were mad at me."

"Noooooo. I'm mad at my brother. Not you. I missed you."

I set her back down, and all Ty did was raise an eyebrow. "Later," I mouthed to him.

"Your girl can hang with the best of them," Ty teased and then knocked back his shot.

Clearly. She smelled like a brewery, and her words were slurring. But still, she had a sadness in her eyes, and I wanted to know what that was about.

"Can you take me home?" she asked. "Please?"

"Where's your coat?"

"Didn't bring one. I drank enough to make me warm."

I sighed. Yup, sweet pea was pretty drunk. I took off my coat and wrapped it around her. We waved goodbye to everyone, and I slipped my hand into hers. I smiled when she swung our arms together.

She asked me how the game was as we walked back to her dorm. I was glad I came to find her because I didn't want her to walk home alone. Might need to ask Ty to watch out for her while I was on the road.

When we got inside her suite, I helped her get out of her costume, and she drunkenly washed off her makeup. I grabbed her water from out of her mini-fridge and her trash can, just in case.

I pulled back the covers of her bed and helped her in.

"Matt?" she asked, her voice a hushed whisper.

"Yeah?"

She gave me those big, blue, hopeful eyes. "Stay?"

"I will. Gimme a minute."

I changed into pajamas and crawled into bed with her. I stroked her hair, waiting for her to tell me what was wrong.

"Noah shouldn't have fought him," she whispered.

I bent to kiss her neck. "I know."

"Now it's worse."

"Between you and Noah?"

She shook her head.

"What's wrong?"

"Jaime texted me."

Rage ran through me. He fucking what? I wished I had fought the guy, too.

"He was taunting me, and he called me...he called me..." She trailed off into a sob. "He said I was just a stupid puck slut. He doesn't even know I'm dating a hockey player!"

Ah. She looked like she'd been crying when she video-chatted with me, and now I knew why.

I cupped her face. "Sweet pea, you're not any of that. Nobody, and I mean nobody, makes you feel inferior. You got me?"

"Oh, Matt. How did I get so lucky with you?"

I gave her a quick kiss. "I'm lucky with you. But I'm mad I didn't rock his shit tonight, though. Fuck that asshole."

"Please don't fight some douche on my account."

I pulled her into my chest. "You're not any of those things your asshole ex said to you. He was trying to get a reaction out of you. You're smart, kind, and beautiful inside and out. I don't want anyone to ever dim your sparkle."

"Matt..." she whispered.

I pressed a kiss to her temple. "Go to sleep, sweet pea. I'm here. I got you."

"You didn't have to come over. I know you must be so tired."

I was. After a game and travel, I was beat to shit. Then I saw the tears in my girlfriend's eyes. I'd never forgive myself if I hadn't made sure she was okay.

I squeezed her against me. "S'okay. I wanted to see you and make sure you were okay."

"I wanted cuddles," she said with a sheepish grin.

"Well, now you've got them. It's late. Let's get to bed. We'll talk more in the morning, okay?"

She snuggled down into my chest, and we fell asleep together.

If I ever faced off against Jaime Chester again, I was dropping the gloves and punching his face in. Nobody made my girl cry. Nobody.

CHAPTER TWENTY-THREE

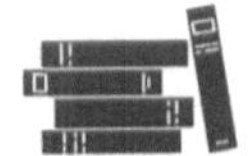

MADDIE

"Are you sure this isn't too much on your plate?" Dinah asked me.

I shook my head as I sat in the comfy chair in the corner of her office with my laptop.

The nice thing about being her PA was that we could meet face-to-face. I had already met with Fi earlier this week to talk about her logistical needs for the signing. To be fair, it was a lot, but I didn't want to let either of them down.

She eyed me. "Maddie, I didn't know you were taking more courses than usual. If you need to work fewer hours or you can't do a beta read for me, say no."

I gave her a smile. "I can handle it."

"I know you can, but I don't want to pressure you into taking too much."

I waved her off. "Be quiet so I can read this and you can get more words down."

She rolled her eyes, but she knew she needed someone

to boss her around to finish writing. That was the real reason I came over after my classes today. She was behind on deadline and needed an extra push.

The other reason was that the team was supposed to come home from the road today, and I selfishly wanted to see Matt. Even if we had to pretend we were just friends.

It had been a couple of weeks since my brother went after my ex on the ice. It pissed me off he was being the annoying protective brother. Matt and I had been arguing again about if we should tell him we were together. It wasn't time yet. Noah wouldn't be prepared if we dropped that bomb on him.

I went back to reading the secret project Dinah was working on. After Fi dared her to try to self-publish this more adult novel, Dinah went to work on it. She finished it, and now I was the first person to have eyes on it. It was so different from her young adult stuff, but I loved it. It wasn't as spicy as the kinky stuff I read, but compared to her other work, it was on fire.

My phone vibrated next to me, and a smile spread across my face when I saw a text from Matt.

MATT: Hey, sweet pea. We're getting in the car now. Can I see you later?

ME: I'm working at the house today. So sorta?

MATT: Okay.

ME: Let's grab dinner later!

"Is that the boyfriend?" Dinah asked.

"Maybe..." I said coyly and set my phone down.

She turned around in her desk chair and pinned me with a knowing look. "When do I get to meet him?"

Guilt lodged in my stomach. I hated lying to Dinah, but my brother said they had a really open relationship and told each other everything. I couldn't tell her and expect her to keep it from him.

"I told you, when your husband learns to control himself."

She frowned. "I talked to him about that. You're not being fair to him right now."

"Whose side are you on?" I grumbled.

"Both of you. He's my husband, but I love you too. I don't like the rift between you. I thought he was getting better about that stuff."

"I lied to you about why I transferred," I blurted out.

"What?"

"My ex sent my nudes to the entire hockey team after I broke up with him. That's who Noah fought a couple of weeks ago. That's why he did it. You know he doesn't fight."

"That's why he was in that fight? Fuck that guy." She walked over to me and sat down on the other reading chair. She put a hand over mine. "I'm sorry that happened to you. That's not your fault."

"I know. He was an asshole. Ma—my boyfriend reassured me about that."

I cringed as I realized I had almost slipped up and said 'Matt.' Dinah narrowed her eyes like she was trying to sus something out. I pushed my hair behind my ear and tried to go back to reading her book, hoping she'd go away, but her stare bore through me.

"Maddie," she said, her tone flat.

"Hmm?" I asked, not bothering to look up at her.

"Why haven't we met him yet?"

"It's complicated. He travels a lot for work."

Not exactly a lie, but not the truth either. I couldn't say 'I can't tell you because your husband will straight up kill him for breaking the code.'

Dinah crossed her arms over her chest. "He travels for work? How old is this guy? Is that why you don't want us to meet him? Is he like your dad's age? I'm eight years older than Noah, and granted, I had some issues with that at first, but nobody cares."

I shook my head. "No. It's not that. He's only twenty-two."

The suspicion marred her face again. "He's only twenty-two...oh my God!"

Before she could call me out about lying to her because I was pretty sure she had figured it out right then and there, the front door opened.

"We'll talk about this later," she said as she walked out to greet my brother.

I had no desire to do that, so instead, I'd avoid coming over here at all costs now.

I went back to my computer and read a little more from her book. The sound of footsteps made me look up. I couldn't help but smile when I saw Matt standing in the doorway.

"Hey," I said.

Noah knew we were friends, so it wasn't weird to be friendly toward him. But I couldn't jump into his arms and kiss him like I wanted to. I didn't want to keep this a secret forever, but I was so worried about what my brother would say. That he'd kick Matt out and try to get him off the team.

"Hey," he greeted back. "How did your test go?"

I frowned. "I don't know. I'm bad at math."

"I'm sure you did fine," he reassured me. He looked over his shoulder and then mouthed. "Meet you in a few hours?"

I nodded, and then he walked down the hallway and toward the basement where he lived.

I worked for another hour until I got to a good stopping point. Dinah was too preoccupied with my brother, and I didn't want to ask questions about what they were up to. I shut down my laptop and put it back into my backpack.

I was hoping to slip out unnoticed, but my brother was in the kitchen when I tried to get to the front door.

"Hey, wait!" he called after me.

I sighed. "What?"

Noah walked over toward me and rubbed a hand over his big, bushy beard. "Can we talk?"

"No."

"Mads."

"Fine," I sighed. "What do you want?"

"I'm sorry."

"For what?"

"Matt told me you felt like I blamed you for what happened with Chester. I want to apologize for that. I don't blame you. It's just... You're my little sister."

I stared him down. "I'm also not a little kid. You don't have to do that big brother overprotectiveness anymore."

He massaged the back of his neck. "You've dated a lot of guys who haven't been right for you."

"That's none of your business. Who I date is of no concern to you."

"Is this why you won't let us meet the new guy? Because I'll scare him off?"

"Yes," I lied.

No, it was so much worse. He had no clue.

"I'm sorry. D kinda gave me the business about that, reminded me about how annoying her brothers were when we first started dating. So, when you're ready, I'd love to meet your new guy. I promise to be on my best behavior."

I stared at my brother. He would absolutely not be on his best behavior. He was going to go through the roof.

"Maybe," I said and shrugged.

He nodded.

"I have to go," I said and turned to leave.

Luckily, he didn't stop me. The guilt was still weighing me down, but I wasn't so sure I'd ever feel comfortable telling him. I knew one person who could help me.

When I got back to my dorm, I dropped my bag on the floor and flopped onto my bed. I pulled out my phone and sent a video chat request to my best friend Ally.

She answered immediately, her blonde hair up in a messy bun. "Hey, you slut! I thought you forgot about me."

I cringed. "I'm sorry. I'm the worst!"

"Mmmhmm. So how's Philly? Has Noah forced you to move in yet?"

I groaned.

"That bad?"

"He fought Jaime."

She laughed. "Douche deserved it."

"I know, but I have a huge problem."

She gave me a concerned look. "What's up?"

"How bad was it when your brother found out you were dating his teammate?"

Ally laughed. "Umm...it was bad, but then they did some stupid alpha male shit where they got drunk together, and it sorted itself out. Why..." she trailed off, and her eyes got big. "Oh no. Are you secretly dating one of his teammates?"

I nodded. "And I think my sister-in-law figured it out."

"Just tell him. What's he gonna do? Forbid you from dating him?" Ally asked with a roll of her eyes.

"It gets worse."

"How?"

I sighed. "He's the rookie who lives with them. You know, the one I told you about?"

Her eyes widened. "Okay, so it's a little more complicated, but...Noah likes him, right?"

I nodded. "Yeah, he's like Matt's mentor. That's what makes this so hard."

She chewed on her lip. "Okay, well, he'll be pissed at first. He might punch him in the face."

"Ally!" I cried. "Not helping!"

"But he'll get over it, okay? Noah's seen all the shitty guys you date, but if he already likes this one, it will be a little easier."

I let her words pour over me. I wanted to believe her, but I wasn't so sure. Of course, Noah liked Matt. He was so sweet and a gentleman, like my brother was with Dinah. Maybe he would see reason since he already knew Matt was a good guy.

"You're such a bitch for not telling me about this," Ally cut into my thoughts.

I grimaced. "I'm sorry. It's been a lot. But I really like him."

"I could tell from your posts. Did he seriously buy you all those books?"

My lips tipped up into a smile at the memory. Matt was such a wonderful boyfriend, and I knew it was weighing him down not to tell my brother.

"So, did you...do the deed?" she asked and waggled her eyebrows.

That made me howl with laughter and miss my best friend. I was a shitty friend for not checking in with her sooner. It had been hard to keep up since I moved to the States, and I'd been busy with my workload.

"I definitely did," I admitted with a grin.

"Get it, girl!"

"Oh, I do."

Then it was her turn to laugh.

"Fucking finally!"

I laughed. "That's what I said."

"I think you gotta tell Noah sooner rather than later. Rip off that band aid. Your sister-in-law will go to bat for you, so what are you afraid of?"

I rubbed my temples. Why didn't anyone understand how complicated this was? "He lives with them. What if Noah tries to get him kicked off the team?"

She shook her head. "He's overprotective, but he won't do that."

I didn't know about that.

We chatted for the next hour, catching up on everything. I was planning on going home for Christmas, so we talked about potential plans. That reminded me I needed to call my mom. I hadn't talked to her in a while. She had texted me, yelling at me about Noah fighting Jaime, but I told her I didn't control him. Mom hated hockey fights. Probably why Noah usually behaved himself.

After I hung up with Ally, I sat down to study before Matt would come over for dinner. He had texted me while I was video chatting with Ally that he went to do weight training and asked if I could handle a late dinner. I was good with that, but I was glad he checked in with me.

Matt was the nicest guy I'd ever dated. I kept thinking back to what Ally said. Maybe it wouldn't be that bad when we told my brother about us. It would be worse the longer I waited to tell Noah. But I kept thinking about how he disapproved of everyone, and I didn't want to jeopardize Matt's career or their friendship.

Maybe Matt was right to resist me. What had I gotten myself into?

CHAPTER TWENTY-FOUR

MATT

Maddie was quiet tonight. She sipped on her beer pensively as we had dinner at Local Hangout.

"What's wrong?" I asked between bites of my burger. I shouldn't have been bad about my diet, but I did a fuckton of weight training with Benny today, and I deserved it.

She rested her cheek on her hand. "I think Dinah knows."

I swallowed my food. Oh, yeah, that. I was pretty sure she knew, too. Especially since she cornered me when I was on the way out the door. Noah told her to lay off me, but her questions about my girlfriend were oddly specific.

I didn't want to sneak around anymore. I wanted to sit Noah down and tell him I loved his sister, that I'd never do anything to hurt her, but there were a couple of things wrong with that. One, I hadn't said those three little words to the woman in question. And two, she wasn't ready to tell him yet. I didn't want to keep pushing her on it. The puck was on her stick about this.

"Is it bad if she knows?" I asked.

"She tells Noah everything."

I took a sip of my beer and thought carefully about my words. "But Dinah likes me, so she'll help us."

"Okay, fair..."

I reached out and grabbed her hand. "I want to be with you, no matter what that looks like. I'd rather not have to continue to lie to your brother, but if you need more time, that's what we'll do."

Her eyes softened. "I'm sorry. I'm so scared about what he'll think. He never likes any of my boyfriends."

"Well, he already likes me. And so does D. Maybe if we tell her, she can help us warm him up to the idea of us?"

She seemed to ponder that for a moment as she took another sip of her beer and a bite of her sandwich. "Maybe," she whispered after a few seconds had gone past. It was so loud in the bar, I barely heard her.

"Sweet pea..."

She pulled her hand away from me. "I don't want to think about it tonight. I missed you so much."

I grinned. "I missed you too."

"I didn't realize how much it sucked to be a WAG."

I laughed.

I changed the subject to ask her how work with Dinah was going. I smiled as her eyes lit up and she told me about the secret project Dinah was working on. I loved the look of excitement in her eyes when she talked about her passions. I worried I was taking up too much of her time, but I wanted to savor every moment I had with her.

When the check came, we fought over it, and I let her win. This time.

"What now?" she asked.

Before I could answer, I heard my name being called. Then, like the whirlwind he was, Ty ran over to us and slid into the booth next to Maddie. She had whiplash from his movement while he stole one of her last fries and gave me a grin.

"Well, look who it is!" he exclaimed.

I gave him a head nod. "Hey, Ty."

He pointed between me and Maddie. "You two ran out at the Halloween party, and I couldn't grill you about this."

I rolled my eyes. "Fuck you, man."

He cackled like the dick he was. Maddie looked amused. He nudged her. "Your boy's so sensitive. You've been chaining him up in your bed? Is that why he's been ignoring me?"

Maddie's cheeks went red at his joke.

"Ty," I warned.

"What? There's nothing wrong with a little bondage. Don't be prude."

"He's not," Maddie managed to squeak out while trying hard not to laugh. God, if only Ty knew.

Ty waggled his eyebrows. "Oh, really?"

"Stop it. What you want, asshole?" I asked.

"Come to the hockey house and party with us tonight."

I looked over at Maddie, silently asking her, and she shrugged.

"You can bang each other later. I haven't seen you in weeks," Ty whined.

I shook my head at him. "Dude, you're needy."

"I am. Hey, Lu-lu said she's coming to visit soon. This is practice for when she gets here."

I gave him a stern look. "You're not, under any circumstances, taking Luna to a kegger. You got me?"

He nudged Maddie. "He's so easy to rile up. Come on, you fools, let's go!"

He whirled away as quickly as he came.

I stared at the empty space where he had just been sitting, and Maddie giggled. "Is he always like that?"

I groaned. "Unfortunately. We don't have to go if you don't want to."

She gave me a bright smile. "I'm down. Could be fun."

"Alright, then let's go."

Truth be told, I felt like a dick ignoring Ty, and he kept hounding me after seeing each other at the Halloween party when I collected Maddie. He put on that party boy front, but Ty was still hurting over his breakup. People assumed because of his personality, he was a douchey athlete who fucked anything that moved, but Ty and Elsa had been together forever. He'd never admit it, but he had really loved her. No offense to Elsa, but I don't think she ever felt the same way.

"Let's go," Maddie insisted. "We never hang out with your friends."

To be fair, we didn't hang out with hers all that much either.

"Okay, let's roll."

I helped her with her coat and slid her hand in mind. We found Ty outside waiting for us, and we walked together to the hockey house.

We could hear the house from a mile away. I did enough partying as a hockey player that I don't think I missed much from not having the college experience. We walked inside, and Ty screamed at the top of his lungs that the party had arrived.

I shook my head.

"Him and TJ would get along really well," Maddie said.

I had thought the same thing multiple times. Probably why I easily brushed off TJ so much. Ty was my practice run.

I took our jackets into the hall closet but lost Maddie at one point. I walked into the kitchen and grabbed us some beers.

"I thought she was off-limits," Ty said from behind me, making me jump.

"She is."

He raised an eyebrow at me. "You're sneaking around? You? Really?"

I grimaced. "Her idea."

"She's cute. You look happy."

"I really like her."

"Then you'll figure it out, man. But it explains why you disappeared on me."

I took a sip of my beer and glared at him. "You know I'm on the road a lot."

He grinned. "I know. Just yanking your chain."

I shoved him. "Dick!"

"You down for some Pong?"

"Yeah. Where'd my girl go, though?"

He waved me off. "Oh, Ari's here. Let the girls chit-chat."

I took his word for it and followed him to the makeshift dining room, where a bunch of guys in backward baseball caps were playing a round of Beer Pong. They nodded at us as they finished their game.

Ty and I were up next, and we dominated like we always did. I had been so focused on hockey and staying in Philly that it made me realize I needed to make time for my friends, too. Maddie and hockey had been all I had time for lately. Not a bad thing, but making time for the other people in my life was important.

As I sunk my last ball and won the game, Maddie sidled up to me. I wrapped my arms around her waist. "Hey, there you are."

She leaned up on her tip-toes, and I bent down to give her a quick kiss. "Sorry. Got lost chatting with the girls. Did you win?"

"Fuck yeah, we did!" Ty told her.

She sipped on her beer, and I felt like a dick because I got her one, but then Ty drank it while we were playing Pong.

"You play?" Ty asked her.

"Sure."

"I'll be your partner, and we can get their asses," a female voice called out.

I turned and saw the blonde from the night I told Maddie I wanted to be more than friends. She looked a little tipsy and had her arm around Maddie's roommate, Ari.

"Yeah! Kiira and I are gonna crush you!" Maddie cheered.

Ari leaned up and gave Kiira a quick kiss. Huh. Interesting.

"Okay, you're on!" Ty said, and we reset the cups.

A little friendly competition never hurt anyone, and since we were all hockey players, we were extremely competitive. The girls proved to be even more than Ty and me, and they completely kicked our asses.

Ty looked at me in disgust as I had to chug another cup, but I shrugged.

"Man, Cally, your girl's showing you up!" Ty teased.

Maddie beamed at me.

"She's lucky she's cute," I teased.

"I heard that," she shot back but gave me a wink. I blew her a sarcastic kiss, and she pretended to catch it.

Ari laughed.

After the game, I refilled our beers, and Maddie dragged me to the dance floor. I ground against her perfect body as she moved to the beat of the music.

As much as I loved our nights in, watching action movies or getting tangled up in the sheets, coming out tonight and hanging with our friends had been fun. We didn't have that opportunity with our relationship being a secret. If she got over her hangups about her brother disapproving of me, we could have this all the time.

I brushed her hair behind her shoulder and bent to her ear. "Tonight was fun."

She turned around and wrapped her arms around my neck. "It was. I love spending time with you, but we don't get to do this often."

Neither of us said we couldn't hang with my teammates without her brother finding out. It was why I always came to her since there was little chance of her brother showing up on campus. Franklin U was like our little bubble where we didn't have to worry.

I slid my hands down her sides and gripped her hips, moving along to the music with her. "We should do it more often. Kiira seems fun."

She nodded. "She's the first of my teammates that really made me feel welcome."

I squinted at her. "Is she the goalie?"

She busted up laughing. "How could you tell?"

"Because the goalie's always weird."

She leaned up, and I met her in a searing kiss on the dance floor. Here, with my girl, was all I cared about at this moment.

"You want to get out of here?" I asked when we pulled away.

She ran her finger down my chest. "You know I do, baby."

"Such a dirty girl."

She shook her head. "Nope, we both know I'm your good girl."

"Damn straight."

Maddie lay naked and spent across my chest, curled into me like she had been for the past fifteen minutes. She needed extra cuddles after the intensity of being together tonight. She brought out the wild man in me, but we both loved it. I was never that growly or demanding in bed with any other woman. It was like her desires to be taken by a big brute made me transform into it.

I ran my fingers through her hair. "Was that too much tonight?"

She shook her head. "No. I loved it. I couldn't touch you at all, being completely restrained, and you were such a tease. It was so hot."

I pressed a kiss to her forehead. "Good."

"I'll tell you if it's too much," she said, swirling her finger around my chest. "But I love how willing you are to try new things. I wasn't sure I'd like my ankles bound too, but I did."

"I want to make you happy."

"Baby..." she sighed.

"What?"

She lifted her head up. "You do make me happy, even without all that stuff. Even if we had boring, vanilla sex, you'd make me happy."

I laughed. "Okay, even when we do have vanilla sex, it's not boring."

She giggled. "No. It's not. Did I tell you I'm glad it was you? After wanting to lose my virginity to anyone, I'm glad it was you." She pressed a hand against my heart. "That you were my someone special."

Her touch set shivers down my spine. Or maybe it was how her words made me feel. Those three little words were on the tip of my tongue, but it was too early for me to say them. She was nowhere near ready for that.

So I changed the subject before my heart took over my brain and I spilled it out. "Hey, are you going to Dinah's brother's for Thanksgiving?"

She shook her head. "Yuck Thanksgiving in November."

I laughed. "You're the weirdo who does it in October."

"No. I'm not going. Why?"

"Because...we'd have the house to ourselves. I could have you in my bed for once."

She grinned up at me. "You have all the best ideas!"

"Tell me that again when we argue over where to go to dinner," I teased.

She rolled her eyes at me, but then she settled back down against me. It would be so nice to cuddle in my bed instead of squeezing into this tiny one. It was getting harder to explain to the massage therapist why my neck was so sore when I hadn't taken big hits in games.

"Wow, it's late," she said when she checked her phone. "Sorry."

"Nothing to be sorry for, sweet pea."

We got out of the bed and changed into pajamas, each doing our nighttime routine. Then we crawled back into bed to go to sleep. Having her in my arms was one reason being on the road sucked. If I didn't love hockey so much, I'd give it all up for her.

CHAPTER TWENTY-FIVE

MADDIE

"So, good..." I moaned into the pillow and dropped face-first into it.

My hands were still bound behind my back, but Matt made quick work of undoing the cuffs. He turned me around and looked me deep in my eyes.

"Okay?" he asked as he rubbed my wrists. He was always so sweet by cradling me or kissing me after sex.

I nodded and pulled him down for a long kiss.

He shifted onto his back, and I crawled onto his chest, letting his big arms envelop me. He stroked my hair and kissed the top of my head, giving me the aftercare cuddles I needed. He was so good at taking care of my needs.

I pulled away after a few minutes to spread out across his bed. His futon bed wasn't that comfortable, but it was better than us sharing my cramped twin bed.

"Where you think you're going?" he asked.

"Baby, we can spread out!"

"I know, but I like cuddles."

I grinned and slid back against his side. "Do you need more cuddles?"

"Yes..." he mumbled.

Matt could be so affectionate, but he rarely told me what he needed as aftercare. I felt bad because he always seemed to go with whatever I wanted. Although, since we started dating and exploring bondage, he came alive. We weren't in a Dom/Sub relationship, but the alpha male came out in him in the bedroom. I loved that. That he could be so sweet and kind but domineering in the bedroom. Some guys thought being an 'alpha' meant being an asshole, but Matt was proof you could be a nice guy and still dominate your partner. *If* they wanted that, and I very much did.

I lay across his chest again and drew circles on it. He rubbed a hand down my arm and pulled the comforter up around us, encasing me in warmth.

See, so sweet.

"This was such a good idea," I said into his chest.

"Mmmhmm."

I knew what he really wanted to say. That we could do this all the time if we confided in Dinah and helped her get my brother on board. But I was scared. Once we told Noah, this would be real. Like really real, and then I wouldn't be able to ignore the way my heart was yelling at me to tell Matt how I felt. Telling him I loved him after so little time dating would make him run away.

"What else do you want to do today?" he asked.

I looked up at him, and his naughty smile made me grin back. But yeah, I was not ready for another round. He had pulled out all of my pleasure, and I needed to recharge.

I frowned. "Actually, I need to study a bit."

"Math?" he asked.

I nodded. I hated this stupid class. I passed a similar one

in Canada, but Franklin was making me retake it for their credits. It was the class that was giving me a heavier load and stressing me out. I had lied to Dinah about my workload. Working for her, Fi, doing my book blogger stuff, hockey, and taking a full course load was a lot. But I'd sleep when I was dead.

"Can I help?" he offered.

"Nah. I need to study and do the work."

"Well...I could review game tape while you do."

I beamed. I loved sitting beside him while we did our own thing. I liked being with him, even when we weren't talking. Sometimes, I think he reviewed tape and studied stats because he felt bad about occupying all my time. I wanted to spend every waking hour with him, so I was more than happy to sacrifice my sleep.

I disentangled myself from his limbs and got dressed. He did the same, throwing on a pair of grey sweatpants that made me reconsider putting my clothes back on. He gave me a stern look that told me to behave.

I put the leather cuffs back into my bag and pulled out my textbook and a notebook.

I lay on my stomach on the bed, opened the textbook, and wrote out problems in my notebook. Matt sat up against the wall with a pillow behind him, watching video on his tablet.

"Is this bothering you?" he asked about the noise.

"Nope."

We worked quietly alone. Matt had his hand on my thigh as I did my math problems, and he watched game tape. I loved these quiet moments with him.

I studied for about an hour, and then I took photos for my social media. I was behind on reviews. I brought a couple of books over to take photos, so I took some shots with my fancy camera and then loaded them into my laptop to make edits.

At one point, I looked up and saw Matt giving me a dopey smile. "What?"

"It's cute how passionate you are about your work."

My face cracked from a too-big smile. "I love it. I figured if you gotta study game tape, I can get things done."

"I was letting you do your thing. I'm ready for the game tomorrow."

"That's good. Can I tell you a secret?"

"What's that?"

"Dinah brought up me starting my own PR firm...for books. I don't hate the idea."

He gave me a supportive smile. "You'd be great at it."

I chewed the inside of my cheek, my worries swirling around inside my head. "I'm swamped this semester, but next semester, I want to start offering PA services to authors. Now that I have two clients, it could be big for me."

He reached out and squeezed my hand. "You're so organized and passionate about books. It would be great."

"You really think so?"

He nodded. "You can do anything you set your mind to. I know so."

My heart did a little dance that he was confident in my abilities. When Dinah brought that up, I waved her off, but something had been nagging me about it. I could start that process. Or at least take more clients independently and then start the business once I had a solid list.

I turned back to my computer and finished scheduling posts. I still needed to finish a readthrough for Dinah, but I'd do it when Matt was on the road this week.

I turned off my computer and put it away so I could pay attention to him. I was going to ask him if he wanted to watch a movie before I had to go home when I heard a car pull into the garage. Anxiety coursed through my body at the sound of footsteps climbing the steps to the main level.

"What's that?" I whispered.

His face had gone white as we heard voices talking upstairs in the kitchen above us.

Oh no.

Oh fucking no.

Dinah and Noah were back already.

"They weren't supposed to be home yet," I hissed in a low whisper.

The terror was marked across Matt's face, and my anxiety rose. I wasn't supposed to be here. This was not how my brother was going to find out I was dating his teammate.

"I'm not sure why they're back," Matt said, but he frowned when he saw the look of horror on my face. "Hey, C'mere."

I jumped off the bed and looked around for an escape. There was a separate door down here that led to the garage, so I could slip out without going upstairs. But would they notice? Or would Dinah and Noah assume Matt had gone out? Worse came to worse, I could hide out behind the closed bedroom door while Matt awkwardly talked to them upstairs.

"Sweet pea," Matt whispered.

"Matt..."

I didn't know what to say. Noah would put two-and-two together as soon as he saw me down here. After watching him annihilate Jaime on the ice, I had one clue how he'd react with Matt. Poorly. Very Poorly was my guess. I should have never taken Matt up on his offer to chill here tonight. This was such a mistake.

Before he could calm me down, I jumped at the sound of loud knocking on the closed door that led into the basement. Matt got up and left the bedroom, going out into the media room.

"Yeah?" I heard him ask.

"Hey, we have leftovers from my brother if you want any," Dinah's voice shouted down to him.

It seemed like she respected his privacy, so it wasn't like she was going to burst in down here and catch us in the act, but I felt frozen in my spot. This was too much. I was not ready for the fallout. This was why we always hung out on campus. How had I been so stupid?

"Thanks, D. I'll come up later if I'm hungry," he called back to her.

"Okay," she yelled back, and then I heard her footsteps walk away.

I found my coat in Matt's closet and shoved it on, rushing to button it up. I needed to get out of here. I put my backpack over my shoulders.

Matt came back to the room, and he ran a hand through his hair in frustration. "We should tell them."

I vigorously shook my head from side to side, the panic rising like bile in my throat. "This is a terrible way to tell them."

"It won't be bad. I promise."

He was wrong. I thought my brother would actually murder him.

"I have to go," I said. I didn't even let him kiss me goodbye, just ran out of there as fast as I could.

The hockey gods must have been on my side because I didn't run into Dinah or my brother on my way out. My heart pounded loudly in my chest as I walked to the subway and made my way back to campus.

Matt called me, but I sent it to voicemail. I knew we were going to have a big, knockdown fight about this, but I wasn't ready for that yet either. I wanted more time to figure out my feelings for him. I didn't know if he felt the same way yet, and the fear of my brother losing it was too much for me to deal with on top of that.

I wasn't sure I'd ever be ready for this.

CHAPTER TWENTY-SIX

MATT

I tried her again, listening to the dial tone as I raked my hand through my hair.

Did I want her brother to find out we were together by catching us in his house when he had been out? Absolutely not. But it was getting to a point where something had to give, and we couldn't pretend forever.

I groaned and slumped onto my bed as it went to voicemail again. She was being immature about this. Noah would be mad, sure, but he'd get over it. The longer we waited, the worse it was going to be.

I tried her again, but this time, it went straight to voicemail without ringing. I tried to text her instead.

ME: Sweet pea, please. We need to talk about this.

SWEET PEA: Fine.

Okay, not great, but a start.

I needed to eat first before talking with her. Telling Noah wouldn't be so bad. Worst case, he punched me, but I didn't think he'd do that. At least not in the face. Even if he did, I'd take the hit. Might lean into it.

I shoved my phone into my pocket, put on a shirt, and climbed the stairs to the main level. Dinah was in the kitchen doing dishes.

"Hey. I thought you went out," she said.

I opened the fridge and pulled out all the Thanksgiving fixings. "No..."

Dinah angled her head at me, studying my grief-stricken face. "Oh my God! You had your girl over here. She didn't have to leave."

I didn't have any reply to that. I grabbed a plate from the cabinet, piled food onto it, and popped it into the microwave.

"Sorry to be a cock block. My mom was driving me nuts about looking to adopt so she could have more grandbabies that we left early."

I nodded at her but hoped she would go away.

The microwave beeped, and I stared at it for a second.

"Matt, what's wrong?" she asked.

I shook my head and took my food out of the microwave. I sat at the large kitchen island and shoveled food into my mouth. Dinah's brother was such a superb cook that even reheated, this Thanksgiving meal was great.

Dinah put a hand on my shoulder. "You can talk to me if you need to, okay?"

"I know," I muttered.

"What happened with the girl?"

"She freaked."

"Why? We're not scary. Noah and I were looking forward to meeting her."

I swallowed hard. How could I tell her they already met her and knew her pretty well? I needed to talk to Maddie. We needed to be on the same page. I was tired of lying to this woman who welcomed me into her home and of brushing off my mentor.

Dinah gave me a little squeeze. "I'm here if you need."

She grabbed two beers out of the fridge and headed up toward the owner suite where she and Noah resided.

I ate my dinner in silence as I thought about what to say to Maddie. I needed her to understand why we had to quit this charade. Noah and Dinah coming home early was the sign I needed. One day, we were going to get caught in the act. It would be so much better if we told Noah on our own terms.

I finished eating and set my plate in the sink. Then I ordered a car and made my way over to Franklin.

The car took longer than I wanted, probably because it was a holiday. Once I got to campus, it was like a ghost town. I texted Maddie I was here, and she came down to let me in, but she didn't look happy to see me.

She scanned us into her building, and we rode the elevator in an uncomfortable silence. Once inside her room, she sat on the bed, playing with a thread on her sweater.

I took a deep breath. We both knew this was the big fight we had been dreading. "I don't like what happened today."

She dipped her head down, staring intently at the floor.

"I can't keep on doing this."

Her head snapped up, and her eyes were cloudy. "What?"

"I can't keep sneaking around with you."

"But my brother—"

"What about him?" I snapped. "Does he control you?"

"No."

"Then why can't we tell him?"

I paced her bedroom floor. I didn't understand her logic. Noah would get over me breaking the code. He had to.

"Matt, you don't understand."

"What don't I understand? Because I love you, and I hate the fact that I don't get to tell anyone that. We can pretend everything's fine here on campus because we think Noah will never see us together. But what happens one day when he shows up out of the blue? What happens then? What are we supposed to do? Continue to pretend we aren't dating until he's on his deathbed? When does it end, Maddie?" I ranted.

She stared back at me, her mouth agape, but she wasn't saying anything.

"I can't keep doing this. Do you know how much the guilt is weighing me down? I just had a conversation with Dinah where she was trying to console me, but I couldn't tell her the reason my 'girlfriend' literally ran away was because that girl is her very off-limits sister-in-law."

"Matt..."

I held up a hand. "No. I need you to hear me. I love you, Madison. God, I fucking love you, and I know it's too fucking early to drop that on you, but that's why I can't keep doing this. I can't lie to your brother. Do you understand how hard that is for me?"

She continued to stare at me, her eyes big and doe-eyed. "You...you love...me?"

I breathed in as the weight of all the words I spat out fell back on me. She looked terrified. Had I misjudged everything? Did she not feel the same way? Was that why she resisted telling her brother? Because I was just her guy for a good time, not a long time?

"If you can't be an adult and tell your brother we're together, then maybe you don't feel the same way."

"Matt...that's not it. I...you... It's complicated."

I glared at her. She was stumbling over her words, but inside, my heart was aching. If she felt the same way, she would agree to tell her brother about us.

"Matt, it's not that simple."

"Yes, it is. You know what?"

"Can you please listen to me?" she asked.

"No, I've listened to your excuses enough. I'm done."

"You what?"

My irrational brain was speaking before I could stop the words from coming out of my mouth.

"Until you decide that you actually give a shit about us, I'm done. When you're ready to be an adult and tell your brother about us, maybe I'll still be waiting."

"What?"

I didn't let her get another word in and stormed out.

I wasn't sure giving her an ultimatum was the best course of action, but something had to happen. We couldn't keep going in circles with this argument. I couldn't stand that every single day, I looked her brother in the eyes and lied to him.

I ordered another car and waited impatiently in the frosty November night for it to take me back to Old City. I didn't feel good about what happened. Not one bit. I didn't want to break up, but what was the solution? If she didn't want to tell her brother, there wasn't a point in continuing this relationship. That didn't stop the way my heart felt like a heavy lump in my chest.

After what felt like forever, a car pulled up, and I got inside. I was pensive on the drive back to Noah and

Dinah's. By the time I got back, I went into the basement, through the garage, and stomped into my bedroom.

I flopped down on my bed, and I looked up at the ceiling.

I made a mistake, but I couldn't take it back now.

No matter how much my brain told my heart we did the right thing, my heart felt like it had been split in two. If she loved me, she'd come to her senses. And if she didn't, then it was better we ended it here.

CHAPTER TWENTY-SEVEN

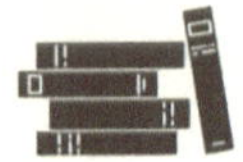

MADDIE

Because I love you, and I hate the fact that I don't get to tell anyone that.

I love you, Madison. God, I fucking love you, and I know it's too fucking early to drop that on you, but that's why I can't keep doing this.

It had been a week since Matt dropped his ultimatum on me, but my brain kept playing back his admittance of love. Why hadn't I said anything? I had been so startled at the confession that it jumbled my brain. Then he broke up with me. I hadn't heard from him since that night, and each time I tried to reach out to him, I froze up.

I had been avoiding going to my brother's. I told Dinah I was busy with school and asked her to cut down on my workload. I tried to bury myself in school and hockey, but everyone on my team saw that something was off with my game. Especially tonight.

"KENNEDY!" Elsa shouted at me from across the ice, pulling me from my distracted thoughts.

I shook my head but realized I fucked up by dropping the pass, and our opponent got possession of the puck. My head had not been in the game lately, and it showed.

I hustled through the play and went back to the bench for the change-up. I didn't look at my teammates, already knowing they weren't happy with me. I was like a robot on the ice for the rest of the game.

We ended up losing 3-1, and Elsa was pissed. Ice Queen was in full force tonight, and I didn't care. I stripped out of my gear and changed into gym clothes so I could shower in my more comfortable bathroom at my dorm.

I left in a huff, not bothering to even give my teammates any sympathetic looks as I walked out. Coach would probably call me into his office to ask me what was wrong with me soon. Not looking forward to that conversation.

It was cold on the walk home, and I wished the skating rink wasn't such a far walk, but my car was still back home in Winnipeg. I was debating bringing it to campus after I went home for break. Parking was a nightmare in the city, and with public transportation and access to my brother's rideshare account, I could manage without. I had been avoiding using Noah's account, though, because that would lead to questions about what was going on with me.

I was trying so hard not to think about Matt, but he filled my brain every second of every day. I was so scared of what Noah would do to him. If I expressed my fears, maybe he would have listened to me and agreed to hold out longer.

Almost getting caught on Thanksgiving had been a wake-up call. Matt was right; we couldn't keep doing this. I had two choices—continue to be miserable without him, or tell my brother and hope he didn't murder my boyfriend.

I missed the way he held me in his arms, or how he purred 'sweet pea' at me, or even how he smiled at me when he watched me work. I missed everything about him, and I hated that I didn't tell him I loved him back. Because I did. I loved him with every fiber of my being, but I was too scared to tell him.

I tried to press the thoughts to the forgotten part of my brain, but they kept nagging me. They continued to nag me when I got inside my suite and while I showered. They didn't let me concentrate when I crawled into bed with a spicy romance book. Especially when I realized it was one of the ones Matt had bought me the day he took me to the bookstore.

There was a knock on my bedroom door, and I looked up to see Ari's colorful head pop in. Then Kiira's blonde head peeked over, too, with Elsa coming up behind her.

What the fuck?

I wiped my eyes and sat up in my bed. "Um, hi?"

"You looked like shit on the ice tonight," Elsa said coldly.

Kiira nudged her. "E!"

Elsa shrugged. "What? It's true."

She wasn't wrong. Harsh, but sometimes the truth hurt.

"What's your point?" I asked.

Ari stepped into my room and opened my closet. She threw some clothes down on the bed. "Get dressed. We're going out."

I raised an eyebrow. "Um, excuse me?"

"We're going out!" Kiira cheered. "Now get dressed because you don't have a choice."

"Kiira's idea," Ari said with a shrug that said, 'what can you do?'

"I'm not doing that," I protested.

"Um, yes, you are because you dropped such a simple

pass tonight, and I've never seen a worse pylon on the ice," Elsa said.

Now that sounded like the Elsa I knew.

Ari pulled me off the bed. "Get dressed, and then you can tell us what's going on with you."

I had a feeling the three of them might have held me down on the bed and made me get dressed if I didn't do it. Or Kiira would have carried me over her shoulder and taken me in my pajamas.

I groaned and got out of bed. "Fine."

Ari shuffled them out of my room and shut the door behind her. I dressed quickly, throwing my hair up in a messy bun, not caring how I looked. I didn't even put makeup on. I grabbed my jacket, and they ushered me out of the suite.

I couldn't help but grin when I saw Ari slip her hand into Kiira's. They were a cute couple but comical-looking. Ari had that pocket-sized artsy thing about her, and Kiira was like an Amazon, but they worked. I had to talk to Ari about how that happened later.

I wrapped my arms around myself as we walked together toward Local Hangout. When we got to the bar, it was packed as always. Elsa spoke with the host to nab the first available table while Kiira brought over shots for us to do.

I groaned. "Are you serious?"

"Just do it, Kennedy!" Elsa snapped. I watched, impressed with the way she downed it like it was water. I was already scared of Elsa, but now even more so.

"Do it! Do it!" Kiira chanted.

I rolled my eyes and downed the shot to her amusement. I set the glass down and pressed a hand against my chest as the alcohol burned all the way down.

The host walked over to us and told us our table was ready. She walked us over to one, and the four of us squeezed into a booth. The server who was always working came around, and we ordered beers. Except for Elsa, who ordered the most fruity drink imaginable.

"What?" she asked. "There's way more alcohol in this than a boring beer."

"So..." Kiira started.

"So, what?" I asked.

"Why did you forget how to score a goal?" Elsa asked.

The girls laughed. Elsa did not mince words, and I had to admire her bluntness.

"Because she's not getting laid," Ari said.

I glared at her. How did she know that?

Ari shrugged. "The Bulldogs only had one away game this week. And...our walls are thin."

I felt heat color my face. That thought had never occurred to me.

Kiira burst out in laughter.

"What happened with Matt?" Elsa asked.

I sighed. "It's complicated."

"Did your brother find out?" Ari asked.

I shook my head. "No. That was the problem."

Kiira took a sip of her beer. "Were you still sneaking around?"

I nodded.

Elsa frowned. "Matt didn't like that, huh?"

I sighed and gulped down my beer. It was nice they wanted to talk it out, but my thoughts were such a mess, I didn't know what to do.

"Maddie," Ari started. "What happened?"

"We broke up," I muttered.

Kiira made a face. "Why?"

I let out a long, drawn-out sigh. "He didn't want to be with me if we didn't tell my brother. He doesn't understand!"

"Then explain it to us," Ari said gently.

So, I did.

I told them the reason I transferred to Franklin in the first place and then how my brother dropped the gloves with the guy who did it. How I was so afraid of what Noah would do when he found out his teammate, who he had taken under his wing, was fucking his little sister. I explained that Matt told me he loved me but then dropped the impossible ultimatum on me before storming out.

Afterward, Ari gave me a sad smile, but Kiira looked confused. Elsa had her arms crossed over her chest and looked pissed.

"So let me get this straight...you love each other but... you're too much of a coward to tell your brother, 'hey, by the way, I'm dating Matt. Get over it'? Sounds like a load of bullshit."

Ari gave me a knowing look. "She has a point. I don't understand the problem."

I gulped.

"You didn't tell him," Kiira said for me.

I dropped my eyes to the table in front of me, guilt wrapping itself tight around my heart.

"Oh, Maddie," Ari sighed.

"You gotta tell him," Kiira insisted.

I looked up at the TV above the bar. The team was in Boston tonight for an away game. They were winning so far, but I had to tear my gaze away. I hadn't been able to bear to watch a game since Matt and I broke up.

"Get over yourself," Elsa scoffed. "You love each other. I don't see what the problem is."

"My brother will murder him," I argued.

She shook her head. "That seems like an excuse."

I looked around at the girls, and they all had similar looks on their faces.

"You love him, right?" Ari asked.

"So much," I whispered.

"Then that's settled. Tell him you love him, tell your brother so you can get back to getting laid and stop fucking up on the ice," Elsa said and took a huge swig of her drink.

I stared back at her. If only it was that simple.

"I–"

She cut me off with a glare. "Fuck off with that brother bullshit. You're scared."

"What?"

"She's right," Ari said. "You're afraid of your feelings that you're making your brother an excuse to drive a wedge in between you when you don't need it."

Kiira nodded in agreement.

I took in all their words and drank the rest of my beer. I loved Matt. I did, with all my heart and soul. Maybe I *was* scared. I needed to think more about this.

"Can we talk about that shitty game now?" Elsa asked.

I groaned.

Kiira laughed. "Is that all you think about?"

Elsa shrugged and pointed at me. "She's the best player on the team, and she showed up tonight like she forgot how to skate!"

Ari looked a little lost at the conversation switch to hockey talk.

"E, if anyone needs to get laid, it's you," Kiira teased.

Elsa bristled at that. "I'm fine."

"Do you miss Ty?" I asked.

She shook her head. "No. We knew our relationship

was over a long time ago. We've been together since fifth grade. We didn't even know ourselves yet."

"Oh. Matt seems to think—"

She groaned. "Matt's so romantic. He thinks we're pining for each other. We're not! I assure you, we're not."

I held up my hands.

"Enough relationship talk. We gotta talk about getting better on the power play."

We all shook our heads at Elsa.

"Never change, E, never change," Kiira said.

We let her rant about how shitty we played, and I felt a lot of the guilt fall on my shoulders. I was half paying attention as I looked at my phone, hoping that maybe Matt had reached out, but he hadn't. I wanted to text him, but my fear still froze me with inaction. Maybe the girls were right to say I was scared, but I wasn't ready for what that all meant.

CHAPTER TWENTY-EIGHT

MATT

I grinned at the petite brunette bounding across the parking lot to Dinah's borrowed car. If anyone could get me out of my foul mood, it was my sister.

"Get in the back," I said to Ty, who sat in my passenger seat.

He made a face. "Why? Because princess has to sit up front?"

I laughed. "You know her royal highness!"

He shook his head with a laugh and got out of the car.

When we were kids, Luna declared herself Princess of Minnesota, and we her two lowly subjects. Ty always appeased her, but I tried to start a rebellion. Now we teased her mercilessly about it.

It had been about a week since I broke up with Maddie, and I was miserable as shit. That was why my sister insisted on coming to visit Franklin U. When I told her I thought Ty or Elsa should give her a tour, she demanded answers, and then I booked her a flight to Philly. I was pretty certain it was not so Ty could show her around but so the two could gang up on me and tell me I was stupid for giving Maddie that ultimatum.

I'd agree with them because I missed her so much. I hadn't heard from her since I laid down the law. Occasionally, I saw the dots pop up in our text thread, but then they would disappear. That hurt even more because I was waiting for her to make a move. For her to get her shit together and tell her brother about us. But now I wasn't so sure there even was an 'us.' Maybe there never was.

I missed her so much. I missed laying in bed with her, watching those cheesy action films she loved, and listening to her talk about the bonkers plot of the latest novel she was reading. I missed holding her hand and her sweet smile that was only for me.

I ran a hand down my face but couldn't help but smile when I watched Luna jump into Ty's arms as he spun her around. Yeah, it was not lost on me that Ty had a thing for my sister. He forgot he told me when we got drunk last night. He might be a douche, but if he ever got his shit together, I knew he'd treat my sister well. It didn't bother me if they ever dated because Luna was her own person with her own opinions.

The only thing good about my breakup was that I was putting all my energy into hockey. It hadn't gone unnoticed, and Coach had been keeping me on the line with Mac and Hallsy, but he also called me into his office and asked me if I was okay because I looked like a robot. I never had a coach like him before. LaVoie actually gave a shit about his players, and not just about hockey. I brushed him off, and he hadn't pressed me more on it.

Luna climbed into the passenger seat while Ty put her bag in the back before sliding in next to it.

"You're grumpy," she said by way of greeting.

I rolled my eyes and tore out of the airport to get back to the city. Dinah and Noah had graciously let her stay with us. They had the room and had been more than happy to host her. We had a game tomorrow afternoon, so Dinah was going to bring her along. Luna had only seen me play on those few times we played the Minnesota Tundra.

Luna turned around to look at Ty.

"Hey, put your seatbelt on," I yelled at her.

I felt her roll her eyes without seeing it, and she did as I asked, but then turned around to look at my buddy. "How bad is it, Ty?"

"Bad Lu-lu."

"Nobody fucking asked you," I snarled.

"She did," Ty argued.

"What did you do?" my sister demanded.

I gripped the steering wheel as I drove and pretended I didn't hear her.

"MATTY!" she shrieked.

"Dude, tell her," Ty urged.

"Tell me what?"

God, I loved my sister, but I could do without her high-pitched screaming right now.

"Tell me!" she demanded.

So I did. I told her the whole messy story. When I was done, we were back in the city and on our way to campus. Luna sat back in her seat and was quiet for a while.

"What do you think, princess?" Ty asked.

"Have you talked to her since then?" Luna asked.

"It's pointless. She doesn't love me."

"I think you're wrong."

I muttered under my breath. I definitely wasn't. If Maddie wanted me the way I wanted her, she would have fought for me. Instead, she was too scared of her brother to give us a real shot.

"But you really love her, right?" Luna asked.

"Yes," Ty answered for me. "That's why he's been so mopey."

I glared at him through the rearview mirror, and he gave me a cheeky grin.

Dick.

"Then I don't understand the problem," Luna said

"She doesn't want to tell her brother. I don't want to be her dirty little secret anymore," I explained.

"Do you blame her? The last guy she dated got his teeth knocked in by her brother. She's afraid for you because she loves you," Luna said.

She never said that, though. When I told her I loved her, she stared back at me in silence, and then I stormed out. Maybe I didn't give her a chance to react, but if she loved me, she would have said something by now.

"That's what I told him," Ty said. "But anyway, princess, you ready for me to tour you around?"

I mentally thanked my best friend for changing the subject and distracting my sister.

It didn't take much longer to get to campus. I found a parking garage and followed behind them as Ty showed Luna all the academic buildings and student services. I worried about her on her own, but Ty still had another year before he graduated, so I knew he'd keep an eye on her.

I hesitated when I noticed he led us to the skating rink. I hadn't been to any of Maddie's games, but I knew they played in the same rink as the men's team. Ty pushed me inside, forcing the argument from my lips.

"Now for the best place," Ty told my sister. "The rink. You want to join the women's team, right?"

The corner of Luna's lips turned up. "I'm thinking about it."

"Come on. E told me we could take a peek at practice."

Luna looked taken aback by that. "You and Elsa still talk?"

Ty nodded. "Not everyone hates their ex."

"I do," she muttered.

"What happened with Chelsea?" I asked.

Luna scoffed. "She cheated on me. Good riddance."

Ty put an arm around her. "Sorry, Lulu. You come to Franklin, and I'll find you a nice guy or girl."

"Or enby," she reminded him.

"We'll find you someone better than her," he told her with a smile.

"Thanks, Ty."

We slipped into the stands, small as they were, and watched the girls hustling down the ice. Maddie's dark braid flowed behind her as she beat Elsa at laps.

"Whoa, she's fast," Luna breathed out, impressed.

"She gives E a run for her money," Ty said.

I pressed a hand against my sternum, feeling like my heart might burst at the sight of Maddie. She was beautiful and fierce as she tore down the ice, reminding me of everything I missed about her. My heart screamed at me that I never should have given her that ultimatum, but I couldn't keep hiding our relationship from her brother.

Luna raised an eyebrow at me, and then her lips parted. "Oh. That's your girl."

I nodded.

"Maybe we should stick around so you two can talk?"

"Nah. Where's the next stop, Ty?"

"Hockey house for a kegger?" he offered.

"No," I said sternly. "Let's head back to Noah and Dinah's and get Lu settled."

"You should talk to her," Luna said.

"Stay out of it, Lu," I warned.

She frowned but didn't press me on it. We parted ways with Ty, and I drove us to Old City. I grabbed Luna's bag when we walked inside. I heard Dinah and Noah in the kitchen as we walked upstairs.

"Hey," Dinah said. "I was just gonna call you to see if you were going to be around for dinner. My brother dropped off a lasagna."

"Ooh, I love lasagna," Luna said.

"Oh, this is Luna," I introduced my sister.

They greeted her, and then Luna took her bag from me while Dinah showed her to her room upstairs. Noah went into the fridge and handed me a beer. The girls came back downstairs, chattering away.

"You ready for the game tomorrow?" Noah asked.

I gave him a silent nod.

I wasn't worried about the game since I had been on fire lately.

"Are you sure?" Noah asked.

"Yeah?"

He studied me. "What's been up with you lately? You're mopey."

I sighed.

"Him and his girlfriend broke up," Luna cut in.

I shot her a glare, and she gave it back like she was daring me to say something else in front of Noah.

Noah's expression was unreadable as he stared at me for a few seconds, like he was waiting for me to say something else. "Well, that sucks. I'm sure you'll figure it out."

Behind him, Dinah stared suspiciously at me.

Noah asked my sister how she liked Franklin, his way of avoiding confrontation. I was grateful for that.

The four of us ate dinner together, and afterward, Noah stood up and grabbed his coat. "Okay, I gotta go."

I pinned him with a look. "Do we have a meeting I don't know about?"

Dinah waved me off. "TJ needs help building a dresser for the twins."

"Do you need an extra set of hands?" I asked.

Noah shook his head. "Nah, I got it. I'll see you later."

As soon as the door shut behind him, Dinah whipped her head around and glared at me. My sister sat up and if she could grab popcorn and watch the show, she would.

"What?" I asked Dinah.

She put her hands on her hips and tapped her foot impatiently. "I'm only gonna ask you once, and I want you to be perfectly honest with me."

"Yeah?"

"Have you been secretly dating Maddie?"

I felt all the color drain from my face, and I stared at her blankly.

"Yes!" my sister answered for me. She gave me an innocent smile. Dinah looked at her with interest. "That's the real reason I came for a visit. He's been a shit."

Dinah barked out a laugh. "That's very true." She turned back to me. "What happened?"

"Did she tell you?" I asked.

Dinah shook her head. "Nope. You two were way too obvious, and she's avoiding me."

I cringed. "Does Noah know?"

She tapped her finger against her lips. "I honestly don't know. What did you do?"

"He gave her an ultimatum," Luna chimed in again.

I shot her another annoyed look. Damn, little sisters could be a pain in the ass.

Dinah raised her eyebrow at me and waited for me to explain.

"I never wanted to hide it. I wanted to tell Noah right away, but she didn't want to."

Dinah blew out a breath. "Okay, I get that. I have three meathead brothers who tried to stare down Noah. He's protective of her, but he likes you."

"D, what do I do?"

"Forget about my husband. He'll get over it."

"Or he'll punch me in the face," I muttered.

She shook her head. "I won't let him do that misogynist bullshit. When was the last time you talked to her?"

"A week ago."

"A week ago..." her eyes widened. "You thought you were getting caught on Thanksgiving, and she freaked, huh?"

I nodded. "I told her we either tell Noah or we're done."

"He fucked up," Luna cut in.

"Quiet you," I snapped at her.

Dinah cringed. "Okay, wrong thing to say. But believe me, I fucked up before with Noah. I had to be the one to reach back out. Maybe you need to do that too."

I frowned.

"Text her and say you want to talk."

"Okay..."

"And Matt?"

"Yeah?"

"You're probably the only guy on that team Noah would approve of. It's almost like he hand-picked you."

"I don't know if sweet pea would like that," I blurted out.

My sister's eyes got soft. "Aw, you call her sweet pea? That's so cute."

"Shut it," I growled.

Dinah laughed. "Okay, I'm done. I knew something was up, and I had to say something."

"What if she doesn't want to talk to me?" I asked.

Dinah waved me off. "Nope. I'll make her come to the game with us tomorrow."

"How?"

"Don't worry about it. I'll handle that."

Luna nudged me. "You focus on winning in front of your girl, and then you can get her back."

"Okay, okay. I'm not sure I love you two teaming up against me."

"You love us!" Dinah cheered.

I shook my head. I did, but I wouldn't give her the satisfaction of knowing that.

Tomorrow. I'd fix it all tomorrow.

I hoped.

When I went to bed, I shot off a text to Maddie.

ME: Can we talk after my game tomorrow?

I didn't wait for a response before falling asleep. I'd find out later if she still wanted me. Or if I was going to be left with this gaping hole in my heart.

CHAPTER TWENTY-NINE

MADDIE

I stared at my phone.

MATT: Can we talk after my game?

He sent that last night, and I still didn't know what to make of it. What was there to talk about?

All my friends had been telling me to suck it up and go talk to him. That I shouldn't care what my brother thought because it was my life. I wanted to believe they were right, but worry coursed through me. Every time I imagined telling Noah, I pictured how he rang Jaime's bell on the ice. Noah wouldn't do that to his own teammate, right?

I was confused about Matt's motives because yesterday, I saw him spying on us at practice. He was with Ty and a girl I didn't recognize, but I felt his stare on me while we ran through drills. They were gone before I finished the next one, so I didn't know what that was about.

My phone buzzed and I declined the call from Dinah. I had been avoiding her, and she knew something was up. I wasn't sure how much longer I could avoid the house, especially since my brother was saying how he hadn't seen me in a while. I kept telling him I was busy, but he'd probably show up here one day demanding what was going on.

I rolled my eyes at Dinah's text message and left her on read.

I furrowed my brow when I saw Ty was calling.

That was odd.

I cautiously answered. "Hi?"

"Hey. Do me a favor and answer your sister-in-law's calls?"

"I'm sorry?"

How did Ty know Dinah?

"Matt's sister called me."

Matt's sister? Why would she...oh shit, she was supposed to come for a visit, and I was going to show her around campus. That was the girl I saw them with. Obviously, Matt didn't call me because we weren't talking to each other.

"Call your sister-in-law back," Ty said, and then he hung up.

I sighed and did as he asked.

"Well, you clearly didn't lose my number," she said, in a way of greeting.

"Hey, D," I said defeatedly.

"Okay, listen up, get your ass in the shower and come to the game."

I groaned.

"I know why you're avoiding me."

"He told you?"

"Yes! But it wasn't that hard to figure out. You think I didn't notice the carpet in my basement in your post yesterday?"

I cringed. "Does Noah know?"

She hesitated for a second. "I don't think so. But...you're gonna come to the game, cheer on your man, and then you're gonna work things out, okay? We'll have my husband drink a couple of beers, and then we'll tell him."

"That's the problem."

"Oh my God! I have three meathead older brothers, and they got over it when I started dating Noah. Matt needs to stand his ground. You better be at the arena, or I'm sicking Rox on you."

She hung up before I could answer, and that lit a fire under me. Roxanne Desjardins was scary, and as much as I wanted to be her when I grew up, I was also kind of afraid of her.

I got a shower because I had been living in my hoodie—Matt's hoodie, actually. The idea of going to the game, of facing Matt again, scared me, but my heart ached. I even went to the health center because I thought something was wrong with me. The hurt inside my chest was all in my head. I could have easily avoided this if I told Matt I loved him too. Or if I stood up to my brother and didn't let him treat me like a child in need of protection. I should have told Noah I was a grown woman capable of making my own decisions, even if they were the wrong ones.

I was swiping lip gloss across my lips when I saw a text from Dinah that she was outside my dorm waiting for me. Um, we hadn't talked about her picking me up. That must have been her insurance plan. For a little thing, she could be pushy.

I left my room a few seconds later, wearing a Kennedy jersey, as I wrapped my big coat around me. Winter in Philly so far was nothing compared to Winnipeg, but it was still cold out.

I got into the backseat of Dinah's car.

Dinah sat in the driver's seat while a petite brunette sat up front. She looked familiar, and I realized that was who Matt and Ty had been with yesterday. That all made sense.

"You hate driving," I blurted out.

Dinah laughed. "True, but it was the only way to make sure you'd actually come."

She sped off toward the arena, engulfing the car in silence for several minutes.

The silent brunette turned around after another few minutes of awkward quiet. "Hi! I'm Luna."

I grimaced. This was not how I wanted to meet Matt's sister after I ripped his heart out of his chest. "Maddie."

She beamed, which confused me. "Oh, I know. So, do you love my brother or what?"

Dinah was laughing so hard in the driver's seat. Meanwhile, I felt the judgmental gaze from Matt's little sister.

"Umm."

"She does," Dinah answered for me. "That's why she came out and put on makeup."

"You didn't give me a choice," I grumbled.

"Stop being such a mope. You two are a pair and annoying as fuck to deal with."

"It was like pulling teeth to get it out of Matt what was going on," Luna agreed.

I groaned. "You know I'm right here?"

"So, do you love my brother?" Luna asked again.

"Yes!"

"So what exactly is your fucking problem?"

"Excuse me?"

"Why did you let him walk away?"

I sighed. "My brother."

"That seems like bullshit."

"Mmmhmm," Dinah agreed.

This was exactly what my teammates said to me. The worst part? They were right. I was so scared of what my brother was going to do to Matt when he found out, but it also scared me how much I loved Matt. When he told me he loved me, I didn't say it back because it shocked me into silence. Then he stormed out, and I never got to tell him how I felt.

"I really miss him," I whispered.

Dinah pulled her car into the parking lot of the arena. She cut her engine and turned around, giving me an annoyed look. "Yeah. We know. He's been miserable lately, so he misses you too."

"He's burying himself in hockey and looks like a robot out there," Luna said.

"Come on, let's go watch our men play, and then you can apologize and, for the love of the hockey gods, get it in!" Dinah said with a mischievous grin.

"DINAH!" I yelled while Luna laughed her ass off.

Dinah gave me an innocent smile. Sometimes, I forgot she could be so blunt, but that's why I loved her. Even if she was being annoying as hell right now.

"Come on," I muttered under my breath as I watched the team struggle to keep the puck out of their zone.

Luna squeezed my arm, and I realized I liked Matt's bubbly sister. We chatted about hockey during the first intermission, and she was excited about the prospect of coming to Franklin. If she got in.

I watched Matt race after one of the Pittsburgh Miners, and I cringed when he slammed into the boards and got knocked down.

Then play stopped, and the whistle was blown.

"What's happening?" I asked. "That was a clean hit."

Dinah stared down at where Mac and Hallsy were talking to the refs. Matt wasn't getting up from the ice. Why wasn't he getting up from the ice?

Horror coursed through me when I saw the medical team race out toward Matt, bringing on a stretcher.

I looked at Dinah. "What's going on?" My voice was shrill, panic rising inside me.

Dinah shook her head. "I don't know."

"Shit," Luna swore as she stared down at her phone. "He's really hurt."

"Fuck, fuck, fuck..." I rambled.

Dinah had her phone to her ear while the arena watched in silence at the medical team getting Matt off the ice. My heart sank to my stomach at his unmoving body. Luna squeezed my hand in comfort, but it didn't help the anxiety building up inside my chest. I sucked in a nervous breath at the sight of the medical team lifting him onto the stretcher, but then I exhaled in relief when he gave a thumbs up to the crowd. That was good and likely meant not a concussion, but if he couldn't get up by himself, something was really wrong.

After a couple of minutes went by, Dinah turned to me. "Okay, let's go."

"Where?" I asked.

"Hospital. They're taking him as a precaution, but they think his leg's broken."

"Oh no!" I cried.

A broken leg meant he would be out for a while. Maybe even the whole season. This was bad.

"Let's go. He's asking for you."

"He is?" I asked.

"Because he loves you," Luna sang with a grin across her lips.

Dinah pointed at me. "Something like this happened to Noah, and I freaked out, so you're not doing that. We're gonna go make sure Matt's okay, and then you two can figure out what's going on between you. You got it?"

"Man, she really cracks the whip," Luna laughed.

Dinah stood up. "Come on, let's go."

I let Dinah take charge of the situation. We rushed out of the arena and got back into her car to head over to the hospital.

All I could think about was how stupid I had been. How I never got to tell Matt how I felt, all because I feared my brother. Now Matt was injured, and I was so scared for him.

When we got to the hospital, they wouldn't let me or Dinah see Matt, but Luna demanded the doctor tell her what was going on since she was family. She had disappeared behind one of the doors hours ago and hadn't returned yet.

I stared down at my phone, ignoring all the sports app push notifications, and instead kept reading back that message from Matt about wanting to talk. He had to be okay. I couldn't forgive myself if he wasn't.

The sound of footsteps approaching made me look up and see Luna coming back over to us.

"How he is?" Dinah asked.

Luna waved us off. "He'll be fine."

"Luna! What's going on?" I cried.

"Broken leg. They had to x-ray it, but my brother's fine," she explained. Her gaze shifted to the exit, and I turned my head to see what she saw.

Noah rushed inside, his coat whipping behind him as he came closer. "What's the verdict?"

"Broken leg," I muttered.

He winced. "Oof. Season ender?"

Dinah cringed. "Not sure yet. Luna, what did the doctor say?"

She shrugged. "He was more concerned with finding out the problem and setting the cast. But...probably. Any time I've broken a limb, that's it for my hockey season."

The knots in my stomach began to untangle. Okay, just a broken limb. It could have been so much worse. Especially in this violent sport we all loved.

"Does he want visitors?" Noah asked Luna.

"Can he have any?" Dinah corrected.

Luna turned toward me. "He's been asking for you specifically. But he won't mind everyone."

I forgot that my brother was standing next to me. Ignoring all the fear that had been tying me down, I sprung up from my chair and followed Luna to her brother's hospital room. My heart plummeted into my stomach when I stepped inside and saw how miserable Matt looked in that hospital bed.

"Sweet pea," he whispered.

"Baby!" I cried as I rushed over to him, pulling him into a hug. "I'm sorry. I'm so sorry."

"I know."

I pulled back, and my heart broke at how in pain he obviously was. "No, you don't know. I was so scared of what

Noah would think. I love you, okay? I'm sorry. How do you feel? What can I get you?"

His lips curved up into a smile. "I'm okay. I just wanted to see you. I missed you. C'mere."

I did as he asked, framing his face as I bent down to kiss him. I put all my feelings into the kiss, trying to show him with my body how much I missed him.

I would have climbed into the hospital bed with him if the loud clearing of a throat hadn't forced me to wrench away.

All the blood drained from my face when I saw Noah standing there with his brow furrowing. Dinah and Luna had already taken up residence in the chairs next to the bed. I think if they had a bowl of popcorn, they would have eaten out of it as they watched. Assholes.

"Does someone want to explain to me what's going on here?" Noah asked, gesturing between the two of us.

Matt opened his mouth, but I held up a hand to stop him and whirled on my brother. "No, you don't get to do that overprotective big brother thing. Matt's my boyfriend, and I love him, and there's nothing you can do to stop that. Don't tell him if he hurts me, you'll kill him. I'm an adult and can make my own choices."

Noah stared back at me in silence.

"And...this was on me. Matt wanted to do the right thing. As soon as we got together, he wanted to sit you down to tell you his intentions, but I wanted to keep it a secret. Until...he couldn't handle lying to you anymore. I'm the one that fucked up. Not him. So if you're gonna be mad at anyone, it's me. But you don't get to dictate my love life, Noah! It's my life."

My chest was heaving as I stared down at my brother.

He raised an eyebrow and glanced over at Matt.

Then he laughed. He tipped back his head and laughed. I looked at Dinah, and she shrugged while Matt looked scared.

Once Noah stopped laughing, he walked over toward Matt. I tensed up immediately. "You love my sister?" he asked Matt.

"Yes," Matt said. His eyes hardened like he was ready for a fight. My heart sang at the idea of him fighting for me no matter what my brother was about to say.

"You good to her?"

Matt nodded. "One hundred percent."

"Okay."

"Okay?" I shrieked. "Just okay? That's all you have to say?"

Noah gave me a hard look. "Mads, did you think I didn't know?"

"Yes?"

I was so confused. What was going on? Dinah said she didn't think he knew, and she didn't tell him about what happened at their wedding.

Noah sighed. "First, you two aren't as sneaky as you think. Second, I follow you on your social media channels, Mads. I recognized you wearing Matt's hoodie in some of your posts and my own damn basement floor."

Oh. That's how Dinah figured it out, too.

"But..." Noah continued. "After I fought Chester, Matt said something to put me in my place about how I've been treating you. But you were pissed and wouldn't talk to me. I figured if I showed up at your dorm, we'd have to talk it out."

"But we didn't. I kept ignoring you," I said.

"Yeah, no shit. I saw you with Matt holding hands,

walking down the street. None of those fucking absolute losers you've dated made you smile like that."

Dinah stared her husband down. "You knew this whole time and didn't say a thing?"

"Gotta keep some things close to the vest, lovey," he explained. He turned back to me. "I've been waiting for you two to finally admit it and be grown-ups about it. Kinda annoyed you hid it, and I appreciate Matt wanting to be upfront. He's a good guy, but I'll drop the gloves if he hurts you down the line."

"No, you will not!" Dinah cut in. "Absolutely not Noah Kennedy."

Noah grinned at his wife. "Come on, lovey, I have to put a little fear in them."

She glared at him and stood up. "Let's give these two some privacy."

Luna stood up too and followed my brother and his wife out of the room.

That was way easier than I thought it was going to go. Maybe all my fears had been for nothing. Or Dinah made my brother see that I could make my own choices.

"C'mere, sweet pea," Matt whispered.

I climbed into the bed with him, careful not to hurt his leg. "I missed you so much. I'm so sorry."

He pushed my hair behind my ear. "Missed you too."

"How bad is it?"

"Broken leg. Probably out for the season. They'll rehab me down in Reading, which sucks, but it is what it is."

"I'm sorry."

"It's not your fault," he laughed. "I'm the dummy who went feet-first into the boards. I'm glad you got to meet Luna."

I smiled. "I hope she gets into Franklin. I'd love to have her on the team."

"I'd love to have her closer. But I don't want to talk about my sister right now."

"No?" I teased.

"Kiss me already," he whined.

I laughed but bent down and kissed him again. I kissed him like I'd never do it again, like this was the last time.

When I pulled away, he was smiling through the pain. "You want me to get the doctor?" I asked.

He shook his head. "No. I just want you."

"I want you too."

"I shouldn't have given you that ultimatum."

I shook my head. "No. You were right. We couldn't keep pretending. I can't believe Noah knew and said nothing."

"I had no clue."

"Me neither."

"I don't want to hide you, Maddie. I never did. I love you so much, it hurt being away from you. I didn't want this to be the way we had this talk."

I nodded. "I know, baby. And I'm sorry about your season. Maybe you'll heal before the end. I believe in you."

"You're my girl again, right?"

"No, I'm your sweet pea," I told him with a grin.

He didn't respond. Instead he pulled my face toward his and kissed me again, and it was like everything was right in the world again.

EPILOGUE

MADDIE
JUNE THE FOLLOWING YEAR

I was trying to be as quiet as possible as I packed up the boxes in the basement of my brother's house while Matt was asleep behind the closed bedroom door.

Last year, rather than go home after my school year was over, I moved in with my brother. At first, I was sleeping upstairs in one of the guest rooms, but gradually, I made my way back into Matt's bed and never left.

Did I love commuting to campus from Old City? Nope, but it wasn't so bad. When Matt and I started looking for our own place, we settled on a low-maintenance condo a couple of blocks away. Besides, with the two other rookies my brother 'adopted' it was getting crowded here.

Matt's alarm blared, forcing him up from his pregame nap so he could get ready for the game tonight. Tensions had been high, and that's why I was working on the packing. We weren't set to move until next week, but there was still a lot to do.

I finished packing my current box as quietly as I could as I heard the sounds of Matt waking up behind the bedroom door. He'd need a few minutes to fully wake up and get dressed before walking out here, and I wanted to give him that space.

I shut the box I was packing and tapped it up. I pushed it to the side with the others and padded across the room for a new box. I opened up a new one and taped it together, then assessed my piles. I might have too many books. Matt joked our second bedroom at the condo would be filled with them, and he might not be wrong. It was his own damn fault. That man loved buying me all the books I wanted.

I grabbed another pile and spent the next couple of minutes loading up more books. It felt like the piles were only getting smaller by a fraction. Moving was no joke.

I was taping up the second box when the bedroom door opened, and Matt walked in wearing the blue pin-striped suit that I loved. He gave me a big smile, and my insides still got mushy at that.

"Hey, baby. You ready for tonight?" I asked.

He scowled. "I told you I'd help."

I waved him off. "You worry about bringing home the Cup tonight. I got this. We're a team, remember?"

He crossed over to me, and I yelped when he lifted me in his arms, but then I melted into him when he kissed me. I wrapped my arms around his neck and clung to him through the kiss. I made a face when he pulled away.

"What's wrong?"

I ran the back of my hand across his bushy playoff beard. "I can't wait for you to win and get rid of this thing."

He waggled his eyebrows at me. "I thought you loved the way it felt between your thighs."

"Um, no, that's you, babe."

"So you don't love my head being between your legs?"

I laughed. "Well, I didn't say that."

He set me back down, and he cocked his head as he spied the application I had lying on the couch. "What's that?"

"Nothing!"

I tried to distract him, but he darted around me and picked up the piece of paper. The one I had been scared to fill out. He scanned it and raised his eyes at me in question. "What's this?"

"It's the business application."

His eyes lit up. "For the PR company?"

I nodded.

I officially had five authors I was PAing for now. Dinah was still my number one, but I had such growth that I decided to start my own PR company for authors, mostly in romance. Matt and I had talked about it at length after I graduated last month. He fully supported my dreams, and I loved that about him.

"That's amazing!" he cheered.

I bit my lip. "You think I should do it?"

"Maddie, you're so good at it. I'm fully in support of this. And don't worry about money, okay? I'll support us in the meantime."

That was something we talked about too. Noah talked about capital with me and whether I wanted to do it on the side or find a full-time job. I was extremely privileged that I had a boyfriend and big brother who could support me financially if need be. For now, I was going to chase my dreams.

He cupped my face. "Love you, sweet pea."

I beamed. "Love you too. And I can't wait to watch you hold the Cup over your head tonight."

"Don't jinx me!"

"I'm not."

He gave me one last kiss goodbye, and then he walked upstairs to have his pregame meal and head out with my brother and the other new guys. I was so glad we were moving out soon. It was nice having our space down here, but our own little place to start our life together was going to be great.

I packed up a few more boxes, and then I sat down and filled out the form. I was actually doing it. I was going to chase my dreams with my man by my side. First, I needed to watch him win the Cup, then we'd find forever.

I chugged my beer while I watched from behind the glass as Matt took the face-off in the Bulldogs' defensive zone. I glanced at the scoreboard, 2-2, with five minutes left in the third period. They needed one final push, and they could bring it all home.

"Come on, baby, you got this," I muttered under my breath.

Matt's sister Luna gripped my hand and gave me a nervous look. We were all on the edge of our seats. After Matt's injury last season, he pushed himself even harder this year. It was a minor setback, but it made him more focused. When the team made the playoffs this year, I thought Dinah was going to have a heart attack. Then they kept on winning. Now, they had to beat the Chicago Renegades one last time to bring it all home.

"They got this," Dinah said.

"I'm nervous," I explained. "Matt told me to stop jinxing him."

"Don't worry," Dinah reassured me.

I turned back to the ice, and I held my breath as I watched my boyfriend on the breakaway.

"Oh my God!" I yelled along with everyone else in the arena.

"GO!" Luna and Matt's parents were screaming on the other side of me.

We were all up on our feet, yelling our heads off and watching as Matt had the puck and deked it around the Chicago defenseman. Benny and Hallsy skated down to join him, but Matt had the opening. I watched in amazement as he slid the puck past the goaltender.

The entire arena went up in cheers, and the goal siren blared.

"Fuck yeah, baby! The motherfucking cup!" Dinah yelled and then promptly downed the rest of her beer.

I laughed at her. I loved my sister-in-law so much.

The cheering on the ice went on for a bit longer as we watched the rest of the minutes tick down. When the game-ending horn sounded, we all screamed our heads off again, cheering for our team.

The crowd kept roaring until both teams lined up for the handshake line. That had always been one of my favorite things about hockey. No matter what, the teams still had respect for each other at the end of the day.

"I can't believe it," Dinah said in disbelief as we watched the Cup handlers bring the trophy down the tunnel and onto the ice.

The Cup was handed off to Riley first, and then it got passed around to the rest of the team. We waited a little while before heading down to the ice since they still needed to do the team picture.

I was vibrating with excitement for my brother and my boyfriend. I was confident earlier when I told Matt he'd be holding the Cup tonight, but deep down, I wasn't sure I'd actually get to see it.

When they finally let the families on the ice, I laughed at Dinah launching herself at my brother. He grabbed her in his arms and spun her around while he was still on his skates. I pretended I didn't see him slip her some tongue when I searched the ice for my boyfriend. Noah looked like Grizzly Adams with his playoff beard. I wasn't sure how Dinah could stand it, but she liked beards, so she probably liked it. I couldn't wait until Matt was clean-shaven again.

My eyes lit up when I saw Matt skating around the ice with the Cup. He grinned when he saw me, and he passed the Cup off to one of his teammates. He said something to one of the equipment managers, but he wasn't coming over to me right away.

He crooked his finger at me, and I slowly walked over to him. Then my mouth hung open when he got down on one knee.

"What are you doing?" I blurted out.

He smiled at me and held open a ring box. Inside was an absolute rock of a diamond. It was so flashy, but I loved it.

"Sweet pea," he said, and I felt the weight of the cameras and stares on us. "I love you so much. I love that we're a team that supports each other through everything. I don't want another day to go by without you by my side. Will you marry me?"

"You don't even have to ask! Yes, of course I will!" I squealed.

He slipped the ring on my finger, and I was giddy at how it sparkled under the lights. It made me feel like a princess. He got up, and even though he was sweaty and still in his hockey sweater, he was the best-looking man I'd ever seen.

His skates made him taller than usual, so he had to bend down a little more to capture my lips.

I never thought when I transferred to Franklin U last year that I'd fall in love with a hockey player. Much less one who was my brother's teammate. I didn't regret anything that happened. Not when the man I loved more than hockey or romance books was kissing me. Not when one day I'd be his wife.

He rested his forehead against mine when we came up for air. "Love you so much, Madison. More than hockey."

"I love you, Matt. More than all my books."

He grinned, and then he kissed me one more time. Matt Callahan was my future, and I couldn't wait for what was in store for the rest of our lives.

ACKNOWLEDGMENTS

When I first set out to write this series, I had no plans outside of it. But I knew I wasn't planning on letting this series go on forever. The release of this book marks two big accomplishments for me — this series is now complete and it's my tenth book published. A lot of people don't even publish one book, so that in itself is a huge feat I'm proud to have met.

I have a lot of people to thank for this book coming to fruition. Once again my editor Charlie Knight for always championing my books and giving me great guidance. I always appreciate your insight and I'm glad you get me. Big thanks also goes to my long-time beta readers Becky and Chris. Your help makes all my books shine.

I can't forget my critique group - Kat, J Lynn, and Sophie. I cherish our daily chats and your input. I am so grateful for your continued friendship.

Finally...to my readers. Without you I never would have finished this series. I can't wait to bring you new books soon and explore new worlds.

ALSO BY DANICA FLYNN

PHILADELPHIA BULLDOGS

Take The Shot

Score Her Heart

Against The Boards

The Chase

The Fake Out

Game On

MACGREGOR BROTHERS BREWING COMPANY

Accidentally In Love

Trapped In Love

Temporarily In Love

THE MURPHY BROTHERS

Protecting Her

Capturing Her

ABOUT THE AUTHOR

Danica Flynn is a marketer by day, and a writer by nights and weekends. AKA she doesn't sleep! She is a rabid hockey fan of the Philadelphia Flyers. When not writing, she can be found hanging with her partner, playing video games, and reading a ton of books.

www.ingramcontent.com/pod-product-compliance
Lightning Source LLC
LaVergne TN
LVHW091114080826
845145LV00008B/1914

9781957494272